SEPTEMBER GIRLS

Also by
BENNETT MADISON

The Blonde of the Joke

SEPTEMBER

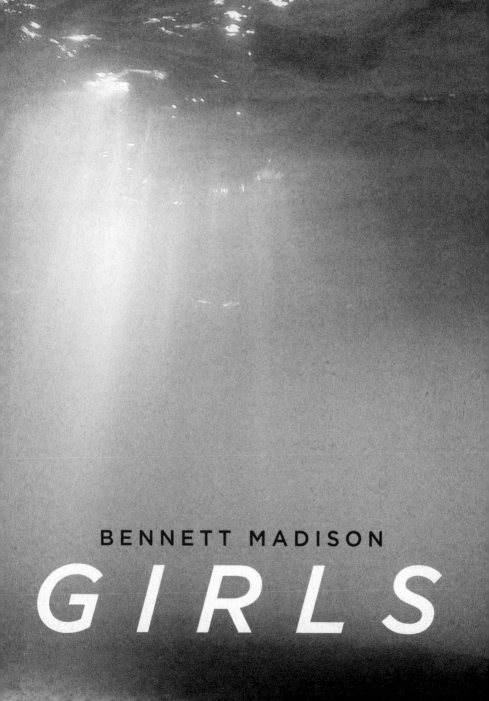

BENNETT MADISON

GIRLS

HARPER TEEN
An imprint of HarperCollinsPublishers

HarperTeen is an imprint of HarperCollins Publishers.

September Girls

ISBN 978-0-06-125563-2

Typography by Erin Fitzsimmons
13 14 15 16 17   CG/RRDH   10 9 8 7 6 5 4 3 2 1
❖
First Edition

For Kathryn Van Wert

ONE

THE SUMMER FOLLOWING the winter that my mother took off into something called Women's Land for what I could only guess would be all eternity, my father decided that there was no choice but for him to quit his despised job and take me and my brother to the beach for at least the entire summer and possibly longer. "A boy should go to the beach at least once in his life," my father declared at the dinner table the night before our sudden departure. This edict was made in a decisive tone that I was more than familiar with by then—one that indicated he had no idea what he was talking about.

Dad had always been prone to vapid pronouncements of this sort, but in the aftermath of my mother's disappearance, the habit had really gotten out of control. He was constantly inventing these half-baked bromides on the spot and presenting them as fact. The most obnoxious thing about them was their tendency to land on the topic of my supposedly impending manhood: that it was time to *be a man, or man up,* or *act like a man,* et cetera, et cetera. The whole subject was creepy—with vague implications of unmentionable things involving body hair—but the most embarrassing part was basically just how meaningless it all was. As if one day you're just a normal person, and then the next—ta-da!—a *man,* as if anyone would ever even notice the difference.

Like you can just instantly transform like that. Like manhood is this distinct thing with actual markers and consequences. Well, maybe it is. But even if it is—if there is any person on this planet who actually knows what it means to *be a man,* anyone who could truly sum it up—I would guess my father to be among the very fucking last to have the tiniest clue.

And anyway! Now he was suddenly saying that a *boy* should go to the beach. Was this supposed to mean that I'd been given a reprieve from the expectation of manhood? If so, it felt like some small victory.

Jeff had the usual reflexive and halfhearted complaints involving his busy schedule and plans that couldn't be rearranged. Dad's scheme sounded fine to me. For one thing, it meant I didn't have to bother studying for my pre-calc test, which was a task I hadn't yet gotten started. For another thing, I was in the mood to go somewhere. Anywhere. Even if it was with my father and brother.

Dad didn't even bring up the fact that I would be missing the end of school. He was apparently now beyond such petty concerns. I wasn't about to argue. I just slid away from the table and went to pack my bags.

My father hadn't been the same since Mom's decampment. She'd left a few weeks after Christmas, and he'd spent the remainder of January as well as February and March in a swamp of discontent, drifting through the house silently, spending entire weekends on the couch, not looking up from his laptop, while I fended for myself and survived on a diet of Mama Celeste and Coca-Cola spiked with whiskey from the ever-dwindling liquor supply.

Looking back, it hadn't been so bad. There are worse things than frozen pizza.

But by April the whiskey had run out (I tried to switch to Malibu, all that remained in the liquor cabinet, but it was disgusting), and Dad had bounced back with a vengeance. He took up *activities*: it seemed that if there was a tear-off sheet on a bulletin board in Starbucks he was willing to give it a try. He took piano lessons and joined a book club. He signed up for cooking class and became a charter member of a knitting circle–slash–men's discussion group at the local library. Worst of all, he began wearing hats.

It was disturbing and bothersome. I quickly began to long for the days when I had been able to eat my pizza unmolested without Dad insisting on sit-down dinners in which he tried to entice me into joining him for things like his Gentle Yoga class. ("It's all chicks," he'd explained excitedly before his first session. But I'd begged off, and when he'd come home he'd been disappointed to report that all the chicks had been pregnant, except for one chick named Nancy, who was an octogenarian and whom I already knew anyway because she'd been my piano teacher when I was very little.)

Now Jeff was home from college, and my father, in his latest attack of enthusiasm, was taking us to the beach. All previous summers had found my family—often excluding Jeff, but always including the frumpy kindergarten teacher formerly known as my mother, now known as Artemis Something-or-Other—spending our cramped vacation weeks in various rocky, misty outposts on the dreary coast of Maine. The beach, yes, but by technicality only. This summer, Dad informed us, we would instead be traveling southward for the Outer Banks of North Carolina. Where the shore was sandy and the sun, so Dad told us, was actually sunny.

It struck me as slightly odd that Dad was so set on yet another beach as, for some unknown reason, he can't actually swim. But I didn't ask questions. It wasn't any weirder than yoga.

When I stumbled down the stairs at five o'clock the next morning, still groggy and sour-breathed, I found Dad waiting by the door, already in his bathing suit and sunglasses, sitting in a folding beach chair, sipping from a thermos and reading a James Patterson paperback. Due to both his wild-eyed smile and the coffee-tinged scent of BO that wafted off him, I suspected he'd been up all night making preparations. "You ready to go, Tiger?" he asked, looking up eagerly.

I didn't answer him. My name is Sam. The first thing you should know about me is that I don't answer to Tiger.

Several hours later we were sitting in traffic on I-95 in the old Honda Accord, because my mother had naturally chosen the Volvo to abscond with. I was trying to ignore Jeff's theatrical groans from the backseat. He had been out all night drinking with long-lost high school friends and was now curled up fetal and hungover with his face in a pillow, acting like a total baby in the customary way of older brothers. Next to me, my father was maddeningly oblivious to the gridlock as he whistled tunelessly, pausing every hour or so to make some remark about how now that our family was "all men" we could fart and scratch our balls without fear of female persecution.

Comments such as these were inevitably followed by loud farts.

My brother had managed to miss out on all the drama of the previous months by being away at Amherst. In fact, my mother hadn't even said good-bye to him. (Her good-bye to me had been perfunctory and inadequate, but I gave her some meager credit for bothering.) And although Jeff had been naturally shocked to learn of the developments that had taken place in his absence, I didn't gather that he was particularly upset by any of it. I guess he'd just been happy not to have to deal. After, Jeff called only infrequently to check in from school and seemed to avoid asking for any actual details on the situation for fear that they might prove unpleasant or—worse—demand action on his part. He ended every one of our exchanges with the same rushed and insincere "Hang in there, bro," and *click*—then I was on my own again.

For hours on the way to the beach, Jeff snored and moaned fitfully while my dad honked and hummed and cursed traffic and strained to lure me into excruciating conversation, asking me about girls and school and needling me to try out for the track team in September and whatever whatever whatever. *Fuck you, Jeff,* I thought. My brother, having already managed to ignore the trouble of the year, was hanging on to ignorance for a few more precious hours. What a dick.

I know I must sound terrible myself—brittle and fussy and totally lacking in sympathy and complain, complain, complain. But I was at the end of my patience. Cut me some fucking slack.

At a certain point, after we'd been traveling for hours, I actually considered getting out of the car and just walking. Just taking off past the Dairy Queens and Waffle Houses and roadside farm stands and whimsically named convenience stores and pushing my way through the ribbons of trees bordering the roads toward an unfamiliar home. Perhaps I'd take a job as a carpenter or a welder. Something with my hands, at any rate.

If I wanted, I could have left Jeff and Dad to fend for themselves. It would have been exactly what they deserved. Just step out of the car and wander an undeviating line until I found a different version of myself waiting for me, bright and open, with an all-new life.

I came so close to doing it. But just as I was about to unlatch the door, my eyes drifted over to my father, whose infuriating mask of cheerfulness had melted into one of collapsed resignation. I looked in the rearview mirror and saw Jeff in the back, scratching his belly under his T-shirt, his eyes sleep-damp and oblivious, and I took pity on them. Because God fucking knows how they would ever have survived on their own. They needed me.

Eventually the traffic cleared up, and soon we were crossing the causeway; then we hit the beach road and finally it was evening and we were crawling our way through strings of vacation developments full of stilted pastel "cottages" that looked large enough to house armies, or at least—judging by the Lexus SUVs in the driveways—shitloads of rich shitheads and their horrible shithead children. Every now and then we'd notice long-legged blondes in bikinis and short shorts ambling along the shoulder of the road, hauling beach chairs and canvas bags, hair still salty and purple in the twilight, and Dad would elbow me and say, "Didn't I tell you this place was gonna be great?" and I would ignore him, although not without taking notice myself.

As the numbers on the mileposts rose, the houses shrank and their electric paint jobs faded to silvery gray. It was getting dark out. Finally, we pulled into a cul-de-sac marked by a sign that read SEASHELL SHOALS.

This end of the beach had seen better days. The house Dad pulled up to was modest—small and dune-brown and worn— and the sand here looked somehow dirtier than usual, although

I know that's a stupid thing to say about sand, which is of course basically just dirt to start with.

"Here we are," Dad said. "Our little piece of heaven!" It was always unclear when he was being sarcastic, or it would have been if I hadn't known he had no capacity for sarcasm. At any rate, crappy as our house was, it seemed to be the jewel of the cul-de-sac, as the stilted houses on either side of it appeared unoccupied and near to collapse. We had arrived.

We got out of the car without unpacking the trunk and climbed the rickety wooden steps to the front door, which opened into a dingy but serviceable family room. I wasn't any more impressed by the inside than I had been by the outside.

The place was all wicker furniture that seemed like it might fall apart if you sat on it, and everything (I mean everything) was plastered with seashells that I could only assume were fake. There was a lamp made out of seashells and another one made out of red wicker. The wood paneling on the walls was (upon inspection) cardboard, and the wall-to-wall carpet that covered every inch of floor was crunchy with sand. The whole place smelled like Lysol mixed with something both mildewy and fishy. It was basically a dump.

Dad plopped onto the couch in the family room, and as soon as I'd dropped my backpack next to a tacky watercolor of a seagull by the kitchen island, he was snoring loudly, his knees pulled to his chest like a little kid, his sunglasses smushed against his forehead. Jeff looked over at me and raised his eyebrows. "Poor guy," he said. I just snorted.

"Give the guy a break," Jeff said. "He's had a rough time. You know that."

"Yeah, well," I said. "You haven't had to live with him."

Jeff unzipped his bag and pulled out a plastic jug of cheapo-looking vodka, which he wiggled at me, grinning. "Come on," he said. "Let's go look at the ocean. Might as well, right?"

"Man, I just want to go to bed," I said. I was exhausted. I wanted to jerk off and fall asleep. (Although I obviously didn't say that.)

"Come on," Jeff said. "Don't be such a little bitch."

How could I refuse an invitation like that?

HOME

None of us remember our home anymore except to know that it's very far away—and to know that when we were home, we were happy. This is not our home. This could never be our home. We have been here as long as we can remember.

We remember our mother, but only a little. We remember that she was beautiful and patient. We remember that we loved her. We have been told that she was a whore, although we can't remember who told us that, and we often find ourselves arguing over the true definition of whore.

Sometimes language confuses us. We search for words and find only shells and sea glass. We search for comb *and find* fork.

We're all afraid of the water. There is an endlessness about it that frightens us, and we know what's down there. (We have a hard time remembering, but we know.) From time to time— afraid or not—we meet late at night on a dark and moonlit beach and strip our clothes off and lounge naked in the tide in orderly rows, not speaking to each other, feeling the freezing cold water lapping at our hip bones and breasts. We stare at stars and pretend they're jellyfish. We don't remember the word for jellyfish.

We're too frightened to swim. None of us knows how to swim, and we know that if any one of us ventured into the water past her thighs she would drown. It happened to Donna, although only one or two of us remember Donna. Sometimes the rest of us wonder if she was ever even real. But it happened to her. We are sure of it.

In the warmth of the sun we are often too frightened to even look at the ocean's horizon. When we venture onto the sand in daylight, we try to keep our eyes on the dunes.

We work as waitresses, checkout girls, hotel maids. We've grown accustomed to the burn of ammonia in the back of our throats. We have grown accustomed to sleeping two to a bunk and stepping over one another on our way to the refrigerator in the mornings. None of us like each other very much anymore. There's too much at stake for friendship. Sisterhood is dangerous.

We are sisters anyway. Yes, we dislike one another, but at least we are comfortable together. We protect one another. We feel uneasy amid the Others: women who speak to us with suspicious contempt and men whose eyes sting like chlorine. We like the boys, but they're few and far between, and they always bring trouble with them—often in the form of older brothers. We hate the girls most of all.

We come and go. Every summer there are more of us; every summer some of us are gone. We barely remember the ones who disappear. Donna becomes Kelly—or was it Brenda?

After a while we stop bothering to keep one another straight. There is really no point. We are not happy here. We are filled with emptiness.

But sometimes, on rare days in the sticky fog of summer, one of us will step off the boardwalk and onto the sand and turn her back to the sea and find herself sinking to her knees in astonishment at the generosity of this place: at the cool wind twisting in her yellow-green hair and the sun on her brow and the bead of sweat that forms at her widow's peak and inches down to her lips, where she licks it away and is grateful for the salt. This place that has lent us what little it has of itself with such forgiving aplomb.

She might look down only to find a piece of sea stone, smooth and perfect, robin's egg, and pick it up and roll it between her fingers and think: I could stay here. She might think: I could be happy here.

That's when she knows it's time to go home.

TWO

JEFF AND I walked to the ocean in the dark, barefoot, passing the jug of vodka back and forth between us. I wasn't used to the taste of straight booze and with every sip had to brace myself to keep from wincing.

The ocean was a block and a half away, across the beach road and a rotting path of wooden planks that cut through the dunes. Jeff and I made small talk as we walked, him talking about his classes (he had been planning on majoring in econ but was tormented by statistics, as if I gave the slightest shit) and about some crazy-sounding girl he was trying to lose. "You sleep with some girl once, and before you know it you're like trapped in her crazy pussy-web," he said, nodding sagely to himself.

I had no idea what the fuck he was talking about. "So I hear," I said, doing my best to humor him.

"How about you?" he asked. "You getting any action these days?"

"Nah," I said. "I've got other things on my mind, *these days.*"

"I doubt it," Jeff said. "You seem pretty hard up."

"Fuck you," I said.

"Dude," he said. "This summer we're gonna get you laid, bro. It'll do you some good."

"I don't see what *we* has to do with it," I said. "Isn't getting laid like something you generally do on your own?"

"There's your first mistake," Jeff said. "You don't even have the basic mechanics right."

I snorted.

"Whatever," he went on. "You should see yourself, dude. You've been working this like constant bitchface ever since I got back from school." When I still didn't respond, he punched me in the arm and laughed loudly. "Turn the motherfucking frown upside down already. What's the point?"

The gravel on the road was digging into my feet, and I was glad when we made it to the beach access, a boardwalk half-sunk into the sand. Jeff pulled a flashlight from the pocket of his cargo shorts and snapped it on, shining it under his chin, lighting his face up like a jack-o'-lantern. "Oooohooooohooooh!" he yodeled, trying to be spooky. "Very scary!"

I looked at him like he was insane. Maybe he was; I once read this book about some lady who caught a case of syphilis and was certifiably nuts for years without anyone noticing.

"Man." He sighed. "I'm working my ass off here. You gotta give me something. I mean, anything."

Then we stepped off the boardwalk, past the blind of the

dunes, and the ocean revealed itself to us: just unfurled as a dark and infinite ribbon curling and waving in every direction. Black sand, black water, black sky, all of it variegated in barely discernible bands, the beam of Jeff's flashlight cutting through it as a bright and pointless wedge. Ghostly, glowing sand crabs scurried in every direction. Jeff said nothing and neither did I, but my muscles tensed and then relaxed in surprise, and I could feel Jeff reacting similarly at my side.

We walked down the sand together and stood in the surf, him bouncing his small light off the crests of the crashing waves. The water was freezing, but it felt okay on my ankles. I wondered if I waded in farther if it might snap me back to life. I chose not to take a step.

"I know I've been a shitty brother lately," Jeff said after a few minutes like that. He took a swig from the vodka and handed it to me. I was already feeling unsteady on my feet, but I chugged anyway. It was starting to taste kind of good.

"Nah," I said. "I mean, it's okay." It wasn't okay, not really, but I was happy that he was finally coming clean.

"Dude, you're gonna be fine," Jeff said. "It's all gonna be fine. You know that, right? It'll be over before you know it. You'll be out of there so soon; you'll put all of this year behind you and never even think about it again. It's Dad that I worry about. I mean, that's his life. I mean, fuck. I can't believe her. What a bitch."

"She's not a bitch," I said. "Everyone's got their reasons, right?"

"It's gonna be fine," he said.

"I know," I said.

"Step one, you gotta get yourself laid," Jeff said. "Seventeen years old and still a virgin. No wonder you're in such a bad mood all the time."

"What makes you think I'm a virgin?" I asked.

Jeff hooted. "Look at yourself, bro."

Before I could ask what he meant by that a wave crashed and swirled around us. As the water receded, I started to realize exactly how drunk I was. I wobbled a little in the undertow and then was on my ass with a splash. "Fuck," I said.

Jeff didn't answer. "Holy shit," he said.

"Dude," I said, looking up at him. "Whatever." But his attention was elsewhere. He had been swinging his flashlight around the water the whole time we'd been talking, but now he had stopped the fidgeting and was pointing it down the coastline. "What the fuck?" he said, practically whispering. I crawled onto my knees in the tide and turned myself around, following the beam of light down the line of the beach.

"What?" I asked. Then I saw what he was talking about. A hundred paces off, in the shallows, was a body. A girl. She was naked. And she was lying in the tide on her back, her arms thrown at weird doll angles, her bare and smallish breasts quivering and beaded with salt water. It was as if she had just been spit out by the ocean.

"What the fuck?" I said.

"Hey!" Jeff shouted. The girl jerked her face toward us. So

she was alive. It was hard to make out her expression, but she looked disoriented, maybe drunk. Then again, we were drunk too. I climbed to my feet, and was knocked down again as another wave hit me in the back of the knees. When I'd finally managed to stand, the girl was gone.

Jeff shoved the flashlight into my hands and began racing toward where we'd seen her. I followed him, but it was hard running in the water. I thought I felt hands grasping at my calves, but that must have been my imagination.

"Hey?" Jeff shouted. As a question this time. There was no answer. The girl was gone. And then I turned the flashlight up onto the shore and saw her again, hastily stumbling up the sand. She was floundering, completely naked, unsteady on her feet and tripping onto her knees every few steps, wet hair longer than I'd ever seen tumbling down her back in wild, sea-weedy clumps. Despite her clumsiness, she was moving fast. I mean, really fast.

"Stop," Jeff called after her, not that loud anymore, knowing that it was pointless. Either she couldn't hear or she didn't want to. "Wait!" he said.

I had stopped running and was just staring at the girl, who was crawling now. I'm embarrassed to admit that Jeff had been right: before that night I'd never seen a naked girl other than on the internet.

This was not at all how I had imagined it; I mean, I'm not sure if it even counted. The girl was paper thin and ghost white. The lines of her body were indistinct and out of focus.

She tried once more to stand and fell and then gave up and was on her hands and knees again, skittering away. Or maybe it was more of a slither.

Jeff splashed out of the water and made a line for her, but although it seemed impossible—in his golden adolescence, Jeff had been captain of the track team—she was somehow outpacing him in her crab crawl. Before he was even halfway up the sand, the girl had disappeared into the tall grass of the dunes and was gone. Really gone.

I moved the flashlight back to my brother and saw him standing in the sand, arms outstretched in midmotion. He stood there like that for a second, totally still, and then fell back onto his ass in defeat, running his hands through his hair.

FIRST

First we are alone. First we are naked. At first, walking is nearly impossible. It remains difficult. We have problems with our feet. They are always aching. Our shoes often have blood in them. We are covetous of the Others' high heels, especially the shiny, patent-leather kind. We can only wear flats.

First we are alone. We're not sure how we find one another, but we do. Then we are still alone, but in the way sardines are alone.

We are given clothes. The first thing we learn is how to balance plates in the crooks of our elbows. We learn to walk without wincing. We learn to take only small amounts from the register. We learn to smoke Gauloises—even though we will never master their pronunciation.

We learn the small pleasures of this place: press-on nails and eye makeup and hair dye, Chinese slippers with sequins and little embroidered flowers. Wine coolers and soap operas. We don't like meat, but we have a weakness for french fries. Not to mention french tips.

We like shiny things. Not only because they remind us of home but because if something's shiny enough it will sometimes offer up a reflection. We collect things that sparkle and hide them in places we'll forget to look.

The first thing we forget is ourselves. People think we're vain because we're always looking in mirrors; they don't understand that we are just searching for clues. We never find any. We don't know the first thing.

THREE

THE GIRLS WERE everywhere here. They were behind the registers. They were stocking shelves and smoking in the parking lot of the roadside trinket shop I stopped in for sunglasses. They were at gas stations, pumping gas into broken-down minivans. They were wearing halter tops and cutoffs and sweatpants and old oversized T-shirts and flip-flops, rolling unwieldy carts of cleaning supplies along the road from beach house to beach house, struggling to keep their carts' wheels from catching on the crumbly pavement, stopping to adjust their tube tops every few feet. They were on the beach, in the sand on their stomachs side by side, faces planted in towels, fingertips grazing fingertips, and tendrils of yellow hair curling into each other.

They were beautiful.

Although I'm normally not an early riser, on the first day at the beach I had somehow woken up before either my dad or

Jeff, just after the sun. Something about the weather must have roused me. I had decided to take a walk, and now I was alone at the edge of the water as it came and went. The sun was hot and high in the sky and it felt good.

It felt good just to be alone, especially after the previous day's cramped and endless journey. I consider myself a sociable person, but sometimes I feel best being sociable with myself. I guess that's why I enjoy masturbation.

The girls were everywhere, but I tried not to look at them. Not because I'm polite, but because there was something about them that kind of creeped me out. They were too much.

There were so many of them; they were everywhere, and every one of them could have been sisters—all with hair somewhere on a spectrum that ranged from blond to blondest, all with full, glossy lips and eyes that floated an inch in front of their faces, suspended in deep pools of liquid liner. They traveled in pairs and threesomes, and they seemed to move as parts of a strange beach machine. Tossing their hair in slo-mo unison, drifting easily back and forth into one another's space as if exchanging bodies.

They were just kind of weird. They reminded me of the clusters of jellyfish I'd spotted floating in the swells.

But they were also really hot. Fuck, I mean really hot. I did my best to pretend they weren't there.

In the heat of the early morning, the beach had changed from the night before. In sunlight it was just different. Whereas last night the shore had seemed stingy in its infinity, it was now open and welcoming and sort of cozy—a little tacky, but in a way that made it unassuming and familiar, even overtaken as it was by these beautiful, otherworldly girls. It was a fat, cheerful aunt in an appliquéd sweater and dangly wooden earrings, all *Every time I see you, you've gotten more handsome!*

And then I'd feel eyes on the back of my neck, and even in the heat I would shiver.

I wasn't totally sure if I remembered the night before. I mean, I remembered it, but had it been real? I was undecided. With the ten o'clock sun beating down on my back as I walked along the shoreline, wet sand squishing between my toes, I felt the girl in the surf receding back into the waves, growing more and more indistinct in my memory, more and more imaginary. Sea foam.

I wasn't walking anywhere in particular. I mean, it was the beach—you could only go one way or the other. So I had picked an arbitrary point on the horizon and was walking toward it. Just to have a destination, any destination. It had started as a coral-pink spot in the distance, and after a half hour of walking that spot was only just beginning to come into focus as a beachfront hotel on a cliff of sand. If I closed my left eye and held my fingers up to judge it, it was about an inch tall.

I started to think of it as if it belonged to me. I could put it in the pocket of my bathing suit and walk away.

A pair of girls walked past me, giggling, leading with their chests. Their legs were long and smooth and tan, and they were each dangling a pair of flip-flops from their fingers and tossing their hair over and over, to one shoulder then the next, and then again. One was young and blond, the other a few years older and a few shades blonder. Even though I tried not to stare, I couldn't help catch the eye of the blonder one, and I swear I'm 50 percent sure she looked right back and smiled.

Maybe I was kidding myself. On the other hand, it's not like it would be totally out of the question.

I can say without too much ego that I am attractive enough (aside from being on the pale and skinny side), but usually feel more awkward than handsome. I'm never sure of how I'm supposed to move. How to put one foot in front of the other without looking like I'm about trip over myself. For most people, I've been told, this is easy, but for me it all requires a certain amount of thought, a certain amount of intention. This morning at the beach was different. I felt the muscles in my shoulders pumping with blood. I felt ocean in my eyelashes and a heaviness in my dick. I felt strong and solid, more myself—the best version of myself, I mean—than I had in a while.

I'm not always as bad as I've made myself sound. I'm told I can be funny and at least up until recently have generally done a decent job of keeping my sourness to myself. I believe I have—at a minimum—the normal measure of social skill. It all seems to count for little anyway.

Well, no, it all counts for something, I guess. While Jeff had been annoyingly accurate in his speculation about the state of my innocence, I *had* had some small successes in that department in the last year—though unfortunately none that involved actual sex or anything even close. The most notable of these triumphs was when I'd succeeded in groping Sasha Swain's chest through her deliberately slutty *Alice in Wonderland* costume during a drunken make-out session at Ryan McIntire's Halloween party, much to the approval of my friend Sebastian, who had been encouraging me for some time to touch a boob.

It could have gone further if not for the fact that we'd been interrupted by Sasha's horrible friend Missy Taylor. And although Sasha had remained obviously into me in the weeks following the party—texting me nonstop and leaving long and pointless handwritten notes in my locker—I'd quickly decided that she was annoying and not even all that hot.

Sebastian said it didn't matter whether she was hot or not, that she was just a "starter," and a "solid seven" anyway, but pursuing it any further seemed like way too much of a pain in the ass. So I basically let the whole thing slide, which resulted in Sasha thinking I was an irredeemable dick and left me feeling unexpectedly sad. Then January had rolled around and I'd had other things on my mind, and Sebastian started dating Alexis Taylor, who was legendary for her blow jobs—legendary, I guess, just for the fact that she gave them at all, or at least supposedly had given one, once, to Jason Jamison—and it was all forgotten.

Maybe this all seems like a digression or even a case of protesting too much, but the point is that I have touched a breast and that I liked it.

* * *

When I finally got to the pink hotel I'd been aiming for, the beach had turned gloomy. The sun, which had been strong all morning, had by then become obscured by clouds, and the water took on a tone of muddiness against the damp gray sand. The hotel itself, which had appeared majestic and opulent as I'd made my way toward it, was depressing up close: the pink paint was peeling and dirty. It was nothing like the palace I'd anticipated.

Now that I'd reached the place I'd been traveling toward for hours I didn't know what else to do, so I plopped myself in the surf and dug for squirming baby sand crabs, picking them from the muck and tossing them into the water as far as I could, which was not very. I thought about Sasha Swain and wondered if she still liked me. I thought about Sebastian and Alexis and wondered if he'd gotten her to give him a BJ yet. (She had given him an HJ a couple weeks before school ended, so I figured the answer was probably yes.)

I considered the future: what school would be like next year if we ever went back home, where I should apply to college, and whether I could guilt Dad into buying me a car now that the Volvo was gone. I considered the horizon. I wondered if I would ever see my mother again.

I found that any prediction was beyond me other than to know that, for the summer, I would be at the beach. The future was clear and placid up to September and then dropped off instantly like ocean at the edge of a flat earth.

I wondered if the earth was flat—and if so, where did the

water go when it tumbled off the edge?

I mean, I'm not an idiot. I'm 99 percent convinced that the world is not flat. But I believe you can't be sure of anything until you've seen it with your own two eyes. And maybe it's just the limitations of photography, but I've seen those pictures of the earth from outer space and it looks flat as a quarter to me.

There was a couple frolicking a few yards away—a guy and a girl—who were probably a few years older than me. The girl was blond and tan like all the other girls around here and was wearing a skimpy red bikini wedged up the crack of her ass, and the guy was muscled and golden-haired, kicking water at her and chasing her as she squealed and feinted. It seemed fake and all for show, but I guess it's the kind of fakery that's sort of nice if you happen to be a participant in it.

As I pretended not to watch, he tackled her onto the wet sand and pushed himself on top of her, kissing her neck and shoulders and finally, her nose and then her lips. I was close enough to see their wet, pink tongues moving in and out of their mouths. The muscles in the guy's back were straining as he ground his hips against hers; his biceps were veiny and popping. For some reason I felt very sad. Maybe it just made me lonely.

I decided to head for home. By the time I was halfway back I could already feel a sunburn forming on my neck, and by the time I was walking up the stairs to the house it was stinging like a bitch. I had forgotten sunblock.

Dad, in a tight-lipped prissy way that was unusual for him these days, was annoyed that I'd gone off for so long. He was hungry for lunch.

"So why didn't you get lunch?" I asked, to which he replied, "We were waiting for you so we could get lunch *together*."

Jeff was on the couch, flipping through a newspaper, looking smug. He somehow seemed to have gotten two shades tanner overnight. "Don't worry about it, bro," he said. "Dad and I needed some time to catch up anyway." He gave me a beatific smile.

So we got in the car and drove off to some random restaurant that Dad insisted on going to because he had supposedly read about it on the internet. "Everything's different down here," he said. "You won't believe what the french fries taste like. It will blow your mind!"

"Fuck yeah," Jeff said, but even he seemed fatigued in his enthusiasm.

"This is going to be a summer you'll never forget!" Dad promised, somewhat desperately.

When we pulled into the Fisherman's Net just a few minutes later, it turned out—despite Dad's promises of an unprecedented dining experience—to just be any old roadside greasy spoon, undistinguished and vaguely seedy, silvered by weather. It was wedged haphazardly between the road and the ocean, constructed on stilts, half on the beach and half over the water, and from the angle it was pitched at I was unconvinced that it wasn't about to fall right into the sea at any minute.

Outside the entrance a girl in black ballet slippers and a tiny pair of denim cutoff shorts was smoking a long, skinny cigarette. Her breasts were straining against the ribbed cotton of her white wifebeater; her hair was wild and tangled and a little bit matted. My dad let out a low whistle and elbowed me from the driver's seat.

"Shut up," I said. "You're so gross."

"Did I say anything?" Dad asked, grinding the car into park. I tried to pretend that he didn't exist as we walked into the restaurant, right past the girl with the cigarette, whom I made a point not to look at because with Jeff right behind me in all his bronze, broad-shouldered glory there was no reason to even bother.

It turned out that the Fisherman's Net took its role as a tourist trap very seriously. It was not content to just be a restaurant: stepping inside, you found yourself at a crossroads. To the right, through a swinging saloon door, the eating area. To the left, a pathetic gift shop the size of a medium-sized bathroom. "Gifts" seemed to include gum, magazines, T-shirts of questionable taste, crossword puzzle books, and, beneath a glass case, a bunch of tacky little figurines and things like sand dollars with tiny shells glued to the surface. (All of which added up to about twice as much seashell as I thought any person really needed in a single tchotchke.) Straight ahead, a turnstile led out to a pier that stretched into water.

Yet another blonde was halfheartedly manning the register

of the gift shop. She was slouched behind the counter with her bare, dirty feet propped on the glass case, looking like the boredest person on earth as she flipped through a terrible-seeming women's magazine called *Her Place*. Although she was sitting directly under a No Smoking sign, she, too, was smoking a long, skinny cigarette. I found myself staring at her, and she looked up from her magazine and smiled. I looked away.

"Howdy," Dad said to the girl. She looked at him like he was crazy. "We're just going to grab a bite to eat," he clarified, to which he received a confused half nod in response. But out of the corner of my eye as I turned to follow him, I thought I saw her wink at me. I brushed it off as just my imagination and decided to look into causes and symptoms of heatstroke when I got home.

We pushed through the saloon doors and took seats in the restaurant, which was decorated to suit a nautical theme. I could actually hear Dad's stomach making angry gurgling noises from across the table. We all just sat there looking at one another. Even Jeff had nothing to say.

After we'd been waiting for several minutes in absolute silence, the waitress finally sidled up to us. She was angular and statuesque and had her hair piled on top of her head with a few ball-point pens in an elaborate origami. Her eye shadow gave her eyes an exotically trashy aspect, and her red spaghetti-strap tank was cut to reveal a supple, copious helping of cleavage in which a small necklace dangled, a curled seashell in sunset colors.

More seashells. Another blonde. She was standing there, poised to take our orders. We stared up at her expectantly. She stared back.

"Hi," I said.

"Hi," Jeff said eagerly.

"I'm Crystal," the waitress said. I was glad she had cleared up the pronunciation, because her faded plastic name tag read "Kristle." *Like gristle*, I thought. The name tag had a blob of dried ketchup on it: a rancid comma. There's nothing sicker to me than the smell of ketchup—dried ketchup especially—but I'll be real with you. Stupid name and dried ketchup or not, she was gorgeous. Maybe a little tan before her time, but hot nonetheless.

"What can I get for you boys?" she asked, pulling one of her pens from her updo without disturbing it in the slightest. She had an accent—practically unidentifiable, but foreign for sure. I looked back down at my menu, still undecided between a burger and a steak and cheese—I was leaning toward the burger because I didn't know about the wisdom of getting a steak and cheese in the American South—and that's when I felt her hand on my shoulder. I looked up slowly and saw both my father and brother staring at me with expressions that were flipping between surprise, amusement, and *what the fuck*. Kristle gave my neck a tender squeeze.

"Got a little sunburn there," she said. I couldn't tell if she was making fun of me.

"Uh, burger," I said, doing that thing where you stare straight ahead and look at a person at the same time.

"One burger," Kristle said.

When she took my menu from me, her fingers brushed against my wrist, and I felt a tiny tingle shoot up my arm and into my chest.

After she'd walked away, my father made an exaggerated face like, *okay now*, and Jeff gave me a look of befuddled consternation.

When we were finished eating, my father and Jeff went down to look at the beach, and I paid a dollar to the gift shop girl for a ticket to the fishing pier. She took my dollar, reached into a drawer, pulled out a ticket, and ripped it in half before handing me the stub. As she gave it to me, it was like she let her fingers rest in my palm a split second longer than usual.

I took it from her, weirded out, and walked away without saying anything.

I walked out to the pier alone, past old grizzled fishermen with leathery brown skin and scraggly beards and those little hats and buckets of bait and everything. When I got to the end, I lingered against the side, just to look like I had some purpose for being out there, like maybe I was waiting for someone to deliver my fishing rod.

I watched my father and Jeff in the distance. They were in the sand together and were now standing and chatting. It was weird. I was so sick of my father, and the last thing in the world I wanted to do was talk to him, but seeing him and Jeff talking so easily I felt left out. It looked like they were having some kind of intense conversation, standing facing the water, Jeff with his arms folded high on his chest as he nodded thoughtfully, the wind whipping his hair in every direction and the late-afternoon sun glowing on his face. I wondered what they could possibly be talking about. Maybe Dad was still talking about how great the fucking french fries were "down here." (Mine had been soggy and unremarkable.)

I watched them for a few minutes and finally—reluctantly—decided to join them. And when I turned around, I saw one of the girls from the restaurant standing behind me. Not Kristle, not the girl at the gift shop, but the girl who had been smoking out front when we'd walked in. She was just standing there, right behind me, not doing anything, just smiling and looking me up and down.

She was prettier up close than she'd looked earlier. Her eyes were green with gold rings around the pupils, and her nose was large and aquiline—the kind of nose most of the girls I went to school with would probably have been begging to have replaced. It made her more beautiful. Her breasts were just as unavoidable as before, and her hair was cascading down her back in clumped, luxuriously greasy tangles. Her shorts were unbuttoned and folded down at the waistband, revealing a half inch of her smooth, sharp hip bones.

"Hi," I said. I wondered if it was a southern thing not to speak unless you were spoken to.

"Hey," she said. She reached into the waistband of her cutoffs and pulled out a package of cigarettes. "Do you have a light?" she asked, placing a cigarette between her full and glossy lips. She had the same accent that Kristle had. It was soft and fluid and could have been French or Scottish or South African or anything really.

"No," I said. "Sorry."

"I think I have one anyway," she said, and, without hesitation, pulled a hot-pink Bic from her pocket. She lit up and took a deep drag. "Do you want one?" she asked.

"No thanks," I said.

She looked me in the eyes and smiled. "What's your name?" she asked.

"Sam," I said.

"Hey, Sam," she said. "I'm DeeDee."

"Hey, DeeDee," I said.

She raised her eyebrows. "You're cute." She blew a puff of smoke into my face. "See you soon, I'm sure," she said as she turned and walked away. "Thanks for the light."

YOU

We have always known you. Before we even saw you, we knew you. We have known you every time. We will know you the next time.

You have been many things and many people. You have always been the same.

We wait for you every summer. We wait to see who you will appear as this time. The line of your shoulders, the arc of your smile. The things that you find funny and the things that trouble you. We are always surprised.

We are always surprised, but one thing is always the same. There is one thing we can count on. You will always leave us. You will always, always break our hearts.

Or is it just the other way around?

FOUR

AFTER A FEW days there was no question at all. The girls had taken notice. Everywhere I went, they smiled at me. They stared. They swiveled their hips a little more when I walked near, pushed their boobs up a little higher. Their hair was always tossing, tossing, tossing; their eyes sparked and pulsed like flakes of mica at the bottom of a creek.

It made me nervous.

It's not that I minded the attention. I was as flattered and turned on as any person would be to have insanely hot girls staring at him wherever he went. I'd be sitting alone on the beach, putting on sunblock or walking to the store or whatever, and suddenly there would be this electricity in the air, and I'd look up and see a girl, unflinching, hair blowing behind her like in a music video, just staring, maybe with the hint of a smile, or, if not, with that fake-o insouciant pucker that people learn from watching television. They were always smiling, always daring me to make my move. They never came near me, though, and never said anything. They were waiting for me.

I don't really like dares, even implied ones. I think if someone wants something from you they should ask directly. Anything else is just passive aggression.

So I did not make any move. I was suspicious. I didn't know what to make of any of it. Girls had never looked at me like this before—they had always turned to Sebastian or Jeff or whoever first, with me as a second choice if not necessarily a last resort. Now, even with Jeff right next to me—even with him casually flexing his pecs for show—it was like I was the only guy left on earth.

If I was the only one who had noticed what was going on that might be one thing—you could chalk it up to my imagination, hubris, wishful thinking, whatever. But Jeff saw it too. In fact, it was pissing the hell out of him. He was used to commanding all attention.

"You wearing some kind of special cologne or something?" he asked. "You're working some crazy voodoo on those bitches." He was trying to sound obliging, but there was annoyance in his voice. In the week since our arrival at the beach, he had started primping before we left the house, taken to wearing sleeveless shirts and swimming laps in the ocean out beyond the breakers every day, going for jogs—the whole drill. He was trying to keep himself in fighting form, maybe attract a few glances of his own. It was no use. The girls wanted me.

Okay, maybe I'm overstating things a little bit. It wasn't *all* of them. The thing that's hard to explain is that there were other girls too. There were girls, and then there were Girls. You could tell the difference. It's hard to say exactly what separated them, except that the *other* girls were just regular girls—I mean, the kind I go to school with. Some were pretty; some were busted. Some were fat; some were thin; some were a little of both. Blondes, brunettes, whatever. They were on vacation. They were with their families, with their boyfriends, walking along the beach, whatever, and they would be leaving in a week or two. Those girls didn't pay any attention to me.

It was the Girls who cared. The Girls who were all tall and blond and a little strange looking, all of them young and beautiful but odd. Who seemed sort of alien, who worked in the stores and the restaurants and at the surfboard rental shacks. These were girls you wouldn't be able to imagine living anywhere else but here, except that they seemed out of place *here*, too. Not just because of that weird accent, but also because of the way they drifted without purpose, hesitant and distracted looking, almost like they weren't ever sure where they were going. DeeDee. Kristle. The gift shop girl. The rest.

When they passed me, they stared and smiled.

Again, it was fucking weird. I couldn't piece it together. So I didn't bother. I just tried to ignore it, just went on doing my thing. For our first week and a half at the beach I continued waking up early and taking walks alone, always to the pink hotel, where I would sit for a few minutes before returning home.

It was a ritual that I enjoyed. I liked the melancholy of it; I liked the solitary feeling of being alone against the backdrop of peeling paint and happy vacationers. It was like being the last survivor of a civilization, like the crowds around me weren't even real but just lingering echoes from other, beachier times. Sometimes I would try to eavesdrop on their conversations, but they all just sounded like squawking birds.

I would often return from my walks to find Jeff in the sand on the shore near our cottage, sometimes asleep, sometimes playing some dumb-ass game on his iPhone, sometimes squinting to read a book (he was halfheartedly working his way through *Infinite Jest*, although when I asked him what it was about, all he said was, "Hell if I fuckin' know"). Something seemed to be bothering him. I figured it had to be the lack of sex, which he'd previously made a point of indicating he was used to on a very regular basis. He had stopped bothering with his plans for getting me laid. He had himself to worry about now.

One morning I woke early, ready to go walking, only to see Jeff waiting for me at the kitchen table with an uneaten bowl of Froot Loops in front of him. The milk had turned a deep and sickening brown. He looked up at me with a woeful, cross expression.

"Hey," I said. "You're up early."

Jeff scowled but at the same time pushed his thick, dark eyebrows together entreatingly. "Where do you go?" he asked.

"What do you mean?" I asked.

"Every morning," he said. "Every morning you're off on some

trip of your own. Where are you going?"

"Nowhere," I said. "I mean, I just like walking. It's not like there's anywhere to go. In case you hadn't noticed."

"I've fucking noticed, that's for fucking sure," Jeff said. And then a pause. "Can I come with you?"

I didn't answer right away. It's hard to be alone when you're accompanied by your older brother, who never shuts up. But the look in Jeff's eyes was bordering on pathetic. "Please?" he asked. "I'm dying here, bro. I can't take a whole fucking summer of this. I mean, I'm lonely. Shit, man, I'm lonely as fuck. Dad . . ." He trailed off. He didn't have to say it.

"All right," I said. "Well let's go, then."

We walked to my hotel. "This is what you do every day for three hours?" Jeff asked.

"Yep," I said.

"Why?" he asked.

"I just like it."

Jeff kicked at the water. "Where do you think she is?" he asked after a while. I was surprised to hear him bring it up. I had assumed that Jeff had been oblivious to my mother's disappearance, but it appeared that I'd been wrong.

I thought for a second before I answered him. "I think she's gone," I finally told him.

"Well, clearly," he said. "But where is she? I mean *where*?"

Where was she? "She's in the land of women," I said. "A place we cannot even begin to comprehend. Don't think too hard about it; it's like staring directly into the sun."

"I can't stop thinking about it," he said. "I mean, you were *there*. You saw it all go down. All I've heard is stories, and I've barely even heard them."

Lucky you, I thought.

"How could she have just left?" Jeff asked. His voice sounded wounded and pathetic. "Where is this supposed Women's Land anyway?"

"She says it's more of a state of mind than an actual location. A state of mind that in this specific case exists somewhere near Cleveland? But look around, dude."

Jeff and I surveyed the beach together. Everywhere we looked were Girls.

"Maybe we're there already," I said.

"Let's go home," Jeff said.

"Okay," I said. So we turned around and made our way back down the beach.

We had not spoken about the girl in the surf since the night we'd seen her. I can't explain why except to say that, for my part, she had grown slippery in my memory. I had to fight to even think about her. Every time I tried to picture her in my mind, I ended up completely off the mark. It was like trying to pick up a droplet of mercury. Had she existed? Had we seen her? I can't say.

We were halfway back home when we saw Dad. I recognized the way he moved before I could make out his face: the defeated shuffle, the head bobbing back and forth like he was trying to gauge the origin of a distant tune. His gray, hairy, and ever-growing paunch jiggling over the waistband of his faded and too-small swimsuit. Jeff saw him too.

"What the hell is he doing?"

I squinted to see what Jeff was talking about, and noticed that Dad was swinging a long, thin rod in front of him, back and forth, back and forth, slow and deliberate like a blind person with a cane.

When we were near enough to see better, Jeff let out a low whistle. "Holy shit. He's gone off the deep end," he said. "I mean, he's really fuckin' crazy."

"*Now* you see," I said.

Our father had evidently bought a metal detector. He was floating along the beach, waving it around, doubling back on himself, moving in circles. He was searching for something. A pink fanny pack dangled under his belly.

"Hey, Padre!" Jeff shouted when we were in striking distance. Dad didn't look up; he was staring intently at the sand. "Pops!" Jeff called out. "Whatcha doin'?"

Dad waved happily and raised his sunglasses, a grin spreading across his face. "Looky what I bought!" he called. "A man's got to make a living somehow, right?" he said. (Did I mention that our father had quit his job of twenty years on a day's notice? All to come *here*?) "I'm already having some luck, too. Look." He reached into his fanny pack and pulled out a pair of rusty earrings, dangling them in the air and waggling his eyebrows like he'd uncovered the Holy fucking Grail itself.

"So you're . . ." Jeff seemed at a loss.

"Looking for buried treasure," Dad said. "There's gold in

them thar hills! I mean this here beach. I found a book about it at the bookstore—apparently this whole beach was settled by pirates. Dollars to donuts, I'll find some of their booty if I just look hard enough."

"Uh-huh," Jeff said.

"Get ready to be rich beyond your wildest dreams! This little device here might just be the key to our future." He grinned hopefully. (Or maybe it was hopelessly. I've noticed lately that there's often no practical difference between the two.)

"Yo ho ho," Jeff said. He didn't seem to be able to muster the enthusiasm required.

I didn't bother at all; I stared at Dad and he just shrugged and drifted down the beach without another word as his metal detector pulled him on his way. Jeff looked sidelong in my direction and dropped to the ground into a set of anxious push-ups. Whatever.

So I turned my back to him and waded into the water, deeper and deeper, ignoring the chill, hopping over the waves at my calves until I was almost up to my nuts. A swell hit me square in the chest, but I didn't move. The waves were crashing and crashing, but I stood firm, one leg in front of the other and bent at the knee. I was solid and unwavering. Like this I blocked the ocean with my body. Then I dove right in, somersaulted into the water, and crawled along the ocean's floor, squinting to see my hands as shadowy impressions in the muck of sand and salt. When I surfaced, everything seemed different in a way I couldn't place. I decided to swim farther out.

I am not what you would call a strong swimmer. I mean, I

know how to do it and everything—if I fell off the side of a boat in open water I probably wouldn't die for at least a few minutes unless I was eaten by an octopus—but compared to Jeff with his wall of swim-team medals and Sebastian with his summer lifeguarding job, I basically suck.

I didn't care. That day, for whatever reason, I was unashamed of my clumsy, amateur stroke. I just swam. I swam a lame-ass crawl out as far as my arms could carry me, over the waves, out to clear and placid ocean, beyond where my feet could touch comfortably—to a place where my toes could scrape the sand for only seconds before the water rose and carried me with it, paddling. I flailed for a while, bouncing on my toes, then floating on my back, then treading water. I knew I was out way too far. I wouldn't even normally be able to swim the length of a swimming pool without having to catch my breath, but somehow I had made it out here, out to where Jeff appeared on the shore as just a speck among specks. (Speck-Jeff was now doing crunches, which is how I could tell him from the rest.)

The world felt light-years away. I felt light-years from myself. The feeling was nothing new.

So I stayed where I was, scrambling to tread water, hoping that if I kept afloat long enough, a mysterious current might happen on me and pull me away, not back to land, but out to some deserted island that was secret and better.

I could have drowned. I mean, I totally could have. And just like on the first night in the surf, it occurred to me that I felt something like hands grabbing at my ankles as I struggled for traction. Maybe it was a whisper in my ear, urging me not to bother.

Out there in the water, just trying to keep my head above the waves, I felt at home, or at least closer to home. I could have drowned. I could have wanted to.

I turned onto my back and floated, staring at the sky, at the clouds, the birds—which that day reminded me of fish in their arcing laziness. I thought about nothing. I let myself float. I didn't try to swim; I didn't try to head back for the shore. I wasn't even trying not to drown. I was just staying afloat.

But then, out of nowhere, I started to feel something pushing me toward land. It wasn't the water itself—not the lucky current I had been waiting for—but instead an unsettling gravity that I can't describe, a pull emanating from a place somewhere deep below the water's surface. I guess it was close to an *intention*: not my own, but something belonging to the ocean that was unhooking the invisible grasping hands from my body and urging me to get my ass out of there. I had the strangest feeling of my mother being nearby. Or maybe not my own mother, but a mother of some kind.

When I turned my head to find the shore, I was suddenly dazzled. The edge of the beach was so bright that I could no longer see Jeff in his calisthenics or the bologna-scarfing blanket-liers, or the umbrellas or the dunes. I couldn't even see the sand. It was all shrouded in a blinding and otherworldly light, a veil of brightness that I knew was there for my benefit. Something was being hidden from me. But also: something was revealing itself to me in the hiding.

I felt a burning in my eye sockets and I wanted to look away, but I didn't. Instead, I squinted, still floating on my back but half sitting up while I made a fist and held it to the slit of my eye, loosening it in the tiniest increments until I could see again, just barely. I was fairly certain that I was hallucinating—that a combination of exertion and sun and lack of oxygen had led me to a temporary insanity. But even if it was only because I had gone totally fucking insane, I couldn't deny what I was seeing. In the dunes, I could see the indistinct but unmistakable silhouettes of what looked like hundreds of figures lined up shoulder to shoulder as far as I could see in either direction. They were nearly identical, and all perfect. They were all the same height, all of them an elegant swoop of shoulders, breasts, and hips. And they were just standing there in a line in the dunes, staring at me, shining on me, calling to me to come back in.

Feeling light-headed, I ducked under the water and when I came back up for air, everything was normal again. I could see Jeff now, more clearly than ever, almost clearly enough to make out his face even. He was sitting in the sand with someone blond and beautiful at his side. He appeared to be laughing.

And soon the waves were rising behind me and I felt stronger, and then I touched my feet to the ocean's floor and I was stronger still, and then a huge wave was curling at my back and I threw myself into it and it swallowed me comfortably. Soon I was crawling breathless in the surf, and I stood in the warmth of the sun and pulled my drooping bathing suit back up over my bare ass. My shoulders felt broader than ever and the sun was hot and I knew that up and down the beach eyes were on me, even if I couldn't see them anymore. I didn't care. I liked it.

So I stumbled up onto the sand, rubbing the salt water from my eyes. When my vision was clear, the Girls were unmistakably gone—as I'd basically known they would be, because after all they were surely just my imagination in the first place. But I saw that Jeff was sitting in the sand with the waitress from the Fisherman's Net. *Kristle.* Rhymes with "crystal." She looked up at me and smiled as I approached. Jeff seemed not to notice.

He was too busy ogling her tits. She had her hand on his thigh but she was looking at me with a hungry glint in her eyes. When I say hungry, I mean literally, like she wanted to actually eat me.

"Dude," Jeff said.

"Dude," I said.

"Hey," Kristle said. She tossed her hair and squeezed Jeff's thigh harder. She inched her hand up toward his package without taking her burning green eyes off me.

"Kristle's having a birthday party tomorrow," Jeff said. "We're totally going. I mean, even *you're* invited."

"Well in that case," I said.

That night, we played Scrabble with my father with CNN blaring on the television. Jeff is the annoying kind of Scrabble player who plays a lot of obscure two-letter words that shouldn't count but for whatever reason are considered legitimate. My father is the annoying kind of Scrabble player who takes hours with his turn and then plays deliberately misspelled words that no one has the heart to call him out on. I am the perfect Scrabble player, both serious and considerate. Obviously I lost by a lot.

There was a hole in the screen door and mosquitos were buzzing everywhere, and it was too hot because the air conditioner only worked a little bit, and that horrible woman on CNN would not shut up about some mother in Ohio who had murdered her entire family with a ballpoint pen. I asked Dad to turn it off but he said he liked "the background noise," so I went out onto the porch just to get away from the blue Paper Mate that was beckoning enticingly from the kitchen counter.

I stood on the porch in the dark, letting the salty breeze moisten my skin. The dusty cul-de-sac of rentals was quiet and the sky was foggy black, the moon obscured by clouds.

I was considering walking down to the beach alone when I started to notice strange glowing points in the distance. At first I thought they were stars, but they were too yellow and too vivid, and anyway they weren't in the sky. Then I thought they were fireflies, but they weren't blinking, and do they have fireflies at the beach?

I squeezed my eyes shut and when I opened them, the glowing flecks were everywhere. They still weren't blinking, but they were pulsing, almost imperceptibly getting bigger, then smaller, then bigger again, and maybe moving, too, like from side to side or bobbing up and down. Some were bigger than others, implying closeness.

They reminded me of eyes staring at me. It would be absolutely stupid to think they were eyes. I couldn't think of what else they could be, though. It must have been my imagination.

NAME

We come here without names. There are the names they call us. But those aren't our names.

The names they call us are not hard to guess. Comehere, Wheresmyfood, Trysmilingsometime, and Suckonthis are four common ones, but the list goes predictably on from there and only gets uglier.

Those are the names they call us. Those are not our names. We choose our own names. We choose names from television reruns and dusty paperbacks and celebrity magazines and names from the sides of packages we like. There are always Bibles around, but we hate the names in the Bible. They feel old-fashioned and remind us of our father anyway.

We name ourselves after shampoos and perfumes and dishwasher detergents. We do have one rule: no one is allowed to call herself L'Oréal anymore. We kept getting in fights over who got to be L'Oréal, so a rule was established. We've since had a few Pantenes, but not enough to cause problems.

You have no idea how important a name is. You have always known your name. You have no idea what it means to be nameless, or to have the gnawing feeling that your name is only an imitation. An approximation of what is unpronounceable, what is unknowable, what is limitless. What's really in the end just inexpressible.

The names we give ourselves are like drawings of God. Well, that sounds dramatic. But that's how it feels. So call us Dramatic. We've been called worse.

FIVE

"WE'RE GETTING YOU laid tonight, bro," Jeff was saying. "I mean, we're getting both of us laid tonight. It's gonna change your life, dude. Dad was hell of right about this place. It's unbelievable. Where the fuck did all these girls come from? I mean, dude. I mean, dude! That fuckin' Kristle, dude."

It was a question I'd had too. Where had they come from? They were everywhere: every time you looked around it seemed like they had multiplied. They were all beautiful. They were all blond, in chest-baring tops, with eyes that changed depending on the light. They all looked like sisters but they couldn't be sisters, because sisters have parents, and the Girls seemed to have none. They were just *there*. Like they had appeared out of nowhere. No, not nowhere. Like they had crawled straight out of the ocean. (It goes without saying that girls don't just crawl from the ocean, but anyway.)

"It seems like they're foreign, right?" I wondered. "Kristle sort of has an accent, you know? It sounds like she might be faking it, I guess. I never heard of a French person named Kristle."

"Maybe it's the Americanized version of Kris*tal*," Jeff said, pronouncing it in the manner of a champagne-swilling rapper. "Very classy."

"Ha," I said.

"Oh, who gives a fuck," Jeff said. "The point is they're hot and they're here. I just hope they're already drunk when we get to the party. I hope they're ready for a piece of *this*." He groped his crotch obnoxiously, and I looked at him like he was made out of shit, wondering how it was possible that I was related to this idiot.

He just laughed. "Have a sense of humor, bro," he said. "I'm just fuckin' with ya. The truth is I'm the biggest goddamn gentleman you'll ever fuckin' meet."

He and I were on our way to Kristle's birthday party. It was close enough to walk—everything around here was close enough to walk, if you had time—so we were walking. The night was warm, and I could feel the damp air soaking in through the hairs on my arms, which were standing on end despite the fact that I was not at all chilly. Jeff was excited as hell about the party, parties being his natural habitat, but I wasn't especially looking forward to it.

I've never really liked parties. I mean, maybe *dislike* is too strong of a word; I guess it's more like I've just never gotten the point. A bunch of people standing around not talking to each other because the music is so loud, all pretending to have a good time, chugging warm beer, and pretending to be much drunker than they actually are. What is really the point?

The event was being held at an empty rental not too far from ours. One of Kristle's roommates was a receptionist for the Realtor and had "borrowed" the key for the night. Jeff had forgotten to write down the exact address, but it turned out to be unnecessary. From a block away I could already feel the bass thumping in my chest, and when we followed the sound of the music and turned the corner into another beachfront development, there was no mistaking which house was hosting us. There it was, at the very end of the block, right on the dunes: towering and Adderall blue and glowing from within, with kids hanging off the porches and trailing out of the driveway into the street. Every few seconds a whoop would ring out and there would be a splash or the crash of shattering glass followed by raucous laughter and maybe an ear-piercing scream or a "Dude!"

"Shit, man," Jeff said. "This is gonna be good." I had my doubts but I'd already made up my mind not to be a complete dishrag. I just smiled and nodded.

Jeff became one with the party as soon as we stepped inside. He surveyed the scene, gave me a quick punch in the shoulder—"You'll be okay, right, bro?"—and then was gone. The place was filled, mostly with men. Or boys, I guess. Or man-boys. All of the above really, because it was all kinds of guys: fratty guys in oxfords and white baseball caps, long-haired sun-leathered beach dudes, wan and dazed-looking out-of-towner preppies in boat shoes and popped collars who looked like they had gotten lost on their way to somewhere else. There was even a clutch of dad-aged dudes standing in the corner sucking down beers and watching the scene from the sidelines, looking hell of creepy.

The Girls were here too, obviously, but they were outnumbered. It was clearly the way they liked it. It was Kristle's party, after all, and her guest list. The Girls were scattered throughout the place, each one holding court individually as the center of her own tiny universe. They were vamping and tossing their hair and shotgunning beers, shimmying their hips to the music, smoking cigarettes with calculated carelessness, while the guys circled them and ogled and competed for their attention. It only took a second of casual eavesdropping to tune in to the stupid jokes the guys were all telling in some dumb competition for the Girls' fakey, too-loud laughter.

The only people who seemed at all out of place (besides me of course) were the few, scattered normal girls—girls with mousy hair and unremarkable scowls who had surmisably not been invited themselves but had simply been dragged along by their oblivious boyfriends. These girls were standing at the fringes of clusters with their arms folded, staring at the ceiling, looking unhappy. Well, at least I wasn't one of *them*. At least I could blend in, sort of.

I cast around, hoping to see someone I recognized, but I did not. I don't know who I was hoping for. It's not like there was any reason I would know a single person here except for Kristle herself, and even that was a stretch. Maybe I had some outlandish fantasy that Sasha Swain or any one of my friends from school—even Sebastian!—would just pop out of nowhere, all

Dude, what are you doing here? You didn't tell me you were coming to this too. It's crazy, right? Look at all these hos! But no. Of course that was totally impossible.

I resigned myself to the fact that I was on my own and pushed my way through the packed crowd of happy, drunk strangers, heading first for the kitchen to grab a beer from the island and then out through the sliding glass doors onto the wraparound porch, where I looked out over the beach and the ocean and sipped slowly. I hoped that no one would notice me standing there all alone. It was embarrassing.

I was alone. I just was. I had been alone for months. I had made a hobby of it.

As lonely as I was, I ignored the Girls who approached me. I'd gotten used to it by then. They'd wander up and stare at me for a few seconds, sometimes openly and sometimes with mild subtlety, but either way they'd go away if I didn't say anything.

It seems stupid that I didn't say anything, but for some reason I just felt like talking to strangers would make me feel even lonelier than I already was.

So a half hour later I was still standing by myself, considering the waves with my now warm and nearly empty Bud in hand, while the crowd around me jostled and chugged and laughed some more. Some shit song was thrumming from the stereo inside, but you could barely make out what it was over the noise.

Everyone seemed to be enjoying themselves thoroughly except me. I wondered if I had been this way forever. Had I always been this big of an asshole or was it a new development?

I mean, I guess it was new. There was a time when I enjoyed Budweiser. There was even a time when I enjoyed Beyoncé. I just couldn't remember when that time was.

I was just considering leaving—fuck Jeff—when I found a hand on my elbow. I didn't turn around. Then I felt breasts against my back, and breath in my ear. It smelled like Malibu. A strand of blond hair curled over my shoulder and tickled my chest through the V-neck of my T-shirt, and then a pair of arms wrapped around me from behind. "Hey," a voice whispered. There was that accent. Where did it come from, anyway? It sure as fuck wasn't French. It was Kristle. "You always this antisocial?" she breathed.

"Usually," I said, still without turning.

She untangled herself and moved in next to me. She lit a cigarette and offered me one but I turned it down.

"Happy birthday," I said. No harm in being polite.

"Thanks," she said. She hoisted her beer can with an amiable raise of the eyebrows and a smile, and we clanked, cheersing.

"So how old are you?" I asked. "Or is that rude to ask?"

"Oh—it's not really my birthday," she said. "My birthday's at the end of the summer. I just like to have my *party* at the beginning. The end of the summer's always so depressing. Who wants to have a party when summer's about to end? What's fun about that?"

"I guess nothing," I said, even though it seemed stupid. I could understand throwing a birthday party a few days or even a few weeks before your actual birthday, but jumping the gun by months was a little aggressive. "So how old will you be on your actual birthday then?" I asked.

"Twenty-one," Kristle said, sighing a big cloud of smoke into the night. I watched it curl away in the moonlight, toward the water. "Legal and everything. I don't want to talk about it, okay?" she said. Even though the cigarette was barely started, Kristle tossed it off the porch without bothering to stub it out. "These things'll fuckin' kill you." And she reached into her bra and pulled out a metal Altoids case, which she flipped open to reveal a neat row of perfectly wrapped joints. "A birthday present," she said, smirking and plucking one from the tray. "I forget from who. Splitsies?"

"Sure," I said. She tossed her hair, placed the joint between her lips, and lit it.

"Where'd your brother go?" Kristle took a deep drag and held it, then passed to me.

"Good fuckin' question," I said. I inhaled. The joint was already soggy from Kristle's lip gloss. Hold it. Burn. Breathe. "He's like what you would call unreliable."

"Uh-oh," Kristle said. "I know the type. But fuck him."

She reached out a finger and dragged her long, red nail from my shoulder down my chest, swaying her hips as she did it. Her eyes were burning: green with gold rings around the pupils. I tried to look away but I found that I could not. I instantly had a raging boner.

"You seem like you could be pretty unreliable yourself," she said.

"Well," I said. "I'm not. Sorry."

"So modest." She took another puff from the joint, holding my gaze as she handed it back to me.

I knew I shouldn't have another hit, but I couldn't see any way of turning it down. So I sucked.

"Thanks," I said after a brief coughing fit.

Kristle was casually half dancing to the beat of a song coming from inside. I studied her.

She was beautiful. I mean, she was beautiful but she wasn't: she was both beautiful and ugly at the same time. Her face changed the longer you looked at it, and the more you looked at it the more you couldn't put all the pieces together. Just as it was starting to make sense, it all fell apart. She was a page in a book in a dream where you can't read.

And she was saying something, but I didn't speak the language anymore. All I could focus on was her lips, her eyes, her large and jagged nose. The landscape of her bare collarbone.

I started to feel dizzy. And then Kristle's hands were on my waist and she was kissing my neck. Then her hands were on my ass and her warm tongue was in my mouth. I mean my tongue was in her mouth. I mean both. She pushed me up against the railing, and before I knew what was happening, my hand was on her breast as she nibbled at the corner of my lips. I guess people were probably watching us, but I didn't even consider it at the time. I was gone. I was flying with cement feet.

"Do you want to go upstairs?" Kristle whispered in my ear.

I didn't know what to say. I'm not sure if I was capable of

speech at that point anyway—I might not have been capable of reciting the alphabet. But I was reaching for something that resembled yes when I opened my eyes and saw my brother standing not ten feet away, staring through the crowd. His mouth screwed to one side, brow furrowed, nostrils flaring—more hurt than angry, I thought, but mostly just shocked. He was standing all alone.

"What the fuck?" Jeff said. Kristle let go of me and turned around.

"That's my little brother," Jeff said, speaking of course to Kristle but in a tone of voice that made it sound like he was talking to himself. "He's fucking fifteen," he said, then paused to consider it for a second. "Sixteen," he muttered. "He's fucking sixteen."

"Seventeen," I managed to say.

Jeff didn't hear me. "What the fuck are you doing?" He wasn't actually making eye contact with me or with Kristle but instead was looking sideways toward the ocean.

Kristle seemed unsteady, flailing. She pulled her fingers through her hair, tucked a strand behind her ear.

I could see that I had no choice but to walk away. So that's what I did: I walked away, and as I did, the chatter on the deck stopped abruptly and everyone stared at me. I stumbled and almost fell as I reached to push the sliding doors open but I recovered myself just in time and stepped inside, over the prone body of a passed-out meathead, back into the party, where things had turned uncomfortably wild. The floor was littered with beer cans and there was another guy nearly passed out on the crappy couch, drooling and mumbling to himself. At the kitchen island people were slamming shots and screaming, led by a raucous blonde wearing nothing but a red string bikini and a baseball cap with her ponytail pulled through the back. She was counting off shots as glassy-eyed dudes chugged. "Five!" she shouted. "Can I get six?"

I tried to focus, to modulate my breathing. I tried to pretend I was watching this all on television. I just needed some space.

I just needed to sit by myself and not think about anything. So I padded away from the crowd, down the dark, carpeted stairs into the sandy depths of the house. In the downstairs living room, things were quieter, sort of. The light was dim; on the couch, a girl in gold, lace-up sandals was straddling the lap of a sandy-haired guy who looked about my age, practically sucking his face off.

I didn't want to stare, but I couldn't not. The boy seemed to sense me watching, and he peered out from behind the girl, meeting my eyes with his. He looked blissful and content, drugged, and I turned away and opened the first door I could find. I hoped it would lead to a dark and quiet bathroom where I could lie down on cold tiles and take a nap.

The door did not lead to a bathroom. Instead, I found myself on the threshold of a sparse bedroom, decorated in beachy floral with a fake ficus in the corner and a busted, tiny two-dial television on a dirty wicker chest of drawers. A girl was sprawled on the twin bed nearer to the window reading *Her*

Place and listening to her iPod. It took me a second to realize that it was DeeDee: The girl I'd met on our second day here. The Girl from the pier.

She looked up from her magazine and took her headphones out of her ears. She didn't seem surprised to see me. "Hey, you," she said.

"Sorry," I said. "I was looking for the bathroom."

"I've read this same issue of this same awful magazine three times," she grumbled, tossing the magazine aside. She touched her fingers to the wall behind her and arched her back, stretching casually.

"I'd never heard of it before we got here," I said. "But it seems like it's everywhere now."

"Yeah, well. It was probably put on this island specifically to torment me." She gestured at me with a blue package of cigarettes. "Want one?"

"No thanks," I said.

"I mean, look how depressing this is." She showed me the cover. It did indeed look idiotic. The photo was of a woman I didn't recognize as a celebrity. She was holding a plate of cookies and tossing her hair with a psychotic grin.

DeeDee read a cover line aloud: "'Ten Steps to the Old You! Rediscover the Gal You Used to Be!'" Then another: "'Snack Happy: Slim Your Waist by Improving Your Attitude!' Give me a fucking break. Who reads this? Besides me I mean. Just once I'd like to find a rental stocked with *The Complete Works of Shakespeare*. Almost anything would be better than this shit.

Not *that* much better, but every little thing counts when you're working on your English."

It seemed like her English was fine, unplaceable accent aside, but I didn't question it. I lingered at the threshold, not sure if I should leave her alone or what. Of course I'd wanted to be alone but now I sort of didn't. I couldn't move. It seemed important to be with her now.

DeeDee's eyes glittered with a private joke as she lit her cigarette. I had the weird, impossible feeling that I already knew her. That I had been here before.

"You can come in, you know," she said. "I'm just hanging out. I could use the company."

"People are, like, practically having sex out there," I said. I don't know why I felt the need to say it. "Like right in the open and everything. Well, not full sex, but . . ."

"Typical," DeeDee said. She rolled her eyes extravagantly and then laughed. "Well then come in already!" So I stepped into the room, closed the door behind me, and sat down on the edge of the bed.

"You're not into the party?" I asked.

"I'm so over these parties," DeeDee said. "It was fun at first, but it gets old. Maybe it was never fun. I can't even remember anymore."

"So like, they throw these parties all the time?"

She sighed a sigh that was both cheerful and annoyed. "You don't even know," she said. "Every week it's another one. Sometimes another three, at least at the start of the summer. What else is there to do here, I guess. No one else really likes them either but they won't admit it. It's what we *do*; how can we not like it? At least I'm honest about it. Usually I just find a bedroom to hang out in by myself and read or whatever, but these rental places have the worst books. That's how I get stuck reading the same issue of *Her Place* over and over. I already got sick of the Bible, which is the one other thing they always have. That and mystery novels set at the beach. *The Haunted Boardwalk* and things like that."

"I've never read the Bible," I said. "I didn't know anyone actually read it."

"Well I did," she said. "Three times. It seems like it's going to be a real drag, and some parts really suck, but it actually has some good sections. I like the parts about hos, even if they always come to a bad end. Eat a fucking apple, you're a ho. Open a box, you're a ho. Some guy looks at you: turn to stone, ho. See you later, ho. It's always the same. The best one is Lilith—also a ho, but a different kind of ho. She went and got her own little thing going, and for that she gets to be an eternal demon queen, lucky her. No one likes a ho. Except when they do, which, obviously, is most of the time. Doesn't make a difference; she always gets hers eventually."

Maybe DeeDee's English wasn't so good after all, since I had no clue what the hell she was talking about. Maybe I was making up the whole conversation. It's true that I was stoned out of my mind. Either way, I nodded, trying to appear wise.

"Is all that really in the Bible?"

"No. Some of it. Well, the ho with the apple at least."

"I never thought of her as a ho."

"Think again."

There was an awkward pause while I tried to figure out what I was supposed to say next. "Well I guess I'll go find the bathroom now."

"No," she said. "Stay. Sorry. I'm just—never mind. I mean, I'm joking, you know. Not to mention sort of drunk. Joking's one of those things that you need a good command of the language to pull off; sometimes it comes out wrong. Did you meet Fiesta yet?"

"Who's Fiesta?"

"Just some ho. But not enough of one, I guess. More the Lilith type, I suppose. She's actually pretty great. It's her going away party. I'm going to miss her."

I didn't think to ask where she was going. Later I would wish I had. "I thought it was Kristle's party."

"Kristle thinks every party is hers." She rolled her eyes again, but this time she was smiling. "That's her charm." Then she looked at me knowingly and cocked her head in amiable appraisal. "Let me guess," she said. "She tried to do it with you already?"

"Yeah," I said. "You could say that." I hadn't completely thought of it like that myself, but once DeeDee put it that way . . .

"God," DeeDee said, reaching for an ashtray and stubbing out her cigarette. I couldn't take my eyes off her. "Kristle can be so ridiculous. But who knows what I'd do without her.

Total ho, by the way—not that I'm judging; I actually like hos myself. Maybe I am one—I barely know what counts anymore. Being blond certainly never helped anyone's case. Hey, want to do the quiz?" She fished a pencil from a hidden place in her tangled hair.

"Are you always like this?" I asked.

She squinted at me. "Like what?"

"Like so direct, I guess. Or something."

A troubled look crossed her face. I'd hurt her feelings. "All I asked is if you wanted to do the quiz," she said. "What's so crazy about that?"

"Oh," I said, still unsure how much of this was really happening. "Okay. Quiz time then."

She cleared her throat and folded back the magazine. "Cool," she said. "Ready?" I folded my hands in my lap and then realized that was stupid, so I let them fall to my sides, but that didn't feel right either so I folded them again. "The quiz is 'How Does He *Really* See You?'" DeeDee announced.

"Who's *he*? Like in my case? Aren't *I* the he?"

"Just imagine yourself as someone else. Imagine yourself as someone very stupid. That's what I always do anyway. It's the only way it works." And she began to read aloud. I tried my hardest to pay attention but it was very difficult. "'It's Valentine's Day and your hubby's working late. When he comes home, he brings you (A) a dozen red roses; (B) a string of diamonds; (C)—' Hey, are you listening?"

It was true that I'd already lost my train of thought. As

she'd been reading, DeeDee's voice had started to cave in until it was unintelligible. Now it was all I could do to remember her name.

"Oh my God, you're fucked-up!" DeeDee tossed the magazine aside. "You didn't smoke one of Kristle's joints, did you?"

I shrugged.

"For fuck's sake. Never smoke Kristle's weed! It's the first rule of everything. You're lucky you're not a girl—you'd have wound up the child bride of some underworld demon ages ago. If anyone ever offers you a pomegranate in his fiery hell-lair *just say no,* okay? Jeez."

I felt a line of nervous sweat forming at my brow. "Wait, what's wrong with Kristle's weed? What's going to happen?"

"Nothing! I mean, it's just really strong," DeeDee said. "Kristle's a total pothead. Her shit will mess you up. She never thinks to warn anyone; I think she actually does it on purpose. Just try to think about something totally neutral and you'll be fine. Here, actually, lie down."

So I lay down next to her on my back and looked at the ceiling, which was suddenly very interesting.

A few minutes later I was feeling slightly better and I turned on my side to face DeeDee. She didn't move.

The small bedroom was filled with smoke and my eyes were stinging. She was reclining next to me, just burning away. The weak light from the lamp on the bedside table clouded with the smoke around her head in a wobbly yellow nimbus. She'd closed her eyes and stretched out, like she had forgotten I was there, but she wasn't asleep. She had a private smile on her face. It all amused her.

I suddenly wanted, more than anything, to kiss her.

I wanted to kiss her to say, you know, I get it. To say, I see how funny and fucked-up it all is too.

Instead of kissing her I stood. "I guess I should go now," I said, hoping she would stop me.

She didn't say anything, but she opened her eyes again and looked at me. I could not interpret her half smile, her slippery gaze. Her languid, curious stretch.

"Hey," she said. I saw several thoughts crossing her face all at once, and I could tell she was about to say one thing and then changed her mind and said something else. "Have fun at the party."

I knew I could stay if I wanted to. And I did want to. I wanted a lot of things, but sometimes it's harder than you would think to take what you want.

"See ya," I said, and left the room.

When I went upstairs, the men were mostly gone and had taken their disgruntled girlfriends with them. It was pretty much only the Girls who were left now, crowded around the kitchen island and jammed together on the couches, intense in their silence, the stereo now blasting Lady Gaga. As they noticed me, a roomful of blond heads all swiveled in my direction in eerie synchronicity.

I looked at them. They looked back at me, expectant. No one said anything.

I moved for the sliding doors that led onto the porch, feeling uncomfortable, but before I was halfway across the room I heard another door opening and turned to see Jeff stepping out of it, disheveled and guilty-looking with Kristle right behind him.

"You ready to go, bro?" Jeff asked, without looking me in the eye. "Looks like the party's kinda shutting down."

"Yeah," I said. "I'm ready to go." We left.

MAGIC

We have been searching for an enchanted mirror.

Where we come from, it's redundant to talk about enchanted mirrors, as all mirrors are enchanted. Around here, enchanted mirrors are scarce. We're not from around here. But you're probably starting to understand that.

The truth is that none of us remember ever finding an enchanted mirror in this dried-out place. There are rumors, yes; some of the older girls think they recall hearing stories. Was it Brenda who discovered one that time? Or was it Kelly? And where was it again? How could we forget something so important?

Once, Nalgene thought she found one in a dressing room at the outlet mall, but it was a false alarm. We sent a delegation to investigate, and it was finally decided that it was just one of those mirrors that makes you look skinnier than normal— which isn't enchanting at all. It's just a way of trying to trick you into buying jeans. Everyone was annoyed with Nalgene for weeks after, but she's not the brightest among us and has always been insecure about her weight, so we eventually forgave her.

We avoid calling them magic mirrors because we don't believe in magic. Enchantment—okay, fine. Maybe. Magic is what our father commands. We don't want to give him the satisfaction of believing in him.

We barely know what we believe. Even though we don't believe in it, we suspect we might have certain magics at our own disposal. Silly magic, nothing useful, but magic nonetheless. We try not to think about that.

Our father is the Endlessness. Our mother is the Deepness. Our brothers are Speed and Calm. (Calm is easier to get along with, but he can be dull.) We don't know who we are.

That's why we need that mirror. If only we could find one. Well, it might not solve everything, but it would make things more straightforward.

SIX

"COME ON," JEFF said as I was emptying the dishes after dinner a few nights after Kristle's birthday. Or was it Fiesta's going away party? And did anyone have a normal name around here? "Get your ass in gear, little bro."

It took me longer than it should have to decide which exact flavor of disgusted look to shoot at him, but after a few seconds I settled on *mortified, could vomit* and was pretty satisfied with that choice. "I don't karaoke," I said flatly. "It's, like, one of my basic guiding principles in life. I don't dump in public bathrooms and I don't do karaoke. Fact."

"Oh no," Jeff said. He stepped behind me, turned off the sink, and closed the dishwasher, then took me firmly by the shoulders and pointed me to the door. "No way. You're not getting away with that. Fact. No brother of mine's going to get away with *not doing* karaoke. It's like saying you don't believe in love."

"I thought *you* were the one who didn't believe in love. Weren't you basically telling me that the first night we got here?"

"Dude," he said disbelievingly. "Dude! Me? I *believe* in love. I just think it's not for everyone. Karaoke, on the other hand, can be enjoyed by all. Including you. It'll change your fuckin' life, little brother. Come on. Let's go." He slapped my back, yanked the door open, and shoved me out into the dark.

I had become aware of Jeff's burgeoning proclivity for drunken, musical showboating in crummy bars based on a few cursory investigations into his Facebook profile, where the last year's worth of photos often depicted him frozen in time with his face contorted into pop histrionics, his eyes always glazed and unfocused, a glowing blue screen hovering around his shoulder. At first it had seemed out of character for him to have developed such an extravagantly lame habit, but then I thought about it a little more and realized that, no, it was pretty much totally something he would be into.

He had shoved me down the steps and halfway across the driveway when it became certain that there was no way I was getting out of this. "Fine," I said. "I'll go, but I'm not singing."

"Everyone says that their first time," he said. "We'll see."

Kristle was waiting for us on the beach road. There was a small part of me that was hoping she'd bring DeeDee, but she was alone. Her eyes went to me first, mild boredom briefly flickering into something else, but then she looked at my brother. I had no idea what she was thinking. "Hey, boys," she said. "I hope you've been warming up your vocal chords."

Jeff did a falsetto yodel into the night and the two of them headed off ahead of me, his arm around her waist. I decided to follow.

Ursula's was packed when we got there, mostly with locals, but there were a few tourists and some of the Girls too. I looked around, sifting through their faces, but none of them were DeeDee. So I thumped down onto a stool at the bar, where a Girl I thought I recognized was tending. Without waiting for my order, she handed me a can of Budweiser, the tab already popped. I moved for my wallet but she waved me off. It was just as well because I was pretty sure I didn't have any cash on me.

"Thanks," I said.

"Don't thank me. Underage boys drink free tonight," she said. "Just Bud, though—don't start bugging me for piña colada this, tequila sunrise that. This isn't *Cocktail*, okay? And anyone who sings 'Kokomo' gets kicked out. House policy."

"Okay," I said, taking a long chug. "I don't really know what any of that stuff is anyway. I saw you at Kristle's party, right?"

"Probably," she said. "I was there. But I've been told that we all look the same. So it could have been someone else, too."

"I'm Sam," I said.

"Taffany," she said with a hurried smile, turning to fuss with a rag over a bunch of glasses. "So what are you singing tonight?"

"I don't sing."

She rolled her eyes. "Oh, sure," she said. "One of *those*." And she slid a big book across the bar to me. The song list. "Every-one sings here," she said. "Even me. And I *really* don't sing, all right? Just remember—*no 'Kokomo.'*"

I shrugged and started looking through the book, but I had barely made it through the first page (10,000 Maniacs; 3 Doors Down; 4 Non Blondes; 5th Dimension, The) when there was a screech of feedback and then a voice over the PA. "Jeff? Do we have Jeff here? Let's get Jeff up here to start the night off with a bang!" I groaned, registering a rustling in the corner of the room, and then my brother was bounding through the crowd to the makeshift stage near the back. I swiveled my stool around to see a leathery guy with a tidal wave of gray hair handing him the microphone. Jeff was clutching a frozen drink with a pink umbrella in his free hand and he began to pogo maniacally, sloshing it everywhere, until the host raised a warning finger at him. Chastened, Jeff lifted his drink to the crowd and the microphone to his mouth.

"Who here *believes*?" he asked breathily. There was a smat-tering of unenthusiastic applause. "This one's for my little brother!" he shouted, and then, more quietly, added, offhand, "Who could *believe* a little more. In something—I don't really know what." At that, he launched into an earnest, caterwauling rendition of "Don't Stop Believin'."

"Of course," I heard Taffany mutter. "Just once in my life I want one of these assholes to surprise me by singing something other than 'Don't Stop Believin'.'"

"That's my brother," I said apologetically.

Taffany looked sympathetic.

I glanced down at the beer in my hands and tried to focus on it, hoping that it would suddenly develop a new fascinating aspect to distract me. The alternative—paying attention to my brother's performance—was too unbearable to contemplate. But as hard as I stared, the beer remained boring. When Jeff was at the part of that song that he had decided called for ear-splitting screeching, Taffany winced and slid me another Bud even though the first one was only half-empty.

"Your brother does this a lot, huh?" she asked as he was doing his post-performance victory lap, high-fiving everyone in the audience who could be bullied into it. "I guess he's the type."

"Apparently," I said.

"Jimmy's gonna get sick of him fast," she said.

"Jimmy?" I asked.

"The host. That's Janice over there." She pointed to a portly, frosted-haired woman stuffed into a coral-pink halter dress, who was standing behind the sound equipment and fiddling with the knobs. "His wife. They've been doing this for years. They don't appreciate showboaters."

Jeff punctuated this with a high-pitched yowl and took a bow before surrendering the mic back to a scowling Jimmy.

I didn't budge from my stool at the bar. Taffany kept the beer coming, chatting me up distractedly. The terrible singing kept coming too, but it wasn't that hard to ignore—not counting the point in the evening when Janice herself abandoned her post at the sound board to perform a bizarre rendition of a song I somehow knew to be from the Broadway musical *Les Misérables*.

Taffany paid no attention; she was obviously used to it all. As Janice and the rest of them sang, she gave me tips for successful karaoke: no songs over four and a half minutes; no Meatloaf; nothing too obscure, they won't get it. I couldn't tell if she liked me or if she would pretty much have the same basic conversation with anyone at all, but I didn't care. At least she was talking to me.

After a while she got distracted by the other customers and left me to my own devices and I just sat there, chilling out alone, sometimes tuning in to whoever was singing, some of whom weren't completely terrible, and other times just drifting into whatever thought occurred to me. More and more of the Girls began to trickle in as the night went on. Some of them tripped the same mild feeling of recognition I'd had when I'd seen Taffany behind the bar, but there was still no DeeDee. Not that I was keeping track, exactly. I hadn't seen her since the night of the party, and I wasn't really expecting to see her again. I just wouldn't have totally minded if I did is all.

At a certain point during a grizzled local's drunken trainwreck performance of "Ruby Tuesday," Jeff plopped himself onto the stool next to me. "So what are you going to sing, bro?" he asked. He raised an eyebrow and gave me a big wink.

"Dude, shut up," I said. "I told you I'm not singing." But he was already scribbling new numbers on slips of paper, evidently planning his next showstopper.

I didn't think about it at all until a half hour later, when I heard my name being called. "Sam? Where's my good man Sam?" It was Jimmy. Everyone in the room began to look around. I tried to sink as low in my seat as I could, but I felt a hand on my back.

"Over here," Jeff called out. He pushed me from my stool. "We've got a winner!"

I looked over my shoulder and shot him the most deadly glare I could muster. "Dude, go," he whispered. "Don't worry. I picked a good song for you. You'll be fantastic."

"I'm going to fucking kill you," I whispered back, but knew I had no choice. I pushed through the crowd, took the mic from Jimmy, and tried not to shake too much as I awaited whatever fate was about to befall me. The music started to play. I recognized the song.

There I was. What else could I do but sing? "'Just yesterday morning they let me know you were gone . . .'"

It was "Fire and Rain," a song my dad had played a million times in the Volvo on family trips, while my mom crooned along in an off-key warble from the passenger's seat and Jeff occupied himself giving me noogies and wet willies, the dusty smell of the AC filling the car, the sun streaming through the windows, and the scenery whizzing by. I hadn't heard it in years—I'd never been a fan, and who was this Suzanne person anyway?— but as soon as the first line was out of my mouth I didn't have to think about it at all, the words came to me without having to follow the bouncing ball on the screen. I could almost hear my mom's voice under mine in a broken harmony, could almost hear my dad's reedy whistle as he weaved in and out of traffic. We were all back in that car again, all of us speeding off toward some destination: my grandmother's house or Hersheypark or camping or somewhere else, anywhere.

Wherever it was we were going, it was a place where we would still be a family. Like we already were; like we always would be. Until someday—now—we weren't.

My turn was over almost before I'd really known it had begun, and when I looked up, I was surprised to see that the audience was still there and that they were all applauding for me. I had been good. Or at least they were doing their best to humor me. I handed the microphone back to Jimmy and stepped aside. It felt like I was stepping into my own body after having been gone from myself for a while.

When I took my seat at the bar, Jeff was looking at me with bemused admiration. "Told you, buddy," he said. "You're a natural. Now to pick the next one . . ."

"Fat fucking chance," I said. But I picked up the book and started flipping through it anyway.

"And now," Jimmy was saying a few minutes later, after a rousing performance of "Like a Virgin" by two recently divorced moms from Philadelphia, "the lovely Miss Kristle's going to sing us one of my favorite tunes." Every single person in the room was drunk now, and even I found myself cheering wildly along with them as Kristle emerged from the crush. Jimmy fastened the microphone onto the stand.

I was surprised at how tiny she looked; she seemed to shrink as she stepped onto the stage, like Alice in Wonderland walking through a doll-sized door. The stand was too high for her, the microphone pointing to her forehead, and as she struggled to adjust it, her eyes darted around the room. She had a shy, barely there smile on her face. "Hi, everyone," she said, looking down at her feet. The strings came in.

"Sea of Love" is a song I've always hated, but now, with Kristle singing it, it was something entirely different from the song I knew. Her voice was thin and wispy but had a deeper timbre than I'd anticipated, hollow and insubstantial but with a vulnerability that was haunting. It wasn't at all what I had expected. The audience had been wasted and raucous when she'd stepped up, but within seconds they were utterly silent, mesmerized by the spell she was casting.

Without looking over to his spot next to me, I felt something in Jeff change. I felt whatever last bit of himself he'd been holding on to leave him. He was hers now.

The sound that was coming out of her mouth was unearthly and far away. We were all hers, sort of.

And then I found my mind drifting over the ocean, suspended over the waves as Kristle's song echoed out into the distance, into infinity. It was empty and black, so big that it was a little scary.

Then, in my mind, I saw DeeDee. She was walking down the shore alone, coming slowly toward me and into view, her flip-flops dangling from her fingers as she dragged her toes in the sand.

I wondered where she was going. I wondered where she had been. I wondered whether she was thinking about me, and why, in this moment, my mind had turned to her. She was barely there at first, shimmery and foggy—just a cloud of blond hair—but as she got closer she became more and more herself. I'd always thought of all the Girls as looking pretty much the same, but as I watched her approaching, Kristle's song still slow and mellow in my head, DeeDee looked nothing like the rest of them. I just couldn't put my finger on the exact differences.

It was just about then that I heard another voice, and I was back on my stool at the bar, watching Kristle sing. Kristle was no longer alone: somehow DeeDee was up on the stage too, hunched over, leaning in close to the single microphone with her like she had hummed out of a gap in the guitars and just materialized, already singing. Their voices wove in and out of each other's, the same but different, and for a while it was impossible to know whose was whose.

The audience was silent, everyone in the bar staring at them, but DeeDee was concentrating only on the song, adding layers and layers onto Kristle's melody until Kristle receded into the background and DeeDee was the only one I could hear. It had lost all resemblance to the original tune, and then I didn't know what the song was anymore at all. All I knew was that it was beautiful, that DeeDee was beautiful.

And even though she wasn't looking in my direction—even though I'd thought of her only in passing since the night of Kristle's party—I had a certain feeling that she was singing only for me.

When the song ended I'd expected the crowd to disperse, as shocked and dazed by what they'd just seen as I was. But Jimmy just introduced another song and things rolled right on.

I found her outside the bar a few minutes later. DeeDee was smoking on the wooden patio that overlooked a muddy patch of grass. She was leaning out over the railing, swaying her hips in time to the song coming from inside, and when she heard me behind her, she looked up and smiled wordlessly.

"You're a pretty good singer," I said. "You should go on *American Idol* or something."

"Yeah, well," she said. "I don't think that's a very realistic goal. Or whatever. Actually that show makes me sort of sad."

"Me too," I said. "It's depressing as fuck; I hate it."

"I liked hearing you sing," she said, dragging on her cigarette with a half smile like she was challenging me to try to figure out whether she was joking or not.

"You saw me?" I asked.

"Duh. Of course I saw. You were pretty good. Most guys are afraid to choose something like that; they're worried it'll make them look too sensitive or something." She shrugged. "You surprised me, I guess."

I decided not to tell her that song hadn't been my idea or that I'd always thought James Taylor seemed like kind of an asshole.

"Okay, cool," I said. "Sensitive boys doing karaoke make you happy. Check. What else?"

She laughed. She was still laughing as she stood up on her

toes and leaned in to kiss me.

The kiss was drunk and smiling and only lasted a few seconds. "That does," she said. Then she was gone.

"James Taylor," Jeff said when I went back inside a few minutes later. "Works every fuckin' time. Don't say you never learned anything from your big brother. By the way, you have lipstick all over your face."

THE KNIFE

We have learned that we are beautiful.

All of us. We are all beautiful. To those who may read this: we are more beautiful. No matter how beautiful you are, we are more. We just are. It's just the truth. We are the most beautiful. No one has ever told us otherwise.

We say this with no pride at all. We say it, maybe, with a little sadness. Our beauty is a gift that we have had no choice but to accept. We would have been happy with another gift— say, a gift certificate to the outlet mall in Duck. Or a Camaro. (Red, please.) But we were not offered either of those gifts. We were offered only beauty. We took it and we use it. It's nothing special. It's how we survive.

Nothing special: where we come from everyone is beautiful, and each one of us is equally beautiful. (Except our mother, who is a different story.) Where we come from, beauty is so ordinary that it's meaningless. Beauty is so meaningless that there's not even a word for it. (Well—except when it comes to our mother. But no one talks about her.)

Since we have no word for beauty, we use the closest word we have. We call it the knife.

Our beauty is only our knife. Our beauty is our only knife. It's just a knife: rusty blade, ordinary handle. But it's sharp. It does its thing. Nothing special.

When is nothing special the most important thing? When it's the only thing. Where we come from, beauty is so ordinary that we don't even know we are beautiful. It is only after we arrive here that we begin to understand the knife that we clutch.

We crawl onto land naked. We learn which clothes to wear. We learn how to do our makeup, how to style our hair. How to toss it with sexiness that appears unconsidered. The women think we're tacky, but we're not interested in the opinions of women anymore. We learned long ago how unimportant the opinions of women are. We are here because our mother could not protect us. We are here because our father had an "opinion."

So. We learn how to use our breasts, our asses, our eyelashes, our lips. We learn how to get what we want.

No. Not what we want. We never get what we want, do we?

We learn how to get what we need.

We crawl onto land naked. We learn to use our breasts (large but not cartoonish), our asses (heart shaped, unblemished), our eyelashes (impossibly long), our lips (smirking, exotic, and always, always glossy). We learn how to dance, how to flirt. How to toss our hair and slam shots and play pool (we are exceptional pool players, but we know it's best to lose on purpose) and how to talk about football. We learn to fuck, yes, but it doesn't take long to figure out that it's almost never the fucking that gets you anywhere. It's the not fucking. Except in certain and very specific circumstances. Thrust, parry, thrust, thrust, kill. How are we to survive?

We learn quickly.

Rather, most of us learn. There are those of us who take a while to figure things out. There are those of us who never quite get it. And now and then there is a girl who is certain (certain!) of her skill until the moment she's gutted by her own blade.

"I leave you with only one thing," our father tells us—so we have been told—just before he casts us out. "I allow you your knife," he says.

A knife is sometimes a tool. A knife is sometimes a weapon. You can eat off a knife if you don't have a fork or spoon. A knife can be used as a mirror, in a pinch. And if you're lost in the woods, a knife is helpful for marking your path on tree trunks. But what the hell good is a knife, really?

Never trust a gift from your fuckface father.

SEVEN

I WAS STARTING to lose track of time. The longer we stayed at the beach, the more impossible it became to figure out how long we'd been here. It could have been a month or two, or we could have gotten here just yesterday. Who knows. And while I could have tried to figure it out, the point is that it didn't matter. Days of the week had become so unknown to me that if someone had asked me to recite them all from a list, I probably would've pronounced Wednesday without dropping the *n*. *Wed-niz-day*. What's that again? When had Kristle's party been? When had we gone to Ursula's?

"Summer" had superseded all other designations. What day is it? What month is it? Tell me the day of the week. The president of the United States. My answer to all those questions would have been basically the same: *It's summer. It's summer. It's summer.* And *How should I know? It's summer.*

For the first time in my life, I was starting to get a tan.

Sometimes I'd fall asleep in the sand and wake up barely remembering who I was, feeling both infinite and blank, nothing more than the sum of my sore biceps and sun-reddened hair and the salt in my ears and the sand in my ass, and end up just stumbling down the beach totally unfettered, without any purpose.

Jeff, on the other hand, had found his purpose for sure. The purpose's name was Kristle. They'd been inseparable ever since karaoke night: she was at the house constantly during the day, eating all our food and lying on the deck (sometimes topless, facedown with her bikini strings puddled at her sides), smoking endless cigarettes and waltzing inside when she was bored of tanning to plop herself in front of the TV even when it was perfectly obvious that I myself was just about to settle in to watch *The Price Is Right*.

Jeff was her shadow. He was usually draped over her as she watched TV—overnight, he had become tolerant of those shows about housewives—and always seemed to be twirling her hair absentmindedly around his finger or rubbing her leg, or else staring at her from across the couch with a goofy and hunch-shouldered grin that I'd never seen on him before. This was so unlike him as to be somewhat disturbing; he had clearly entangled himself in the dire pussy-web he'd warned me about on our first night here. I had to say I was disappointed in him, if only for abandoning his own repulsive principles in such casual fashion.

Jeff was obviously smitten, but Kristle was harder to figure out. The way she looked at him was different from the way he looked at her. I'd catch him in a rare moment of distraction, reading the funny pages or whatever (Jeff was an unapologetic fan of both *Garfield* and *Marmaduke*), and Kristle would be leaning against the refrigerator a few feet away, Budweiser in hand, gazing at him with a curious and crooked look of beleaguered affection. A halfhearted hand on her hip. Was it love or something opposite? Was there a hint of contempt in the upturned corner of her mouth? Or was I just being paranoid?

Sometimes she noticed me noticing her, and she'd look up at me and shrug like, *Well what the fuck do you want me to say?* And I would just turn.

And then, more rarely but still regularly, I'd be scavenging in the cupboards for something to eat or sitting on the couch reading an old copy of *Her Place*—thinking of DeeDee as I scanned through the quiz—and I'd feel a tingle in my groin, only to slowly turn and see Kristle behind me, appraising me with an unembarrassed up-and-down, arms folded across her chest, mouth puckered, and eyes sparking with intensity.

She wasn't the type to look away. When I caught her staring, she'd just hold my gaze until I flinched. It never took long.

Jeff seemed to have completely forgotten the entanglement he'd recently caught us in. I remembered it myself only in a vague way, like it was something that had happened to someone else.

Even so. I hadn't kissed that many people in my life, and having shared with Kristle what I am probably embarrassing myself by characterizing as an intimate moment, it was kind of unsettling to have her now constantly in my midst, making ostentatious time with my fuck of a brother and ogling me creepily when I was just trying to go about my business in my own fucking house. I couldn't figure out her game. So I tried to just avoid the two of them as much as I could.

Kristle would not be avoided. One day I was digging some milk out of the refrigerator and turned around to see that she had appeared out of nowhere. She was sitting on the kitchen island, swinging her feet, wearing only a pair of tiny mesh shorts and a bikini top, and staring at me. I jumped. She smiled.

"Hey," she said.

"Hey," I said. "What's up?"

"Just waiting for your brother," she said. "He went to get us coffee. The stuff your machine makes is nasty."

"I think it tastes okay," I said. I poured some milk into it and took a big sip without even stirring. "Mmm," I said. "Delicious." But she was right; it did taste waterlogged and gross.

"If you say so," she said.

"So how's your little sister?" I asked, mostly just for something else to say. Well, no, actually, that's not totally true. I had been wondering. I had been hoping I'd run into her ever since karaoke and had even poked my head into the Fisherman's Net a couple of times hoping she'd be working, but she hadn't been there.

"Oh, you mean DeeDee," Kristle said. "Yeah, she mentioned you guys hung out. She's actually not my sister, you know; we just sort of look alike. Forget her; she's a bitch. I'm not trying to be rude. I'm just saying."

"Oh," I said. "Well she didn't seem like one."

She shrugged. "You know, Sam," she said, "you don't have to feel nervous around me. Just because I'm into your brother or whatever." She slid off the island and took a step closer to me. "What I have with your brother is its own thing. But you and I could have our own thing too." Her breath smelled like salt water. "You're a good kisser, you know."

I panicked, expecting Jeff to walk in at any second. "I have to go get a newspaper. I promised my dad."

Kristle looked over to the newspaper sitting right on the counter, raised an eyebrow, and flipped her hair. "Have fun," she said. "Don't forget sunscreen."

I skipped the sunscreen, slid on some flip-flops, and was out of there. I walked the mile to Cahoon's, where I bought a pair of sunglasses. I didn't really need a pair of sunglasses, but I was there; I had to buy something. I was sort of relieved that the woman at the register was well into her forties; Kristle had freaked me out and I didn't want to be reminded of it by another one of her creepy friends.

I couldn't figure out what she wanted from me. On one hand, I didn't want to know. On the other hand, she was hot, so obviously I had spent a fair amount of time considering unspeakable possibilities.

After having walked all the way to the store I was thirsty. I considered getting a soda, but that seemed like the biggest waste because we had plenty of soda at home, so I kept walking to the 7-Eleven that was wedged into the pie-shaped junction where the bypass met the beach road. The Slurpee machine was mostly broken and only had banana flavor, which I normally hate and which was only half-frozen, but I bought it anyway.

When I came out of the store, there was a boy around my age in the parking lot, just sitting there on one of the pieces of rotten old wood that marked the spaces. The guy was barefoot, his sneakers lying next to him on the asphalt, and he had a dazed expression on his face, not like he was lost, exactly, but more like he'd lost something. Like he'd misplaced himself.

A car zoomed by, close enough to toss the boy's hair across his face, but he was oblivious to it. He was shirtless and tanned like he'd been lying in the sun for months, and when I got a good look at him, I recognized something familiar. I knew him from somewhere, but I couldn't place him.

There was something about him that bothered me: the way his eyes were sharp and watery, the way he was casting around like he was looking for something he knew he wasn't going to find. There was something about him that I could relate to. He reminded me of someone who could have been a friend.

I would have ignored him anyway, but he caught my eye as I was about to turn in the other direction, and I felt like I didn't have much choice but to say something. "Is everything okay?" I asked.

"I'm fine," he said. "Thanks."

"Do you need money or something?" I dug in my pockets.

"I've got a bunch of quarters." Then I felt like a dick, because why would I assume he needed money, and anyway, what's anyone going to do with a bunch of quarters other than buy a Slurpee?

He didn't seem to care. "It's just—I forgot how to swim," he said.

"You can't forget how to swim," I said. He had revealed himself as a crazy person, but it was weird to think of someone who looked so much like me as crazy, so I didn't walk away yet. Maybe he had sunstroke or something. "You either know or you don't."

"That's what I thought," he said. "But I forgot. So maybe you can. I went in the water this morning, and I couldn't do it. I was on the swim team back home. I'm a good swimmer. Or I was. It's so weird."

He really didn't seem crazy. Something was happening. He was saying something important.

"It's not just that either," he said. "I forgot something else, too. But I can't remember what; all I know is it seems important. I don't know why I'm telling you this."

"It's okay. Did you forget which house is yours? They all sort of look the same around here."

"Nah," he said. "I remember that. I basically don't feel like going home right now. I actually don't want to talk about it."

"I'm sure you'll remember," I said. "Anyway, no one forgets how to swim. Maybe you need some sleep or something. Here, have my Slurpee."

"It's fine, man," he said.

"No, seriously. It's banana. I don't even like banana."

He took it and slurped practically the whole thing in one gulp.

"Thanks," he said. "Maybe I'm dehydrated. This place is fucking weird, though, huh?" He stood to go.

"Yeah," I said. "It is."

"Don't trust them," he said, turning.

"Who?" I said.

"You know who," he said over his shoulder as he walked away. "I can tell you know."

"Oh," I said. "Maybe."

Then he stopped for a second, like something had occurred to him, and turned back to face me again.

"Actually, it's worth it," he said. "On second thought—you can't trust them, but you can't not trust them either. And it is worth it, I guess. No, it is. Yeah."

He'd left his shoes behind, white Converse low-tops. "Hey!" I said, calling after him as he wandered across the street. "You forgot your shoes."

He looked back one more time and waved me off. "They hurt my feet," he said, and then I remembered where I'd seen him before: he'd been at Kristle's party, making out with the girl in the living room right before I'd found DeeDee. Just as I figured it out, a car sped by, almost running him over as it curved into the bypass and headed for the bridge to the next island, and when it had passed, the boy was stumbling off into the dunes.

His shoes were lying there and suddenly I had to turn away. I don't know what it was; I just couldn't look at them. My hand was still in my pocket, absently jangling at my change. I found myself staring at a pay phone on the edge of the parking lot, sticking up out of the yellow, dried-out beach grass at a crooked angle like a half-dead sapling. It looked like it was either from the future or the past or both. A cloud passed overhead; the sun bounced off the receiver. It seemed to me to be a sign.

So I picked up the receiver, dropped a quarter in, and dialed my mom's number. She'd never really gotten the hang of using a cell phone; she was always forgetting to charge it or forgetting to pay the bill or forgetting to bring it with her when she left the house or forgetting to turn it on or leaving it buried in her purse where she couldn't hear it ringing. Even when it did happen to be otherwise functional and in her possession she tended to have a hard time figuring out which button to press in order to answer it. So it had been no surprise at all after her departure when I'd tried to call her once or twice and it had gone straight to voice mail. I hadn't left messages; I knew she never listened to them anyway.

But even just hearing her voice on the machine would have reminded me that she still existed. Really, I think I wanted to remind myself that *I* still existed. This time I would leave a message just to prove it, I decided. "I was here," I would say.

After a minute of static, the phone rang once, and then I heard a robotic voice—not my mother's—in my ear. "To complete this call, please deposit two dollars."

I dropped the quarters into the slot obediently, feeling more and more like an idiot with each rattling plunk. Finally there was ringing on the other end. One ring, then two, then three. And then, unexpectedly, my mother herself was talking.

"Hello! Hello! Is anyone there?"

"Mom?" I said.

"Hello? Who is this?"

"Mom, it's me, Sam."

"Sam? Hello? I can never figure out how to use this damn thing. Can you hear me? Where are you?"

"Yeah, I hear you," I said. "I'm at a pay phone. Where are you?"

"Where am I? I'm at home of course. I show up here, the place is a wreck, the car's gone, and no one even left a note. I'm still your mother, you know; you can't just go running off to God-knows-where. I've been worried sick for the last three hours! Where are you?"

"We're at the beach," I said. "The Outer Banks."

"Tyra Banks? What does she have to do with anything? Can you hear me? Sam, tell me exactly where you are. I was about to call the police!"

"Don't call the police," I said. "We just went on vacation. We're in Nags Head."

Then the robot voice came on again. "Please deposit two dollars to continue this call." I dug in my pockets for change, knowing that I didn't have any more.

"Sam! Sam! Don't you dare hang up!" Mom was saying. "How do I trace this call! Oh, God, how do I use this thing? Siri, trace this call! Sam, stay on the line!"

"You don't need to trace the call," I said. "And I don't think Siri does that anyway." Then, not knowing why I was saying it: "We're at milepost fifteen. You should come. I mean, if you're just sitting around at home anyway. It'll be fun."

The only reply was dial tone. I had no idea why I'd told her to come. She probably hadn't heard me anyway. It was just as well.

But she had returned home. She had been gone for more than five months. Where had she been all that time, and what had made her come back for us?

EIGHT

MY FATHER DIDN'T even look in my direction as he came down the driveway. He was speeding along, metal detector over his shoulder, his face distant and determined.

"Find anything good yet?" I asked as I passed him. He looked surprised to see me.

He brightened a little at my interest but didn't slow his pace. "A few things, Tiger," he said. "Here and there. A few things. You never know what's out there."

Dad had become more and more obsessed with the idea of finding treasure since we'd first spotted him combing the beach. He was rarely in the house during the day now and when he was, he was preoccupied, sifting through his spoils for hours as if he was expecting to find something he hadn't noticed before. I can't say I minded; it meant that he had mostly abandoned his efforts at male bonding and that I could now be left to my own devices. But there was a part of me that sort of missed his cheery, reliable harassment.

I had to wonder what he was actually looking for. The way he would pick up certain items after a long day of searching—an old makeup compact, a stainless steel spoon, an aluminum box of breath mints—and turn them over in his hand, examining them as if waiting for them to reveal themselves to him. You'd ask him what he was doing and he'd mutter something you couldn't quite get about Blackbeard, who I guess is different from Bluebeard, and then he'd just go back to his distraction.

"Hey, bro," Jeff called from somewhere above my head. I looked up to see him and Kristle leaning over the edge of the deck, Jeff shirtless and her in a bikini, both of them radiating gold, both drinking from clear plastic tumblers, their chests gilded with thin layers of sweat. "Hey," I said. Kristle waved at me with a smile like nothing had happened, and I made my way up the stairs, hoping they would leave me alone and let me sneak inside.

Jeff wasn't going to make it easy. Although the onset of Kristle had made me even less inclined to hang out with him than usual, it'd had the opposite effect on Jeff. It was becoming a losing battle to continue rebuffing his increasingly aggressive geniality.

"Where'd you go?" he asked. "It's like we never hang out anymore. Want a drink?"

The day was beginning to slip away, and although the sun wasn't near setting yet, the blue sky was developing a certain periwinkle fatigue that made a drink seem acceptable—not that I cared whether it was acceptable or not. "Okay," I said. My voice came out the same color as the sky.

Jeff didn't seem to notice. He grinned and slapped me on the back. "G and T okay, little guy?"

I'm not personally that into drinking anything that tastes like a pinecone, but he seemed so enthusiastic about it that I couldn't say no. "Sure," I said. "Whatever."

"I make a mean G and T," he said. "I took that bartending class last summer, you know." And he bopped through the sliding doors into the kitchen, humming the first bar of some song as he went. I rolled my eyes as I plopped myself onto the wooden chaise. Then I felt that tingle in my groin again: Kristle had turned to face me. We were alone again.

She was leaning with her back against the porch rail, drink in hand, her hips jutting out and legs crossed at the ankles. Her hair was blowing very slightly in the breeze, and she reached into her drink and pulled out an ice cube with her fingers and dropped it into her mouth, crunching on it loudly. She didn't say anything. This time, when she noticed me looking at her, she looked away.

"What the fuck?" I finally said. "Seriously, what the fuck?"

"What?" she said, with a final crunch. Then she fished for her lime wedge and, having extracted it from the bottom of her glass, was sucking on it, eyebrows raised. The juice from the lime dripped down her chin. "What?"

For some reason I was actually emboldened by the way she was looking at me, by her hair and her hips and her breasts, quivering in her bikini. It had made me shy and nervous before, but now it just made me want to know who the fuck she thought she was.

"So what was that about?"

"What was what about?"

"Earlier today. You know."

It was the first time I had seen her seem nervous. "You're such an American. You all make such a big deal about everything. It wasn't remotely a big deal. I was just trying to be friendly. I just wanted you to know we were friends. That you can trust me."

"Funny you should put it that way," I said. "I met this guy today. He was weird; it was like he'd had his heart sucked out through his nose. I didn't even know him. I barely said anything to him. But you know what he told me?"

"Let me guess," Kristle said. She didn't guess.

"He told me not to trust you."

Kristle hooted. "Me? He told you not to trust me? That's a laugh. I don't even *know* any guys other than your brother. I only know girls and assholes. How should some random guy I've never met know anything about me?"

"He wasn't talking about you specifically," I said.

"Oh, not me *specifically*. Of course. So who was he talking about?"

"You know who he was talking about. All of you."

"All of us."

"All of you. He said not to trust any of you."

"And I'm the one getting blamed for some unknown, untrustworthy thing *all of us* supposedly did? I don't even know who this person is. Like I said: you're such an American."

"I never trusted you anyway," I said. "I don't know if you're trying to fuck with me or fuck with my brother or if you just like fucking with everyone or what. It doesn't take someone telling me to make me think you might not be so trustworthy. But it does help."

She recoiled, wounded and angry. "You have no idea what I'm about," she said, and she turned out to face the ocean and leaned over the street, balancing her weight on her palms and lifting her heels into the air. "Some people have no fucking clue."

That night, Jeff and Kristle decided to sleep at her place—wherever that was. While Jeff was gathering his stuff up, Kristle cornered me one more time.

"Listen to me," she said. "Listen carefully. I want you to know that I really like your brother, okay? Like, I really like him. Please don't mess with that."

"I'm not the one messing with it."

"I know," she said. She tugged at her hair, and she really did look sort of upset. "I know. But still."

I stared at her for a few seconds. "Okay," I finally said. And then: "Can you tell DeeDee to say hi sometime?"

Kristle tilted her head one way, then another, considering it. "Yeah," she said. "Sure. Fine. I mean, it's not like she listens to me ever. But fine, who cares? If that's really what you want. But did you ever think maybe it's not me you need to worry about trusting?"

Then Jeff appeared with his backpack, ready to go. "Hey," he said with a cocky wink, "you hitting on my girlfriend, bro? Uncool."

"I'm nobody's girlfriend," Kristle said. She was smiling and Jeff just laughed in his usual dopey, good-natured way, but I could tell he was bothered.

At first I was pleased to have them out of my way for the night, but after I'd been sitting alone in the living room for an hour—watching TV and picking sand from the crevices of the couch, getting slowly drunk by myself—I started to get bored. I decided to go for a walk on the beach. I took the flashlight with me and headed to the ocean, still just in my bathing suit.

When I got to the shore, the moon was behind a cloud. I didn't remember that it had rained during the day, but the sand was damp. I sat down anyway.

I thought of my father with his metal detector and the fact that we were seeing him less and less lately. I thought of myself, and how untethered I felt, like I could float away at any moment. I thought of the boy outside the 7-Eleven, wandering off into the dunes, his shoes still lying in the parking lot.

I thought of the girl we'd seen on the first night here, and I cast my flashlight out to the ocean, wondering if I'd see another one heading for land. But I didn't see anything. Instead I heard a voice behind me: "Hey, you." That slow and twisting accent again, but this time with a different, still familiar timbre.

I turned. It was DeeDee, standing in the sand with her shoulder cocked awkwardly, her hair wild and blue. I should have been surprised to see her but for some reason I wasn't; I wondered if I had been expecting her this whole time. Maybe Kristle had told her to come find me after all. I sort of doubted it though.

"Can I sit down?" she asked. "I just got off work. Sucky day."

"Yeah," I said. It was so dark that she probably couldn't see me smiling, but I was in fact smiling. She had found me. "I had a sucky day too. Or at least just weird." I had already forgotten about Kristle's warning not to trust her.

"Weird is good. Weird is at least interesting. You wouldn't believe how boring it gets here," she said. "We watch a lot of TV." She plopped down next to me in the sand with a sigh.

"Yeah, I've noticed. Kristle's really into those shows about the housewives."

"Who isn't?" DeeDee said. "Being a housewife seems like it could be a lot of fun, right? Anything's better than waiting tables—except maybe being a maid. Either way, housewives don't have to do any of that. I mean, they're free. Who could be freer?" She took off her cheap Chinese slippers and shook them out into the sand before placing them in her lap.

"You should get more comfortable shoes," I said, not bothering to comment on the relative freeness of housewives or the pure shit my mother had spouted about something called "the feminine mystique" in the weeks leading up to her escape.

"I've tried," she said. "It doesn't help. These are actually the best. I have problems with my feet. We all do."

"If you were housewives you could just sit around all day with your feet in footbaths full of Epsom salts," I said, half sarcastically. I only knew about the existence of Epsom salts at all because they were something my mom had been really into. I didn't quite understand what they were.

"Exactly," DeeDee said. "We talk about that all the time."

We sat there in silence at the very edge of the surf, the cold water creeping up on our ankles every few seconds and then receding. I'd already discovered that when DeeDee started talking she could talk forever, but I was surprised to discover that she was pretty good at being quiet, too.

I was playing a game with myself where I tried to time my breath to the in-and-out of the water, but the truth is that I'm terrible at holding my breath.

"Can you explain Kristle to me?" I asked.

"What about her?" DeeDee asked.

"She confuses me," I said. "For one thing, is she your sister or not? Do you guys hate each other or are you friends?"

DeeDee didn't reply, and I looked over at her curiously. I could see vague reflections of waves rolling in her eyes. Her expression was blank and very far away. She appeared mesmerized. I wondered if I should kiss her again; I felt slightly guilty that she had been the one to kiss me at Ursula's. But it seemed wrong to kiss someone who may have forgotten I was even there.

I was still debating it when she snapped back. "Ugh," she said. A cigarette had appeared between her fingers, seemingly from nowhere, and she had to fuss with her lighter before it would light. "I hate the ocean. You want to, like, go somewhere?"

"Like where?" I asked.

"I don't know," she said. "We could break into the mini-golf course."

I'm generally a law-abiding person. Not out of any sense of morality, but because I'm sort of a pussy. I don't even like skipping class; it makes my stomach hurt. But I looked over at DeeDee, who wiggled her eyebrows in a way that was at once sarcastic and entreating, in a way that made lawbreaking seem totally worth it, and I was just like, "Okay."

She sprang up and dusted her beautiful ass off. She forged a curling and mysterious trail up the beach, cigarette burning from her fingers, and all I could do was smile and scramble behind her. It didn't strike me then that a person can get lost even when following a path.

NINE

"SO TELL ME about you," DeeDee was saying. "I want to know everything."

The golf course was closed for the night—we'd crawled in through a hole in the chain-link fence—and now we were bathed in the eerie, bluish, almost underwater light of the garden lamps as we perched atop a fake lagoon overlooking the seventh hole of Cap'n Redbeard's Hole-N-Fun. Between us, a fiberglass mermaid reclined in a way that was meant, I think, to be seductive but actually made it look like she had a problem with her spine. DeeDee had pulled a small flask of whiskey from her bra, and we were passing it back and forth.

"Like what?" I asked, more drunkenly than I would have preferred. "Like what should I tell you?"

DeeDee looked over at me with an exasperated smile. "I don't know," she said. "God, you're hopeless. Tell me anything. Take a shot and then you have to tell me one thing about yourself, without thinking. Something secret."

She passed me the flask and I swigged. For the first time, I didn't flinch at the burn of the undiluted liquor.

"Um," I said, seizing the first thing that came to me in my wobbly state. "When I was little, I went through this phase where I peed in the sink all the time. You know, like instead of the toilet. Afterward I would always feel super-guilty about it—I thought there was something really wrong and maybe perverted about me. But then it turns out that it's a thing that basically all guys do when they're little. My friend Sebastian *still* does it when he goes to parties, because why not? It's like, primal, one of those things left over from when we were monkeys that evolution forgot to get rid of. Also pinkie toes and male nipples."

"Of course. I love how when boys have a completely unacceptable habit like peeing in the sink, science actually goes to all the trouble to come up with a justification for it."

"Well it's true," I said. "It's a biological imperative." Although then it occurred to me that I didn't even know if it was true at all; Sebastian was the one who had told me about the whole Darwinist theory behind pissing in sinks, and he wasn't the most trustworthy person.

DeeDee grimaced. "God. Last summer I was stuck cleaning houses. Houses with little boys were always the worst of all— you know, even if you rinse it down, piss eventually starts to leave a smell that's impossible to get out. I'm lucky I got the job at the Fisherman's Net this year. Waitressing sucks too but at least I'm not dealing with body fluids very often."

"Do you ever get sick of it?" I asked.

"Of what?"

"Of you know, cleaning houses and waiting tables and stuff? Of working all the time I mean."

"Of course we get sick of it. Wouldn't you?"

I was embarrassed that I'd asked. I hadn't meant it as an insult. Her life was so different from mine; I should have thought of that. But I realized I hardly knew anything about her—I didn't know where she had come from or why she was even working in the first place. I didn't know what had brought her here or where she was going. "Sorry," I said. "Obviously. But, like, what are you going to do next?"

"Right this minute? I'm going to drink some more whiskey." She reached for it and took a sip, then tossed it back to me, and I drank too. I could taste the mild flavor of her saliva on the spout.

"I meant with life," I said. "After you're done waiting tables. Like are you going to go to college or whatever."

"I try not to think too far ahead. I'd like to see France someday. But that's just a fantasy."

"So the accent's not French?"

"Russian," she said, a beat too quickly. It didn't sound Russian to me, but I guess Russia's a big place. It stands to reason that not everyone from there would talk like a James Bond villain.

"What's it like? Russia I mean."

Her face turned vague. "Oh, I don't know. It's been a while. Where are *you* from anyway?"

"The suburbs," I said. "Basically the least interesting place on earth. I mean, I *was* from there. I'm not sure if we're ever going back or what. My dad quit his job and everything. So maybe I'm not *from* anywhere anymore."

She was looking at me quizzically. "Never mind," I said. "It's your turn. Tell me something about you." I pushed the flask into her hands again.

"I already told you I'm from Russia. What else is there to know?"

I raised an eyebrow. "What do you mean? C'mon. I can think of so many interesting things. Don't be stubborn."

"There's nothing that interesting."

"I told you my darkest secret and you're not going to tell me a thing?"

"That's your darkest secret?"

"Just give me something," I said.

"Fine," she finally said, and took what started as a sip, became a swig, and turned into a gulp, before eventually settling at a chug. DeeDee let the flask clatter onto the lagoon before wiping her mouth with the back of her hand and letting out a small belch. "I don't have a mother," she said. She pushed her hair over her shoulder. "Good enough?"

I paused and cocked my head and started to say a bunch of different things but couldn't decide on which. "Where'd she go?" I finally asked.

"Long story," she said.

"They always are. I don't have a mother either. Well, maybe I do. But not really. It's no big deal."

"It actually is a big deal," DeeDee said. "To me at least. Anyway. I don't like to talk about the past—I mean, my past. Other people's are fine. What happened to yours?"

"You know how it goes these days," I said. "It all started with Facebook."

"I've heard of Facebook," DeeDee said. "But I've never used it."

"Really?" I said. "You're serious?"

"Totally serious. We don't have good internet here. You have to go to an internet café and even then it's super-slow. It's not really worth it."

I had noticed the internet problem myself. I hadn't checked my email since we'd left. The thing is that I didn't even miss it.

"Well *that's* something interesting," I said. "You're not missing much though; I'm not sure how my mom got so obsessed with it anyway. It's pretty dumb. For a while she was just happy making all these embarrassing comments on my wall—that was bad enough, but it didn't last. Then she starts playing these games where you have to make a farm and collect chicken eggs and that type of thing, and she's, like, totally into it. She's down there in the basement on the computer all day and then she comes up for dinner and all she wants to talk about is her farm, which made no sense, but it was sort of a relief because it meant she finally was leaving my wall alone. But even with that it was only a matter of time. Soon she started making all these *friends*, and that's when things actually got bad."

"Wait, she had a farm? Where was the farm?"

"Just ignore that part. The point is, all of a sudden she's sending all these messages to these strangers in weird places and next thing you know she's in the basement with a box of wine twenty-four-seven, chatting with them, I guess. Or something. You know, whatever people do on Facebook. And she was different. She got all interested in this weird crap that she wouldn't have been able to tell you the first thing about before. She's reading all this poetry; she has a Tumblr, although I avoided looking at it. She won't shut up about this thing called the *SCUM Manifesto*. . . ."

"Society for Cutting Up Men?"

I was surprised she'd heard of it, but I guess you learn about a lot of crazy stuff watching all that cable. "Yeah, that's the one. Some book some lunatic lady wrote about how much she hates all dudes; it sounded psychotic."

"It's actually pretty funny," DeeDee said.

"Wait," I said. "You've *read* the *SCUM Manifesto*?"

DeeDee looked a little nervous. "Oh," she said. "Yeah. I guess they had it in one of the houses or whatever."

"Oh," I said. "Weird." It was no wonder people were so strange around here, with no internet and only *Her Place*, the Bible, and the *SCUM Manifesto* to read.

"Valerie Solanas was misunderstood," DeeDee said. "Her sense of humor was too sophisticated for most people. Although, true, she did end up shooting someone. But that's sort of beside the point."

I think I sort of looked at her funny but didn't press the issue. "Yeah, well, the *point* is, Mom starts getting all these crazy ideas. We barely see her anymore—she's just on Facebook—and when we do, she's talking about this 'cutting up men' stuff. Then one day I'm getting ready for school and she knocks on my door with a bag packed and she tells me she's going to live at something called Women's Land, where no one ever has to talk to men. And then five minutes later she's gone. As in, completely gone."

"Huh," DeeDee said. "That sucks."

"The craziest part is she'd deleted her Facebook profile."

"When did it happen?"

"I dunno, like six months ago."

"Oh," DeeDee said. "Sorry. That sucks."

"What about your mom?" I asked again. "Where is she? Is she dead?"

"No. Not really. It's hard to explain. She's *around*, I guess. She's just very distracted or something."

"Come on," I said. "Tell."

She dodged the question. "I want to show you something." And before I could say anything back, the flask was in her bra again and she was dangling from the mermaid statue's fins and clambering down the lagoon into an inch-high moat. "Come on," she said. I jumped down and followed her across the golf course to the large pirate ship that faced out over the bypass. It was held aloft over the third hole by two fake rocks, creating both the vision of a spooky shipwreck and the more practical effect of a little tunnel for mini-golfers to putt through.

"Can I have your flashlight?" DeeDee asked.

I tossed it to her and she caught it, flicked it on, walked into the tunnel, and shone the light toward the underside of the ship. "Here," she said after a second, and reached up, unlatching something. A trapdoor swung down.

"Help me in," she said. She was a little shaky and so was I, but I managed to hoist her through the hatch, into the belly of the pirate ship. I had some trouble making it myself—upper body strength is not something I've been blessed with an excess of—but DeeDee grabbed me under my armpits when I was halfway in and pulled me the rest of the way.

It smelled like mildew. I sat up and crawled farther in, feeling my way and stumbling a little over some unidentified detritus. Behind me, I could hear DeeDee pulling the door closed.

I squeezed my eyes shut, and when I opened them again, DeeDee was reclining against the curvy wall of the ship's interior. She'd tossed the flashlight to the floor, and the light was bouncing through the place in unexpected patterns, creating odd shadows. She was smiling, glowing warm and yellow, and I crawled over to where she sat, collapsing next to her. The ship was spinning a little—even though it was fake, I felt seasick.

"Look," she said. She picked up the flashlight and began flashing it around so I could really see the place, which was small and narrow—not much bigger than a very large bathroom—and stuffed with junk.

It was everywhere. It was actually hard to tell what all the stuff was since it was scattered and piled in jumbled heaps, like that show *Hoarders*, but I could pick out clothes and comic books and crappy paperbacks and all kinds of stupid trinkets like votive candles and flatware and Fiestaware dishes. And looking closer under the traveling beam of the flashlight: crappy jewelry and high-heeled shoes and plastic action figures, their poor arms and legs twisted in uncomfortable directions. Propped against the wall at the opposite end was a large mirror with a crack straight down the middle.

"Look at this stuff," DeeDee said. "Isn't it neat?"

"Yeah," I said. "Neat. Is all this yours?"

"Nah. I wish. It's Nalgene's. It's her secret hideout. Like her *lair* or whatever. She works here, you know—at Hole-N-Fun, taking the money and handing out scorecards and clubs and stuff. Anyway, she hides in here sometimes. She doesn't know I know about it, but I saw her climb up in here one day as the place was closing, so I waited for her to leave and then checked it out for myself. Sometimes I use it too. Like I'll come in here just to hang out or to take a nap or whatever. Nalgene would murder me but I don't actually care. It's nice to have a place to be alone. It's important. Next summer I'm hoping she'll work somewhere else, and I'll get to take over here and this'll be mine."

"Where'd she get all of it?"

"Well," she said. "She has, um, this problem. There's always been something a little wrong with Nalgene; Kristle says it's

low self-esteem, but why would her self-esteem be any different from the rest of ours when we're all basically the same?
Taffany thinks she's just a little stupid, but I don't know about
that either. Whatever it is, she has, like, a shoplifting thing.
You have to watch out; she's always trying to pick something
up. She doesn't mean anything by it—it's just what she does.
She could be digging around in your pocket for a quarter or
a piece of gum at the same time she's hugging you. So I guess
this is all stuff she stole. Or, you know, *found*. Or both. I don't
actually know where any of it comes from, but it's got to come
from somewhere, right? All I can say is that I guarantee she
didn't pay for any of it."

"But what's the point?" I asked.

DeeDee looked at me blankly. "What do you mean, the
point?"

"I don't know," I said. "Why bother having all this junk if
you're just going to hide it away and never use it? It looks like
she's never touched any of it."

"The point is just to have it," DeeDee said. "To own something."

"Oh," I said, still not really getting it.

"It makes a lot of sense to me," DeeDee said. "When you're
all the same, all you have is what you own. And we don't own
a lot."

"You don't seem the same to me," I said. "You and Kristle
are nothing alike."

"Don't be so sure," DeeDee said darkly.

116

"Wait. You still haven't told me anything about you. I told you I peed in the sink and I told you all about my dumb mom. And you told me about Nalgene. But I still barely know anything about *you*."

"Maybe there's nothing to know," DeeDee said. "Have you considered that?"

"No," I said. "I reject that premise."

"Fine," DeeDee said. "Well maybe I need you to tell me, then."

"Tell you what?"

"Something about myself. Anything. Just something."

"You're funny," I said. "But you seem sort of angry about something too."

"Funny," she said. "That's how I would describe you."

And then she tossed the flashlight aside and I was kissing her. I don't know, I mean, we were kissing. I'm pretty sure that I was the one who made the first move this time but I could be wrong. Even if I had been, it wasn't something I did intentionally. It was just like we were sitting there looking at each other, and then we were kissing each other and it was a pretty equal thing.

It was different from when Kristle had kissed me. (Had that really even happened?) It was different from when I had kissed Sasha at that Halloween party too. Most of all, it was different from the silly, off-the-cuff kiss after karaoke, which I was pretty sure was really meant for James Taylor. Kissing DeeDee in the hold of the fake fiberglass ship, surrounded by all of Nalgene's crazy plunder, I felt like I was on an expedition to the edge of the world. I felt life unfurling itself in lazy and salty spirals in the water below my feet, revealing itself as something I would never have guessed.

It was perfect.

And then DeeDee's hand was on my boner, and I felt my spine straighten, my shoulders tense, my tongue stiffen in her mouth. I don't know why I was so taken aback; I know that as a seventeen-year-old boy, a girl's hand on my boner is supposed to be one thing that I cannot resist. And yes, it felt good. But my heart was pounding and, okay, I was afraid. So fucking kill me; I pushed her hand away.

"What?" she whispered, biting my ear.

"I don't know," I whispered back. "Not yet." Jesus Christ. What was wrong with me?

"Okay," she said, but then her hand was creeping up the front of my shirt.

"Can we just wait?"

"Okay," she said. "Okay. I'm tired anyway. Let's just sleep." She gave me a warm peck on the cheek and let me go, curling herself into a ball in the bow. I moved behind her and wrapped my arms around her chest and she murmured something happy sounding, and the summery, saltwatery smell of her skin enveloped me as we drifted off together, forward, into whatever unknown ocean.

OCEAN

We don't know how to swim.

We don't really even understand swimming. We see the Others in the water, flailing around, jumping and diving and flopping backward into waves, and we are confused. They call it swimming, but it doesn't look like swimming to us. Maybe we're mistranslating.

We have learned to use our bodies. We have learned to walk without wincing, to stand upright and put one foot in front of the other, to stumble from one place to the next. We have learned to do the other things required of us in this place, too.

But we have forgotten as much as we have learned.

We have forgotten the ocean: what it looks like from below the surface, the mysteries it holds.

We have forgotten how to navigate by the stars.

We have forgotten how to survive on salt. (Though we continue to enjoy salty food.)

We have forgotten almost everything.

The feeling remains, though. That is what we remember: The weightlessness in our toes and the velocity in our fingertips. The way the water once carried us, and how our destination always ended up lying somewhere halfway between our own desires and the intention of the ocean.

We remember waves and currents.

And we remember the knowing. The knowing that as deep as you travel, there is always a deeper wreck to be discovered.

The knowing of our own names.

The ocean frightens us now. We are frightened by how much we miss it. We are frightened as much by what we remember as by what we don't. We are frightened by the way it sings to us, calling us back to depths we know we can no longer survive.

An ocean is large. It's so large that it's probably dangerous to think about its largeness for too long. This may be the reason that we are crazy. Spend too much time contemplating something beyond comprehension and one can start to lose what one had in the way of marbles.

You can see why we would be afraid. It's too easy to get lost. Even just sticking a toe in is dangerous. And an ocean can swallow you, even when you can swim.

TEN

I WOKE UP in Nalgene's lair achy and dry mouthed and a little hungover. I guess we'd had more to drink than I'd realized. Plus I'd slept inside an attraction at a miniature golf course, which never helps. DeeDee was gone. I had also inexplicably managed to lose one of my socks.

I tried not to invest too much significance into her disappearance. She probably had to go to work. Or whatever. But I still felt sort of abandoned and stupid as I dropped out of the trapdoor at the base of the ship and onto the golf course, ignoring the stares of a vacationing family playing through the third hole, and walked right past Nalgene—who was occupied separating colored balls into canisters and not paying attention—out through the front entrance onto the beach road to head home.

No one was at the house when I got back, and my head was killing me, so I poured myself a giant bowl of Lucky Charms, sat down in front of *The Price Is Right*, and was asleep in two seconds. I didn't wake up until I heard Dad clanking around the kitchen after a long day's treasure hunting. He was milling around the room, shirtless and whistling as usual, hauling this big-ass plastic bucket behind him.

"Wanna help me sort through the day's spoils, Tiger?" he asked hopefully, wiggling his eyebrows.

"Are you talking to me?" I said, being unnecessarily prissy just for the fun of it. "No thank you."

"Suit yourself." Dad took his bucket and dumped it out over the dining table, all his scavenged metal crap clattering out in a messy pile. I couldn't tell exactly what he'd scored, but it looked like a lot of aluminum cans and maybe a fork or two.

"Anything good?" I asked, curious in spite of myself.

"We'll see," he said. "One man's trash is another man's treasure."

"Yes, but which man's treasure is it?" I asked. "Yours? And if so, why exactly? To me those look like a bunch of sandy fucking Budweiser cans."

Dad was hurt. "We'll see," he repeated. "Anyway, I hope you're having fun at the beach, Tiger."

"I am," I said.

"Where were you last night?" he asked. I turned around, surprised.

"What do you mean?" I asked. Okay, obviously I knew what he meant, but I was still surprised.

"You think no one notices when you're out all night?"

Actually I did think that. While my father had once been

mostly normal—inquiring as to the state of my homework, smelling my breath when I came home from a party to see if I'd been drinking, objecting to me staying out all night with no explanation—those days felt like a very long time ago. In recent weeks I'd almost entirely forgotten that in addition to being an avid scavenger of metallic bric-a-brac, he was charged with the parental duty of keeping track of my whereabouts.

"Next time I'll tell you," I said, and I took a beer out of the fridge and went to sit on the porch, knowing there would be no objection. It was mostly for show. I didn't even really want the beer.

As soon as I had time to actually sit and think, I was over-taken with humiliation at the events of the previous night. I had a sneaking suspicion that when a girl actually did finally deign to grab your hard-on that it was an unpopular and pos-sibly completely pussified choice to ask her if she could please stop. No doubt she had fled in disgust—Kristle and Jeff were probably right this minute sitting with her and speculating about my potential homosexuality—and if I ever saw her again it would only be for long enough for her to look away awk-wardly, trying to suppress a sneer.

I had a feeling DeeDee was probably not going to be kissing me again.

The moral of the story here is that if you're ever offered any-thing that seems like it might lead to sex, there is no turning back. You just have to take it as it comes or you will remain a virgin for life.

At least, that's what I thought until I heard DeeDee's voice and looked over the edge of the porch to the driveway, where she was standing in an old white T-shirt and a pair of cutoffs, using her hand as a visor.

"Sam!" she shouted.

"Hey," I said. "How'd you know where we're staying?"

"I asked Jeff," she said. "Come on, I want to go to the beach."

"Just a second," I said, my chest swelling as I fumbled for my shoes. I was happy to see her. I didn't bother to tell my father where I was going.

It was getting late-ish and the sun had that perfect, golden quality that means it will be getting dark in no time. People were packing up their umbrellas and coolers and drifting toward home. There were still a few stragglers fucking around in the surf, but you could tell that they would be gone soon too. DeeDee offered no explanation as to where we were going; we just turned right on the shore and started walking. We walked in silence for a few minutes before I decided that I had to say something.

Sebastian always advised me to ask questions when in doubt. "Girls like to talk about themselves. If you can't think of anything to say, just ask some dumb question about nothing, and if you're lucky she'll go off and you won't have to say anything else for another ten minutes and she'll think you're a *great listener*."

"So why do you guys come here?" I asked.

"Come here?" DeeDee asked, surprised, like she'd never

considered it before. "What do you mean?"

"Well, Russia's kind of far away, right?" When Sebastian had formed his theories about girls, he obviously hadn't met one as guarded and evasive as DeeDee. "Why come all the way here?"

She paused. "Oh, I don't know. There's not really a lot for us to do at home. They let us come to work in the summers. Like an exchange program. It's good money—well, not that good, but good enough. And of course the weather's nice. Much nicer than Moscow. Then we stay here through the winter, because why bother going back? Even in winter, the weather's not so bad either. It would be a waste to go home and lose our tans. Not to mention all the English we've picked up. This is my second summer."

"But you still think of there as home?"

She shrugged. "What's home anyway?"

"I guess you get used to it," I said.

"Well, yeah. But look at us. We don't belong here either."

I know she didn't mean it literally, but I looked at her anyway, took in her whole everything. I tried to imagine that I was seeing her for the first time, which wasn't so hard because she had already changed to me since the first time I'd seen her.

She changed every time I saw her—became more formed. She became both more complicated and also easier to understand. And it was true that she and the other Girls stood out here, with their wild hair and strange parties and floating, undersea eyes. True. But I couldn't imagine them anywhere *other* than here. Maybe it was just my lack of imagination, but it made no sense to me that they could call another place home, especially a place as cold and gray as Russia.

"I'm glad you came and found me today. I kinda thought I would never hear from you again."

She frowned and raised an eyebrow. She seemed genuinely surprised. "Really? Why?"

"You know, because of last night. Because I wouldn't—you know."

And she just laughed—a real laugh that was warm and sincere—and put her arm around my waist. Her hand was resting against my hip bone.

"Skinny," she remarked. "You're so dumb."

"It's hard to explain," I said. She hadn't asked for an explanation, but I figured I owed her one anyway. "Say there's this thing you want, this thing that seems more important than everything, this thing you've been *waiting* for because it will make you into something else. And then you get a chance at it and it's almost as if you don't want to change. Because you'll miss the person you were before."

"That makes more sense than you know," DeeDee said. And then, after a pause, she changed the subject and asked a question I was not expecting: "Do you miss your mom?"

I looked at her. Why would she ask something like that? "Uh," I said. "Yes. I mean no."

"Same," she said. I didn't know what she meant. Which was she agreeing with? Yes or no?

"I've found that mothers can be very unpredictable," she said.

"In the end, they can't protect you."

"Same," I said.

"But I do miss her," DeeDee said.

"Same," I said. It might have been the first time I had admitted it. I don't know if it was even true. "I don't know what I miss. She was so different by the time she left. I think she must have been really unhappy. Maybe I just miss being little and not understanding anything."

"Yeah," DeeDee said. "I don't really have a good memory for that type of thing."

The beach had grown increasingly narrow as we'd walked, and the people had begun to disappear until they were gone entirely, and then the shoreline ended right in front of us. Well, it didn't end exactly: there was a rocky outcropping growing out of the dunes and stretching fifty feet into the ocean, blocking our path. It was unusual; this was not really a rocky kind of beach.

"Here we are," DeeDee said. "This is what I wanted to show you. Come on."

Then she was scrambling ahead over the rocks and I tried to climb up after her, unsure of my footing, trying not to slip. The boulders were steep and sharp and there was no obvious path; I was instantly clumsy. I was still feeling my way up the first few rocks by the time DeeDee was already at the top of the ridge, looking down at me in amusement, cheering me on, and cracking up every time I stumbled.

But after slipping a few times and nearly twisting my ankle,

I finally found myself at the top of the climb and it was worth it: I stood next to DeeDee and looked out to the other side and saw an empty crescent of shoreline, bounded on all sides by rocks, forest, and tall dunes. The water was calm and horizonless and bluer than it was anywhere else at this beach.

"What do you think?" DeeDee asked. I didn't bother replying; it was obvious how extraordinary the cove was. "This is where we come, sometimes," she said. "I don't like the water, but it's peaceful here. Just to sit on the sand. It feels private, you know? I mean, it *is* private. Nobody else knows about it, besides us."

Somehow I knew that when she said "us," she was referring to the Girls.

"How can it be secret?" I asked. "It's right here on the beach. You just walk far enough and here you are."

"I don't know," she said. "I guess it's harder to find than you'd think."

Without hesitation, she made the fifteen-foot leap to the sand below, landing in a crouch before flopping onto her ass. I was about to jump when I decided against it and instead made my way down the rocks. I scraped my knee as I went, but it didn't really hurt.

The sun was setting. We went to stand in the surf. It was like we'd found the edge of the world.

"Do you ever feel like there's something unusual about this beach?" I asked. "Like it's not quite real or something?"

"Have you heard of *The Lost Colony*?"

I didn't know what *The Lost Colony* had to do with anything, but I had seen billboards for it on the highway when we'd been driving here. "Sort of," I said. "It's a play or something, right? Like based on a true story?"

"Yeah, a really boring play that no one will ever shut up about," DeeDee said. "They put it on for the tourists. It's been going on forever. Andy Griffith was in it years ago, before he was Andy Griffith. Whoever Andy Griffith is—some kind of local celebrity, I think. He's another thing no one will shut up about."

"So?"

"So, it's all lies."

"Andy Griffith wasn't in it?"

"No, he was. I mean, I assume that's true. But the play itself is all lies. They say it's a true story but it's all bullshit."

"You have a lot of opinions," I said.

She tossed her hair crossly. "Well why shouldn't I?"

"No," I said. "I like it."

"Oh, *thank you*," she said. "I'm so glad you approve of me having a thought in my brain." As usual her annoyed scowl barely covered a grin. She meant it, but she was also just fucking around.

"Sorry," I said. "Just tell me about the lost Pilgrims."

"Thank you." DeeDee put her arm around my shoulder, I guess as a conciliatory gesture.

"So, okay, they lived here; they had their whole little colony thing set up, doing whatever colonists do. Tormenting natives or whatever. They're here, everything's going good. And then one day, they're just gone. Their houses were still standing like nothing had happened, but it was like the people just vanished into thin air. Like they'd been zapped. Where did they go?"

"I remember the story now," I said. "We learned about it in school when I was little. They were kidnapped by Indians. I don't know why people still think it's a mystery."

"No," DeeDee said. "That's where you're wrong. That's the exact part that's bullshit. Of course the Indians are the ones who get blamed for everything; it's typical but it's also fake. It's crap."

I had put my arm around her now too. Talking to DeeDee felt familiar, like talking to someone I had known forever. It had been a long time since I'd had that feeling with anyone.

"Okay, so what happened to them?" I asked. "And also, what does this have to do with anything?"

"You asked what was wrong with this place," DeeDee said. "So think about this. Why does everyone assume that something had to *make* them disappear? Why couldn't they be capable of their own disappearance? It's this beach. It's what it's all about. This is where people come to disappear. Isn't it obvious?"

It wasn't obvious at all: I didn't know what to say.

"But it's also more than that. It's also where people disappear *to*. Many of the people you meet here have already disappeared from one elsewhere or another."

"Like who?" I asked.

She cocked her head and crossed her arms at her chest, leaning back in satisfaction. "Like *you*, maybe?"

"I don't feel like I've disappeared," I said. "I feel like I'm right here. Wherever here is."

This time I knew exactly what I was doing when I kissed her. This time I didn't hesitate.

We were entwined in the sand when I heard the sound of a throat clearing, just over the roar of the waves. DeeDee and I broke away from each other, first rolling over onto our backs and then, realizing not only that we'd been discovered but also who had discovered us, standing up quickly. It was Jeff and Kristle. Jeff was smirking of course, waggling his eyebrows at me like a total idiot, but Kristle looked pissed, her arms folded and hip cocked, eyes placid but cutting.

"Well hello there," she said. "What are you two up to?"

"Ha-ha," I said.

"Hey, Kristle," DeeDee said. She grabbed my hand and squeezed it and then dropped it, like she'd decided it was a bad idea after all. "We were just . . ." She trailed off.

"I can fucking see what you're doing," Kristle said. As if she hadn't been the one who had just asked.

"What's the big deal?" I said. "It's a free country."

Kristle looked at me only long enough to roll her eyes. "There are things you don't know about my little sister," she said, then went straight back to staring a hole in DeeDee.

"Yeah?" I said. "Well there are things I do know about her

too. So who cares?"

Kristle finished with me, though. "Did you tell him about us?" Kristle asked DeeDee. "Does he know what happens?"

"Just shut up," DeeDee said.

"Tell me what?" I said. "What happens?"

No one said anything. Jeff was looking quizzically from me to DeeDee to Kristle and back, and Kristle's face was even more stony. She was glaring at DeeDee as if to challenge her.

DeeDee was staring at the ground as if she'd actually done something wrong. I wasn't sure why she wasn't just telling Kristle to fuck off. So I did.

"Fuck off, Kristle," I said.

"Listen," she said. "DeeDee and I need to have some girl time. A woman-to-woman chitchat."

"Um," I said. "And you're in charge why?"

"It's okay, Sam," DeeDee said. "I'll see you tomorrow." But she didn't make a move to leave, and then Jeff was taking me by the shoulder and leading me away. "Come on," he said. "Let's give these two a chance to claw each other's eyes out. Or whatever it is girls do during girl time."

ELEVEN

WE FELT THE first drops of rain as soon as we jumped onto the main beach from the cliff of rocks that bordered DeeDee's cove. The sun was nearly gone, but it was still light enough out that we could tell there was a dark cloud hovering over our heads. "Well shit," Jeff said. "We're gonna get soaked."

There was a bolt of lightning out over the ocean, spidery and silent, tinting the whole beach in eerie neon purple. Jeff put his hands on his hips and looked out at the horizon in concerned contemplation, as if he had some say in the matter of weather. The crack of thunder came several seconds later, and then the rain really started to come down—it just started pouring. We were drenched before we even had the chance to cover our heads with our arms. I can't exactly say I minded. The rain was warm and felt good.

"What, we're just gonna stand here?" Jeff asked, and he began to race down the empty beach. I followed him, but soon we were both out of breath, the rain didn't seem to be letting up in the slightest, and anyway we were as wet as we were going to get. I slowed first, but Jeff only had a minute or two on me and pretty soon we were walking along in silence, side by side with our heads down, staring at our feet to keep the water out of our eyes.

"So," Jeff said after a while. "Kristle's little sister, huh? Good going, bro." He punched me in the shoulder. "Saw that one coming a mile away. Not as hot as Kristle, but close. This place is treating us well."

"Whatever," I said. "Her name's DeeDee. And I don't think they're exactly sisters—not technically at least." I didn't feel like being congratulated by my brother, whose next remark was sure to be something gross and obliviously degrading.

"Still, it's kinda like incest, though, huh? Two brothers fucking two sisters? Look, I like you, bro, but let's watch our step here."

"I'm not *fucking* anyone," I said. "And by the way, Kristle's a total slut, so I hope you haven't caught anything from her yet."

I should have known better. (Although Jeff was not usually the type to take offense at much, so come to think of it, why should he care?) Either way, before I knew what was happening, my brother had tackled me into the sand with something between a grunt and a scream. He pinned my shoulders against the soggy ground, his knee against my nuts. "Fuck you, fuck you, fuck you," he said. "You little fucking prick." I got his spit in my eye and squirmed, tried to wipe it away with my shoulder, but just ended up getting wet sand all over my face.

"What the fuck?" I yelped. It came out more girlishly than was my intention. I felt like a little kid again.

"Don't fucking call her that," Jeff said. His face was an inch from mine and I could smell Kristle's cigarettes on his breath. "Who the fuck do you think you are?"

"Okay, she's not a slut," I said testily. "Just a skank." I don't know why I was being such an asshole, but I couldn't help myself. All you had to do was look at her to know she couldn't be trusted. The way her pupils seemed to float a few inches in front of her eye sockets when she talked to you. The way her face rearranged itself the longer you looked at it. And everything else. I couldn't believe that Jeff was falling for her succubus bullshit.

"Just to remind you, she's the one who tried to fuck *me*," I said. "Your little brother—like two minutes before she actually *did* fuck *you*. From what I understand, at least. Now that's some fucked-up shit. And let's not even get into what she said to me yesterday."

Jeff looked physically pained and outraged at the same time; I only remembered seeing this look on his face once before, years ago, when I had hit him in the head with the remote control in a skirmish over possession.

He pressed his forearm across my chest and shoved with all his weight. "You fucking shit," he said. "Say you're sorry."

"Or what?" I wheezed. I could barely see Jeff with the storm coming down. Water was streaming from his hair into my eyes.

There was another crash of lightning and this time I could feel the thunder in my rib cage.

"Or I'll fucking kill you."

I almost laughed but caught myself. Also I didn't have enough oxygen left for laughter. While I struggled to escape, the sad truth is that I knew it was no use. My older brother is probably close to twice my size. He threw his weight against me with another grunt, and nearly knocked the wind out of me. "Well?"

"Fuck!" I said. "Okay, I'm fucking sorry! What's your problem?"

"Thank you," Jeff said, and just like that a conciliatory smile crossed his face. He stood up, slicked the hair from his face, and waited for me to collect myself. I took a moment, stood, and tried to dust the wet sand off my ass.

"You just don't get it," Jeff said. "I can see why you'd think so, but she's not just some slut. Things are complicated for her."

"Yeah, I'm sure," I said. "'Which dick am I gonna put in me today?' It gets *complicated*." I knew I had gone too far—I was disgusting even myself—and half expected a punch in the face. I would have deserved it this time. But Jeff was over fighting. One of the nice things about Jeff is that he has a mind like a goldfish and can't sustain anger for more than about three seconds.

"You don't understand," he said. "She's had it hard. She's not from here, you know."

"Yeah, so's DeeDee," I said. "But you don't see DeeDee acting like some nympho bitch."

"DeeDee's younger," he said. "A lot younger."

"What does that have to do with it?"

"It doesn't fucking matter," Jeff said. "It's different for her. Kristle's fucking tough, okay? You don't even know what she's been through." And then, seeing my dubious look, "I think I'm, like, in love with her." He looked away almost shyly and scratched his jaw. "I mean, I think."

You have to know my brother to know that this kind of admission on his part was just flat-out unheard of. Or maybe you know him well enough already to figure that out. The nicest thing I'd ever known him to say about a girl before was that she had an ass he'd like to smother himself in.

"Uh," I said.

"I don't know what's happening to me," Jeff said. "It's totally possible I'm going completely insane."

"Uh," I repeated. But before I could formulate an actual thought, he was stretching his arms to the sky, screaming at the top of his lungs as the rain swept through him. He leaped into the air and landed on his knees in the sand with a triumphant fist pump.

"Uh," I said again. "What are you doing?"

"I'm just so fucking in love!" Jeff screamed, his face gargoyled into a googly and shit-eating grin. I felt humiliated on his behalf. Come on.

"Get ahold of yourself," I said. But Jeff didn't seem to hear me. He cocked his head in a look of startled curiosity, putting out an open palm to the sky.

"Look," he said, climbing back to his feet. "The rain stopped."

He was right. I stretched my hand out and felt nothing but sky. When I looked up, the stars had appeared and were bright and shining and unobscured. I had to admit that it did seem fairly miraculous; like someone was answering him. So maybe Jeff really was in love. Even if he was, I couldn't approve of a display like that. It was unseemly, not to mention so out of character as to be a little scary.

We walked home in agreeable silence. I didn't ask Jeff about Kristle's hard life or what she'd said about *what would happen*. Actually I might have forgotten some of that stuff anyway. All I was really thinking about was being with DeeDee in the sand, how it had felt to be with her, how I hadn't felt nervous or uncertain. I had just been happy and amazed. Like that, the summer had transformed itself. I'd thought I'd known exactly how it would go and now, in just a few minutes, everything had changed.

I thought of the person I had been yesterday. I thought of who I was now and who I would be tomorrow and the next day and the next, and I realized that even though each of those people were different from the others, they all felt like me. I could draw a straight line from one to the next.

"Things might get a little weird from here on out, pal," Jeff said as we were crossing the beach road back into Seashell Shoals. "There's a lot more to these girls than you know."

"I know," I said. "That much is obvious."

"I just mean there's something about them. They have this thing about them. Right? Am I right? But that probably applies to all girls. All the good ones, at least. And, you know, who cares? I think it might be worth it."

I would have pressed him on the matter, but I was distracted by the Volvo sitting in the driveway of the cottage. It had a new bumper sticker on it: MY OTHER CAR IS A BROOM. Jeff and I exchanged a nervous glance as we climbed the stairs to the door.

MOTHER

We have been learning about mothers. Since we don't remember our own mother, we have little to go on, but we try. We do try. Mothers are everywhere: there are books and movies and television shows about them and magazine articles and the woman named Angelina Jolie and something called baby bumps. We soak all of it up, gathering information, making guesses, wondering if any of these mothers could be our own, or at least know her. It seems unlikely. We suspect that our mother has no interest in land mines or Burma/Myanmar or even Meals On Wheels. But you never know with her.

Mothers are everywhere except when they've disappeared. The disappearance seems to be a common routine, but where do all these disappeared mothers go? Is there an island somewhere?

Well, even when they've disappeared, these mothers are still around. They never seem entirely gone. They remain as shadows in corners and as untraveled hallways and as ladybugs crawling across mirrors. You never know where you might find someone's mother. She could be the lucky penny in the street. You never know what somebody's mother might be up to. She could be the bad penny just as easily.

Consider the amateur sleuth Nancy Drew. Could her dead mother be the one behind the many mysterious happenings—

the missing jewels and kidnapped heiresses, the inexplicable lights flickering on the cliffside? Could Nancy's mother be the one pulling all those criminal strings, safe in the remove of her own shadowy elsewhere? And could that elsewhere be just around the corner, under a manhole, or behind the Employees Only door in a smoky, disreputable bar in the bad part of town?

These are the things we consider. We are motherless.

Or are we? Because the thing we sometimes forget to include is that our mother did not disappear. It was we who disappeared, and that makes her failure almost worse.

She could not protect us. Or, consider it another way: she would not protect us. Being the Deepness, our mother has many tricks at her disposal. She has more than tricks, really—our mother commands vast and untold power, all of which seemed to do us no good when it mattered. As here we are, in the land of the disappeared.

Why did she fail us? Well, she must have had her reasons. It's been suggested by a few of our number that she may secretly have been happy to see us go—but we put that notion to a vote and rejected it soundly. She must have had her reasons—good ones. One of us (Taffany? Chanterelle? We can never be sure) pointed out that it's all the same in the end anyway. As here we are.

Here we are. But where is she? Is she still with us, in some small, pointless way? Sometimes we think we see her, when we cover our faces in our hands and spread our fingers and squint out at the ocean's horizon.

Sometimes we think we see her in the bathtub drain, or in soapy clouds in buckets of dirty mop water. Once, we thought she might have been a contestant on The Bachelor. (Or is it contestantette?)

It doesn't seem so farfetched to suppose that she could be nearby. If so, is she watching over us, or is she setting booby traps? Does she love us? Did she ever love us?

It doesn't matter. We don't actually care. We miss her. We know she'll have us back, if only we can get to her. Wherever she is, it's not at the bottom of some bucket.

TWELVE

"WELL, DID YOU miss me?" our mother said from the couch when we stepped inside. Dad was standing at the kitchen island, shell-shocked, clutching a glass of wine in midair. Mom was smiling maniacally. She had her shoes off and her feet up on the coffee table and was wiggling her toes.

"Color me surprised when I got home and you guys had just taken off. It was like Pompeii! You know, you left half the lights on. I guess I'm the only one who cares about conservation."

I knew it was my fault that she was here, but even so, I was first surprised and then annoyed to see her. I hadn't been expecting her to show up at all, I don't think, but I'd at least figured that if she was going to go to these lengths to return to us, she would also have had the grace to offer up some small impression of penitence. I'd figured that she would do us the favor of trying to be her old self.

But the opposite was true: she had been a changed person in the days before she'd left and in her absence she had changed even more, to the point that I was only about 60 percent certain that she was my actual mother at all. She had pierced her nipples—the hoops were obvious through her sheer, long-sleeved T-shirt—and her scoop neck revealed an elaborate tattoo, a blue, scaly snake that curled across her collarbone. Her graying tangle of hair was now a bob streaked with fire-engine red.

"Hellooooo," she was saying as she hopped up from her perch and scrambled over to me and Jeff to wrap us both in a single hug. "I've missed my little guys," she said. She stank of patchouli and sebum.

"I thought you weren't allowed to talk to men anymore," I said when we had extricated ourselves from her embrace.

"Oh, that," Mom said, rolling her eyes. In her excitement to see us she had dribbled red wine down the front of her shirt, and she bunched the fabric to her lips to suck up the spot. When she let it drop, all she had done was leave another stain—the sloppy print of plum-colored lipstick. "Let me tell you, Women's Land isn't all it's cracked up to be. They kicked me out after—what?—a week and a half? I thought the whole point of going there was to stop being bossed around by every Tom, Dick, and Harry. Well, meet Tina, Donna, and Harriet. And you should have seen the bathrooms! Oh, Lord."

I felt Jeff press a tense fist into the small of my back. "Jesus fuck," he mumbled. It was just for me to hear, but I saw Mom shoot him a sharp glance. Dad hadn't moved since we'd walked in; he was still standing at the counter with his wine at his chest, his face plastered with a frozen grin.

"I like your tattoo," I told my mother when no one had said anything else. It was obviously a total lie, just me trying to cover the awkwardness. The old mom had been a kindergarten teacher prone to chunky sweaters with appliquéd ducks all over them.

Mom beamed at the compliment. The room around us seemed to exhale and then hold its breath again. "My friend Gonzo did it. He's a genius, G-E-N-I-U-S. A real artist, you know. I've been staying with him since my banishment from the land of the ladies. Or, I was. It was much better there—the shower actually drains. Who would have thunk?"

"Who would have thunk?" Jeff echoed.

"And look at this one!" she exclaimed, lifting her sleeve and extending her forearm, which was covered in illegible tattooed text. "It's Sharon Olds. Brilliant."

I hadn't gotten a chance to look at Jeff's face and had no graceful way of turning for his reaction. But I could pretty much picture it. "Fucking unreal," he said. A moment later, I heard the door slam. He was gone.

"Well someone's in a bad mood," Mom said. "Jeez Louise."

Dad shook his head and wandered off and then it was just me and Mom, staring at each other. She sighed and collapsed back onto the couch, splaying out dramatically. I wanted to leave too—just go somewhere—but I felt sort of bad for her. And where was there, really, to go? So I just hovered.

"Was this a bad idea?" she asked.

I shrugged.

"At least you want me here," she said. "At least I've got my old pal Sam."

"Why did you come back?" I asked.

"You told me to. I could tell you needed me." She slugged the last of her wine. "'Winter, spring, summer, or fall . . .'" James fucking Taylor again.

But it was true. I was the one who had summoned her. Maybe I could have done it all along. Maybe if I had asked her nicely she never would have left in the first place.

DeeDee had asked me if I missed her and I said I didn't know, but I had; I had missed my mother. Even this strange person sitting in front of me with her tattoos and her striped hair and whatever else: I didn't even know her and I had missed her.

She had tried to do something. She was trying to do something. She was my mother. She had come back for me. At least, that's what she said.

I left her sitting there and walked outside. Jeff was crouched in the driveway and I squatted down next to him. We didn't have anything to say to each other. If he had been DeeDee I could have told him anything. I could have pretended she didn't speak English and just confessed everything, things I didn't even know I had to confess. But Jeff was Jeff, and I didn't know where to find DeeDee, so we just sat there in silence.

"Crazy day, bro," he finally said, after we had sat there for what must have been an hour.

"Crazy," I said.

We both went back inside and went to sleep.

Jeff's voice was the first thing I heard the next morning. "Hey," he whispered as I groaned in my sleep. "Let's get the hell out of here. I can't be in this house with these people."

I sat up in bed and rubbed my eyes. Somewhere in the distance I could hear strange noises. Well, strange if murder can be considered strange—it sounded like someone was being killed down the hall.

"Are they having sex?" I asked.

"Never you mind, little brother," Jeff said. "Let's just go."

I considered fleeing in my pajamas, but in the end decided to throw my bathing suit on. I met Jeff in the driveway, where he was smoking and fidgeting with his hair.

"Since when do you smoke?" I asked.

"Oh," he said. "I don't. Come on, let's walk somewhere." We went to the beach because that was pretty much the only place to go around here.

On the shore, I could feel restlessness rising at my ankles. When I tried to picture Sebastian and school and even Sasha Swain and our house in the suburbs in my mind, I came up with hardly anything. Would any of them remember me when I got home? Was our house still ours, and if we ever returned to it, would I be the same person when I got there? If so, who exactly was that person, again?

It suddenly occurred to me to wonder why I hadn't heard from Sebastian. It wasn't like him; normally he would have been texting to the point of nuisance. Of course, I hadn't been in touch with him, either. It was almost as if there was a force here holding us separate from the rest of the world. But it also probably had something to do with the impossible cell phone reception and not having Wi-Fi in the cottage.

I considered the notion that we had been swallowed, and that the longer we stayed here, the less likely it would be that we would ever be able to return home. That if we tried to cross the causeway back to everyday life, a hurricane might come from nowhere and push us right back to where we'd started. I thought of the Lost Colony, and what DeeDee had said. *This is where people come to disappear.*

Mom had tried to disappear herself, and somehow she had disappeared herself right back to our makeshift lost colony anyway.

Many of the people you meet here have already disappeared from one else-where or another. Was I really one of them?

"So why do you think she's back?" Jeff was wanting to know. We were making our way along the coastline, walking in the damp sand left by the receding tide as beads of sweat formed at the nape of my neck and trickled down my spine to the cleft of my ass. "Is she really even back?" he said. "Or is she going to be gone again by the time we get home? How did she find us?"

I didn't tell him that I had some vague notion of the answer to that question. I was ashamed that I had ever called her, although I couldn't name the reason why. "Is it even her?" I asked. It wasn't just a distraction technique; I was truly sort of uncertain.

"It's her," Jeff said. "I'd know her anywhere. Even with Sharon whatever tattooed all over her whole fucking arm. Even with everything."

"I know," I said.

"I wonder if she'll stay," Jeff said. "Dad's so spineless. He should have told her to leave. How could he even let her in the door?"

"How could he not?" I said. "Really, how could he not?"

"You wouldn't have."

"Yes I would have," I said.

"Well that's different," Jeff said, and he was right about that part.

Neither of us had discussed a destination, but as we continued our trek, it became clear exactly where we were aiming for. We passed the pier at the Fisherman's Net and then three more piers after it, passed through the crowds to the edge of the rental developments, where things were thinned out; we passed the pink hotel and continued along through the narrow and almost empty coast that abutted a gnarled, unpopulated wilderness. Without saying it, we were looking for the hidden cove, but it was eluding us. It hadn't taken this long with DeeDee yesterday. Once I thought about it, I realized that yesterday it hadn't taken any time at all. Or, it hadn't felt like it had.

But Jeff and I walked for hours, ignoring the sunburns creeping at our shoulders. We talked about a lot of things but mostly about nothing.

After the brief initial foray into the subject of our insane mother, we were now pointedly avoiding all matters of substance, which included the topics of DeeDee, Dad, and Jeff's recent queerification at the hands of Kristle. It was nice, though, just to be able to talk to him—I mean in a casual, unguarded way—for what was pretty much the first time in forever. It made me remember that he had once been a good older brother, when I'd been younger and he had been tall and smiling and very impressive.

We never reached DeeDee's beach. It was like we had never been there, like it had never existed.

Eventually Jeff dropped to the sand in frustration. "Motherfucker," he said. "This is weird, huh?" He pressed a finger to his shoulder, which was glowing angry red. "Shit motherfuck," he said.

"There's something funny about this whole fucking place," I said. "And not funny ha-ha either."

"I know," he said. "I already knew, but this pretty much confirms it, huh?"

"What should we do?" I asked.

"I guess go get something to eat?" Jeff said. "I'm starving." I was glad he suggested it. I wanted to see DeeDee again, but it seemed like going to find her on my own would be pushing my luck. If Jeff was suggesting that we go to the Fisherman's Net there was no harm in going along with him. It wasn't my fault that she worked there.

"God," I said, trying not to sound eager. "There's really not much to do around here, is there?"

After our endless walk out to the middle of nowhere in which we had found ourselves it only took a few minutes to walk back to the Fisherman's Net. Kristle was out front smoking like she'd been expecting us all along and was annoyed that we were late to our appointment.

"Hey, babe," Jeff called.

"Hey, babe," Kristle said. So they had reached babe status.

He went to her and put his hands on her hips and pushed her back against the silvery shingles of the restaurant's exterior. She wrapped her arms around his neck, cig still in hand, and they tongued each other hungrily in the salty, late-afternoon sun.

I stood and looked on awkwardly. Their slurping went on for much longer than I considered reasonable, especially given the fact that I was just standing there. When it got too gross to take anymore, I snuck past them into the restaurant, looking for DeeDee.

Instead I found a girl I didn't recognize pushing through the swinging kitchen door, overflowing plates of fried crap balanced on her forearms, a sour expression on her face.

"She's not here," Kristle called from behind me. Jeff plopped himself down at the nearest empty table and was ostentatiously snapping his fingers for service.

"Who?" I asked.

"*Who*, he says. All I can tell you is she better come back soon," Kristle went on. "Olay's a disaster. Just watch, I bet you anything she screwed up every one of those orders."

I didn't really care to watch. "Where is she?" I asked.

"Waitress!" Jeff was calling. "Could I get some service?"

Kristle ignored him. "She called in sick. Some kind of bug, I guess. Want something to eat? It's on me."

"Nah," I said. "Maybe I'll go find her. See how she's doing. Where do you guys live anyway?"

"Oh, I wouldn't do that. She's really not feeling good. She wouldn't want you to see her all gross and everything."

"Maybe I'll bring her some chicken soup or something." Kristle let out a guffaw, and I felt my already-sunburned face flush.

Jeff had tired of being overlooked and wandered out of the restaurant again, probably onto the pier. Kristle dropped a hand to my hip and smiled a smarmily sympathetic smile.

"Listen," she said. "I'm sure you'll see her around at some point."

"I'm sure," I said.

"But you know," she continued. "She's pretty busy. So you might not."

"Uh-huh," I said.

"Honestly, she and I had a talk last night. Just us girls. And the thing is that—listen—I don't want you to get your hopes up or anything."

"What do you mean?"

"Oh, who cares about DeeDee anyway? What's so special about her?" Kristle placed a hand on my leg but jerked it away as Jeff poked his head back through the saloon doors. "Babe. I'm not hungry anymore," he said. "Wanna go get a drink or something? You won't believe what fucking happened yesterday."

"Sure," Kristle said. "Taffany's working tonight. You wanna come too, Sam? She never cards." She winked almost imperceptibly.

Jeff looked from Kristle to me and back, arching his eyebrows and cocking his head, silently communicating that he would kill me if I took her up on her invitation. Kristle grinned bigger at me in a silent challenge.

"Uh, no thanks," I said. "I'm really tired."

"Suit yourself," Kristle said. She tossed her hair over one shoulder, then the other, then smoothed it with the back of her hand. "Another time."

"Tell Dad I'll be back tomorrow. If I feel like it," Jeff said, and Kristle smacked him on the ass in mock indignation.

"I don't know who you think you are!" She giggled.

Jeff looked back over his shoulder at me as they left together. Olay, the new waitress, was staring at me as she went about her business, but I didn't say anything to her and she didn't say anything to me.

At home, the stereo was blasting. I could hear it from the stairs to the kitchen door, and when I got inside, my mother was dancing around to Beyoncé, singing along to "Single Ladies" in her usual caterwaul. She was shaking her hips and sloshing a half-full tumbler of ice-and-something. There was an open bottle of Beefeater on the kitchen counter.

"So are you a single lady now?" I asked, but before she could answer I went out onto the porch, where I sat and looked out at the setting sun.

Out there, I made the decision not to be bothered by what Kristle had said about DeeDee—about *not getting my hopes up* or whatever. DeeDee didn't even really seem to like her; there was no reason to think that Kristle would have the faintest clue what she thought about anything.

Instead, I found myself wondering about DeeDee's mother. I wondered if she looked like her. If you could study the gold rings around DeeDee's pupils and catch a glimpse in the way they glittered of the mother who'd let her go. I tried to project DeeDee's face into the future, dress it up with lines and weight, thinking maybe that would reveal someone. But all I got was a blank where an image should have been. A shimmering, slippery lacuna.

I wondered if her mom missed her. I wondered if she even knew who she was now.

Or maybe she'd never even had a mother in the first place. But everyone has a mother.

I was still trying to imagine DeeDee's mom when an image of my own mother came to me in a memory I had never stumbled on before. In the memory, I was younger—little—and Mom was younger too. She was happy and sun touched, her hair long and wavy, untroubled by gray, and she was wearing a pair of high-waisted jeans and a loose plaid shirt. It was spring and she was teaching me how to ride a bike, because my dad was too irritable and easily frustrated to teach anyone how to do anything. Mom was standing at the end of the driveway of our house in the suburbs, and she was laughing as I picked myself up off the ground after another spill and hopped back on the bike and finally nailed it. I sped past her into the street as she clapped her hands and said, "There you go, pal of mine; you've got it now."

I was older now. We all were. It wasn't that simple anymore.

THIRTEEN

WHEN I WOKE up the next morning, the house was empty and reeked of cigarette smoke. The TV was on, tuned to some soap opera, and the volume was blaring. I noticed a coffee mug sitting on the end table, stuffed with barely smoked butts, the filters emblazoned with thin green rings and stained at the ends with plum-colored lipstick blots.

This from a woman who once told me that if she ever caught me smoking a cigarette she would send me to live with my grandmother in Shreveport. The worst of it is that I had believed her. A part of me still sort of did.

I poured myself some cereal, switched the channel, and flopped onto the couch to finally watch *The Price Is Right*. This had been my original plan for the summer before it had been rearranged in front of me, first by my father and then by DeeDee.

But *The Price Is Right* was not the same as I'd remembered it.

That day, the old ladies squealing as they *came on down* weren't as amusing as they had once been. I no longer felt my usual swell of vicarious happiness when the army vet won the Subaru. Even Plinko had lost its luster.

I wondered if my boredom at all this meant I had finally become a man after all.

No, I decided. I just had my mind on other things. The whole time I was watching the show I was wishing DeeDee were there with me. She'd been a maid last summer; she would surely know exactly how much Windex cost. And I had this feeling she would have an appreciation for a good Showcase Showdown.

A woman was jumping up and down and weeping after winning a dinette set, a Ski-Doo, and a trip to Reykjavik, and, feeling nothing but antsiness, I gave up. This waiting around was hell.

I was going to go find her. She would be working, probably, but I could at least say hi. So I made the walk to the restaurant hoping that she would be there and wondering how I would find her if she wasn't. I can't say that Kristle's warning the previous day wasn't bothering me at all. As much as I tried to put it out of my mind, every time the *Price Is Right* buzzer had sounded, I had imagined DeeDee looking me in the face and opening her mouth to speak and only that loud, awful buzz coming out. *Too high, buddy, try again next time.*

But then I'd remember the way she had looked at me when I'd walked in on her at Kristle's birthday party, and the way she had laughed when we'd been drunk on the mermaid statue at the golf course. The two of us in the sand with the sun setting on a beach that belonged only to us. There was no way all of that hadn't been real. Kristle was just full of shit as usual.

She was back at the restaurant. I saw her beyond the saloon door as I approached, beyond the always-abandoned hostess station, distractedly taking an order from a sullen family and looking sullen to match them. Something about how she was fidgeting with the pen at her ear—the pensive way she was biting her lip—made me almost rethink my plan. I just had a bad feeling.

But in my hesitation, DeeDee looked up and saw me and gave a weak smile. It seemed in that moment of uncertainty that she was gathering herself. There was no turning back now. She glanced to her customers apologetically and then up at me again and raised an index finger in my direction—*wait*.

I waited. She disappeared into the kitchen and reemerged a few seconds later and came toward me. Her smile had a hint of a wince to it.

"Come outside for a second," she said. "I told Olay to cover. We'll see how *that* goes." And I followed her outside the restaurant onto the end of the fishing pier, the same spot where we'd first met.

She lit a cigarette and leaned back on her elbows on the railing but then changed her mind and stood, lifting her chin and straightening her back.

I shuffled my feet. I had been expecting something different. Maybe things were not what I had thought after all.

"Are you feeling better?" I asked awkwardly. "Kristle said you were feeling sick."

"Yeah," she said. "It was just one of those things."

"My mom came back," I said. "We got back to the cottage and her car was there and . . ." I trailed off. DeeDee's eyes were unfamiliar.

"The thing is," she said, "I have to work today. It's really busy in there. Kristle's playing hooky with your brother and Olay's a disaster."

"It's cool," I said. "Tomorrow or something?"

She shrugged. "Maybe? Let's play it by ear, okay?"

"Cool," I said. "Definitely. For sure."

DeeDee gave me a kiss on the cheek and walked back down the pier toward the restaurant. I climbed over the rail and dropped into the sand, where I lay for a while before getting up and moving on.

When I came upon Dad a mile down the beach, his metal detector was lying in the sand. He was kneeling, digging a hole. He didn't see me coming and soon I was just a few feet away, standing over him in his labors. He was concentrating hard, flinging handfuls of sand into a pile next to him, his mouth clenched, brow furrowed. His forehead was dripping with sweat. I was waiting for him to look up and see me. He didn't.

"So what are you actually looking for?" I asked after a while, when it was clear that he might keep going forever without ever realizing I was there.

Dad startled at the sound of my voice. He was thrown off-balance and fell back onto his haunches, where he looked up at me sheepishly like someone who'd been caught at something.

"Hey there, Tiger," he said, trying to play it off. "How's your day going?"

"Terrible actually," I said. I didn't want to talk about it. I didn't want to think about it. "What are you doing?" I asked again. It wasn't rhetorical, even though it seemed that way. I was starting to get the feeling that the treasure-hunting thing was more than just another one of his stupid hobbies. It was different from the yoga and the knitting circle and the book club, all of which he'd given up in a matter of weeks.

This time he had committed himself, falling deeper and deeper into it every day. He was truly searching. And not just the general kind of searching either. Seeing the way he was digging, it dawned on me that he was trying to find something specific—something more than the piles of gold he'd mentioned when he'd first started his quest.

"What are you looking for?" I asked him when he didn't answer me. "What's the treasure?"

Blackbeard's treasure," he said, sounding both pleased that I was interested and mildly frustrated that I had to ask. "People have been looking for it for centuries. It's got to be around here somewhere."

This was getting ridiculous. "All that stuff you've been bringing home doesn't look like Blackbeard's treasure," I said. "Or anyone's treasure. Don't you think you'll know it when you find it? It's got to be sort of impressive."

Dad was still digging. He would humor me, but he had more important tasks at hand than answering my dumb, obvious questions.

"You know, Tiger," he said, looking up at me for just a second as he tossed a handful of sand. "This isn't the first time I've been here."

I was surprised. I'd figured that my father had picked this beach as our destination spot through one of his usual decision-making methods: a Groupon or a flyer posted on a telephone pole or a travel segment on the local news channel. It hadn't occurred to me that he had wanted to come back to a place that had once been good to him.

"Really?" I asked.

"Yep. About thirty years ago, Tiger. Hard to imagine I was ever your age, huh?"

"I guess," I said.

"That's when I first heard about the treasure. People were always talking about it but supposedly no one ever found it. But over the years I've been thinking. What if the treasure was disguised somehow? What if someone *did* find it, but it wasn't what they expected? Maybe they thought it was junk and tossed it right back?"

"So what you're saying is that the priceless treasure might be an old fork or a screwdriver or a crappy earring? Or whatever stuff you've been finding out here and hauling back to the house in that dumb bucket?"

The big orange bucket Dad had taken to carrying around with him was lying on its side next to the metal detector. I picked it up and perused its contents. There was only one thing in it so far: a small coin. I took it out to look at it more closely: it was a euro, probably dropped in the sand by some German tourist.

"Well at least it's *money*," I said, letting it clink back into the bucket. "If you ever go to France you can use it to buy a fancy French gumball. It's a start. But I don't think they even had euros in the days of pirate legend."

"Legendary, Tiger. *Legendary*. That's exactly the right word. The treasure is legendary. But you can't trust a legend. First rule of treasure hunting, buddy. Legends get confused. There's always some truth to them, but if you get too hung up on the details, you'll usually miss what's right in front of your face. Unless you remember that, you'll miss something in a place like this. There are lots of legends around here."

"Like the Lost Colony?" I asked.

Dad tipped his head like he'd misheard me. Then he beamed.

"Exactly like the Lost Colony. Exactly." I had finally gotten his attention, and now he stopped digging. He looked up at me expectantly, prideful and thrilled, all *that's my boy*.

A sense of hopefulness hung in the air as he waited for me to say something else. But when I didn't, his face fell again and he went right back to his work, resigned to the fact that I would never get it.

I didn't care at all what he was talking about. Dad's treasure hunt was obviously a total waste of time. But wasn't everything around here a waste? "Want some help?" I asked. Why not? Without DeeDee or *The Price Is Right* to occupy me, I now had nothing but time to kill.

He looked at me suspiciously. He had gotten used to me trying to trick him with good humor.

But I wasn't fucking with him this time. I got down on my knees and started to scoop. We began to dig a hole together.

It was harder work than I'd expected it to be, but after a few minutes the task became more and more satisfying. I started to see how it wasn't as much of a waste of time as I'd thought—I still didn't expect to find anything, but at least we were *doing* something, making some kind of measurable progress. The pit was deeper and deeper by the second, the two of us working together. After a summer of walking in circles, thinking I was going somewhere always to wind up back where I'd started, it was nice to be doing something that was resulting in a basic, straight line, getting straighter and longer, even if in the least useful direction imaginable.

So we kept digging, uncovering nothing. The sun moved overhead. My muscles were aching and my back was sore. I kept going. I wasn't actually planning on stopping. I wasn't expecting him to stop either. But finally he did.

"Aw, fuck it," Dad said. "Your old man's not as young as he

used to be. There's not anything here. I'm never going to find it." A week ago I would have told him he was right, to just go ahead and give up, but now I didn't want to see him disappointed.

"It's all right," I said. "Maybe not today, but you'll get there eventually." I stood and Dad stood too. He thumped me on the back and looked over his shoulder.

"Come on," I said. "I'll walk you home." I picked up the bucket, and he picked up the metal detector and slung it over his shoulder. He looked like an old, tired Huck Finn. We started back for home. Dad was whistling, which normally drove me crazy, but at that moment I didn't care. I may have even whistled along with him myself.

Eventually the song petered out and we walked for a bit in silence. "So what's going on with you and Mom?" I asked. "Why do you think she's back?"

"Oh, I don't know," he said. "She won't even tell me how she found us." He looked at me sidelong, posing a question.

I wanted to ask him about DeeDee, but I knew that I couldn't deal with the monologue that would inevitably follow if I did. "Do you want her to stay?"

"I want her to do what makes her happy," he said. "That's all she's trying to do. I actually admire her for it, sort of."

"Give me a break," I said.

"You'll understand when you're my age," Dad said with a shrug. "One day you look around and realize all the choices you thought you were making might have been the wrong ones.

That they might not have even been choices at all. Actually, I hope you don't understand. That's why I brought you here, I guess."

I had stopped paying attention. I was only thinking of what I had done wrong. Of how I had found the thing I had been looking for and how I had lost her so quickly.

FOURTEEN

I STAYED AWAY from DeeDee like she obviously wanted me to. If there's one thing I'm good at, it's getting messages. I had misjudged the situation at first, but now I understood. Just like Kristle said, I'd gotten my hopes up. DeeDee had blown me off the way I'd blown Sasha Swain off a million years ago. And if DeeDee didn't want to see me I wasn't going to be a stalker about it.

It was annoying, then, that she was the one who would not leave me alone. In fact, she was more present to me these days than ever. Even if only in an imaginary way. I hadn't seen her since she'd blown me off at the restaurant a week ago. I kept expecting her to come find me, but she didn't. I was thinking about her all the time.

Every time I came out of the surf I'd look up into the distance, hoping to spot her approaching through the dunes. Several times I thought I saw her rolling from the waves, even though I knew she couldn't swim. Every time I smelled cigarette smoke, I thought it might be hers, and when I turned around and saw that it wasn't, I would wonder: What was she doing now? What about five minutes ago, or five minutes from now? She seemed capable of existing in past, present, and future all at once, as if it was no thing, as if the linear notion of time was something she brushed off as silly and irrelevant—*oh, that?*

Was she at the Fisherman's Net, wandering irritably from table to table, or was she taking the trash out, or was she walking up the beach with Kristle, both of them running their fingers through wet hair, their backs to the sun as they bickered? Maybe she was on the pier. Or pushing a shopping cart through a dusty aisle at Seamark, thinking, *Today, frozen waffles and granola bars*, or *Why not brussels sprouts for once?* Or dancing at some party, arms in the air, throwing her head back. Wait, no: that wouldn't be her. More likely she'd be sitting alone on a balcony or secluded away in some bedroom reading a dusty old paperback and waiting for other boys—stoned, confused, a little drunk—to stumble in and find her.

I wouldn't flatter myself to think that maybe she would be waiting there for me. But of course, I couldn't help wondering anyway. Even during the middle of the day when there wasn't any party happening.

And just when I thought I'd managed to put her aside for a minute, an hour, I'd close my eyes and see her face again.

I wondered what I had done wrong.

I thought about talking to Jeff, asking his advice, but he was no help anymore. He never had been, but there was a moment when it had seemed possible that he could be. That moment had passed. Jeff was barely at the house anymore. His excuse was that he didn't want to be around Mom, and maybe that was half-true, but I wondered if it had something to do with me. He'd stop in every now and then just to brush his teeth or pick up some clothes or eat some cereal or whatever, none of which really counted. The times that I'd tried to catch him in conversation, he'd extricated himself as quickly as possible.

Was it Kristle? Was it something else? I couldn't believe I'd thought I could count on him.

I actually thought about calling Sebastian for advice, but I could practically hear his voice: *Wait, this is all over some girl? Don't be such a fucking vagina, dude! I mean, dude! You go to the beach for a month and you turn into a human tampon!*

I was lonely again. Before, being lonely had felt romantically belligerent—a satisfying fuck-you to everyone—but this time it was just loneliness. It was prickly and cold.

Which was maybe or maybe not an explanation for the dream I had when I fell asleep on the beach on a day that was one in a string of many identical, aimless days since I had tried and failed to enjoy *The Price Is Right* and had gone to see DeeDee at the restaurant.

In the dream, DeeDee and Kristle and Jeff and I were all in the sand together, but I was somehow in two places at once: standing in the sand, but also observing myself from a perspective a few paces behind, a few feet above. The four of us were standing there in a row, just looking out at the sun setting on the horizon, our fingers grazing one another's in silhouette like we were a string of old-fashioned paper dolls. The sun doesn't set over the Atlantic Ocean—even my dream self knew that—but I supposed it could have been a different ocean as it swallowed the pink, sinking sphere.

Without saying anything, the Girls stepped forward. They began to wade into the water. Toes, calves, thighs. The waves were hitting hard but they kept walking. Hips, breasts, shoulders. They didn't stop.

I tried to look over at Jeff and found that I couldn't. I tried to speak but I couldn't do that either.

I wanted to chase after them. I wanted to shout at them both to come back. I just wanted them to turn around and look at me, just look at me long enough for me to reach out and stop them.

The water began to crash over their bodies, but they walked on until they were nearly out of sight.

I was outside myself and I was paralyzed. They faded off into nothing. From every direction, I could feel glowing eyes on all of us.

Then the sun was gone and the water wasn't much like water anymore. It was black and tarry and dangerous, and my mother was walking out of it. The color returned slowly as she approached, and I realized the sun was out again. I wasn't dreaming anymore. Mom was wearing this sort of old-fashionedy bathing suit that I hadn't seen her in before, black with white trim and a halter that tied at the neck. It didn't look like the sort of thing that they'd approve of at Women's

Land, but it didn't look like anything that Gonzo the tattoo artist would pick out for her either. I didn't know where she'd gotten it. I supposed it was something that was just hers. In the sun, the inky snake splayed across her chest appeared to squirm.

I thought of what my father had said: about the choices she had made and the ones she was still making. She had decided to take action. Even if it had been pointless, even if it had been the wrong thing, even if it had just only led her back to us eventually, it was still action and that counted for something.

She didn't notice me looking at her; in fact she seemed to be half somewhere else entirely. She was standing alone in an awkward spot not quite far enough from another family's huddle and was staring off into middle distance, fiddling with her hair. Out of nowhere I felt an overpowering affection for her. Well, she was my mother.

LOVE

We have heard a lot about "love." We have a hard time understanding it, but we don't feel too bad; we have heard that it's a difficult concept for many people.

Without a full understanding, it's hard to decide whether it's real. We are divided. Among those of us who do believe, we are divided again as to whether it's a good thing—a gift, a miracle—or a corruptive force.

One thing we have reached consensus on is that—real or not, whether from the Deepness or the Endlessness—love is strange and dangerous. There are many reasons to love someone, reasons that are not often discussed. It's not as simple as one is led to believe.

It makes little difference to us. We don't love anything or anyone. Nothing. This is an unspoken promise that we have made not only to ourselves but, more importantly, to one another. Selfishness is our one true law. It provides order. Our knife must stay sharpened.

But every once in a while we'll be walking along the beach road together, off to some house to be cleaned or another shift at another restaurant, and we might turn at the same time and find ourselves facing each other, pausing in rapt fascination at the sight of a familiar and beautiful face. It is a face from a magazine, filtered through a dream; it's a face that has been passed down, a face we invented.

We might find our breath catching at the way the sun hits the other's hair, the way she pauses for a moment and thinks before laughing. The way she reminds us of our many selves and the way she is different and singular.

Sometimes—rarely, but sometimes—it occurs to us that we would do anything, sacrifice anything, for her.

We never discuss this. We hope it doesn't count as love. The worst thing we could do is love one another.

FIFTEEN

KRISTLE WAS IN my room and she was naked. I thought I was dreaming at first, but I rubbed my eyes and sat up in bed, and she was standing motionless, arms at her sides, her body hard and glowing like a statue made of moon rock.

"Shh," she said. "Your brother's asleep on the couch."

"What the fuck?" I said.

"Shh," she said. "It's no big deal. It's just sex." And she crawled into bed on top of me, her nipples scraping my bare chest, and started kissing me on the mouth.

I pushed her off. "This is so fucked-up," I said. "What are you doing?"

"Shhhh," she said. "Just relax. Don't make it such a big deal."

"You're my brother's girlfriend," I said.

"We don't believe in girlfriends around here," she said. "It's one of many things we don't believe in."

She took my hand and placed it between her legs. It was moist and warm and soft with downy hair, and I'm ashamed to say that this time I didn't recoil. One can only resist so much, okay? "See?" she said, beginning to grind. "No big deal." Her hair was brushing my face, and I felt my breathing get shallow. "I've seen you staring at me," she said. "Be a man."

Be a man. Most things had changed since the beginning of the summer, but this was a constant: I still had no idea what it was supposed to mean. Maybe I was even less certain now, having found myself in this strange kingdom of Girls. Everything was ruled by dream logic around here; it made the entire concept of manhood seem pathetic and, well, flaccid. Not that it hadn't seemed that way already.

Kristle had moved the covers from my body and was straddling my midsection with her hand inside my underwear, where my dick was aching. My fingers were inside her, and she had her head thrown back, lips parted halfway in a look that implied concentration more than pleasure.

Then there was a crack of light coming from the hall, and I looked up to see my brother silhouetted in the doorway. He didn't say anything, but I pushed Kristle off me and threw the sheets back over myself.

"Sam?" Kristle said. "Look, I won't if you really don't want to, but . . ." Then she saw that I was dumbfounded, and she looked over her shoulder to where my brother was just staring, frozen in place.

"Shit," she said, scrambling to her feet, still naked. "Jeff!" He was gone and she was chasing after him. All I could think to do was just try to fall back asleep and hope it had been my imagination.

SIXTEEN

I WENT TO find DeeDee. She'd never told me where she lived, but it wasn't hard to track her down. I waited till Tuesday, her day off, and followed a trail of Girls up the beach road until I found myself standing in front of the pink motel that I'd walked to on the first morning here. Like many things here, it made backward sense that this was her home.

There was a blond Girl in the parking lot, another one of them, leaning against a car and smoking of course. "Do you know where DeeDee lives?" I asked, knowing that she would.

She looked up and her eyes darted with recognition. She twisted her neck and brushed her hair from her eyes, tucking it behind her ear. "Why do you want DeeDee?" she said. She gave a long blink. Her tongue darted out as she moistened the corner of her mouth.

"I found something of hers," I said. "I want to give it back."

"What is it?" she asked. "I'm Jenuvia, by the way. You're Sam, right?"

"Yeah. But can you just tell me where she lives?" I said.

The Girl gave a disgruntled shrug. "Four-A," she said. "But she's in a terrible mood. She's been sick. You sure you want to talk to her?"

"Thanks," I said.

"Wait," the Girl called after me as I was walking away. I turned to face her again and she was different now; she was burning with something I recognized, something I had seen in both DeeDee and Kristle. "Come back. You don't want DeeDee. I know how she treated you. Come talk to me instead. I'm headed to the beach. I've heard a lot about you."

The thing is I almost believed her. For a minute. Worse: I almost went with her. I don't know why. But I pulled myself away just as she was moving for me.

A blonde I didn't recognize answered the door. She was wearing a ratty white T-shirt that barely reached the tops of her thighs and a pair of underpants that looked like they might have once been pink but definitely not for a really long time.

She looked at me expectantly.

"Hey," I said. I was trying not to stare at her near-nakedness. I don't know why it made me so uncomfortable, since she didn't seem to care at all. I swallowed hard. "I'm looking for DeeDee," I said. "Is she here?"

The girl seemed disappointed. "Oh," she said. "Who cares

about her?" But when I didn't reply, she craned over her shoulder and yelled: "DeeDee! Someone's here to see you!"

A scream came back. "Who is it!?" I recognized DeeDee's voice.

"What's your name?" the girl asked me. She put a hand on my hip and gave me that look again. This time I was prepared for it; I stepped past her into the apartment without hesitating.

"It's Sam," I called. The girl turned around, gave me a *whatever* hair toss, and wandered off, leaving me alone to wait.

The place was a complete dump, dim and cramped and a tiny bit smelly (of sweat and old food and maybe garbage that hadn't been taken out in a few days), and littered with junk. I'd entered into a small dining area with a table on which no surface was visible, as it was covered with newspapers and cigarette cartons and dog-eared copies of *Her Place* and stacks of old dishes. There were a few flies buzzing around.

Past the dining table was the living room, or what had once been a living room. I didn't know what it was now: clothes were strewn everywhere; there were T-shirts dangling over the sides of chairs and a tangled up pile of bras lying on a dingy old couch. Several sleeping bags were balled up on the floor next to a few boxes that had been turned into a makeshift coffee table. It made me sad to think that DeeDee lived here.

But there she was, standing next to an open sliding glass door that led out to a balcony, arms folded, hair a mess. Something had distracted her while she was putting on her eyeliner, I guess, because she'd only bothered to smear it on one eye.

"Hey," I said.

"It's my day off," she said.

"I know. That's why I'm here."

"Well try to be quiet; Pucci's asleep in the bedroom and Taffany's hungover and thinks it's her right to be a big bitch to everyone."

I was looking around the place. I wasn't going to criticize or anything, but I guess she could see that I thought it was pretty gross.

She rolled her eyes. "Sorry I didn't clean up for you. Most of the other girls spend all day cleaning; they're not about to come home from work and be neat freaks here, too. Your brother doesn't seem to mind the mess—actually, it wouldn't kill him to lift a finger himself. Here. Come out on the balcony. It's the only place with any privacy." So I stepped over a pile of clothes and through the sliding door to a tiny concrete terrace, which looked out over the parking lot. The girl who'd directed me to DeeDee was gone.

"It's not ocean view or anything," DeeDee said. "But at least it's something. I try to be positive about it. A parking lot is more exciting than the ocean anyway, right? You can see everyone coming and going. What does the ocean do? Just sit there!"

"It's cool that you get to live on your own," I said.

"Ha," DeeDee said. "On our own. Do you realize I sleep in a bunk bed with three other people? Two on top, two on bottom. It's ridiculous."

"I'm sorry," I said.

"Luckily Activia is small," DeeDee said. "And she sleeps

pretty soundly. It could be worse; last year I bunked with Jessamee and she was a kicker. Next year I'll be eighteen, which hopefully means I'll get my own bed."

"How many people live here, anyway?" I asked.

"I dunno," DeeDee said. "Including me? It changes sometimes. There are others all over, of course—Blair and Tresemmé and them have that whole house on the bypass, and there's Franzia and hers in Duck and some more that I don't even really know, but in this unit it's twelve or thirteen, depending on whether you count your brother. Of course, it changes, like, daily."

"Where does he sleep?" I asked.

"With Kristle," DeeDee said. "Duh. She gets her own bed 'cause she's the oldest, but it's causing problems. Everyone wants to know why they can't both live at your place for now. Then Taffany could take her bed and everything would be a lot less cramped."

I leaned over the railing and craned my neck to the sun. There was a flick of a lighter and a plume of smoke curled past my face and into the air.

"So," I said.

"So," she said.

"Kristle tried to do it with me," I said.

DeeDee didn't flinch. "I know," she said. "She told me. Typical ho."

"You don't think that's kind of fucking crazy?"

"We're not from around here," DeeDee said.

"That's all you're going to say?" I asked.

"I told you my favorite stories were the ones about hos."

She was cool and matter-of-fact, revealing no sadness or anger or regret or anything. I could see why she smoked so much now; the cigarette was a helpful prop for looking distracted and careless. "This is just us. This is how we are."

As much as I wanted to reject that explanation—it was sloppy and stupid—I could see that by believing it she had made it true. In that moment, the person I was looking at wasn't the same girl who had shown herself to me in the bedroom at the party and then again in the ship on the golf course. DeeDee was gone now—she had flown off—leaving behind another Girl no different from the rest of them. Beautiful and tan and radiant, but hard eyed and complacent and a little empty, too. A girl who had no idea who she was; a girl like an Eskimo who couldn't find a single word for snow.

She stubbed out her cigarette in an overflowing ashtray and picked up a copy of *Her Place* that was lying on a deck chair. "Want to do the quiz?" she asked, folding the pages back. "This is a good one: 'Are You In Love?'"

"Please tell me what I did wrong," I said. "I'll leave you alone, I promise. I just want you to tell me." I knew I was being pathetic—that Sebastian would have probably disowned me as a friend if he had seen me behaving this way—but I was far past caring.

"Sam, I can't explain. I'm sorry, okay? What do you want me to say?"

"I want you to say what you mean."

"I don't want anyone to get hurt," she said. "I don't want *you* to get hurt."

"What kind of hurt are we talking? Broken arm? Traumatic brain injury? Scraped knee? I mean, it makes a difference. I'm already hurt anyway."

"Sam," she said with a grimace. Something about the disgust in her voice made me hopeful—she sounded angry again. She sounded almost like herself. But she sighed and ran her fingers through her hair. "Oh, Sam," she said. "You wouldn't understand."

"I should have listened," I said. "I never should have trusted any of you."

The funny thing is that no matter what I said and no matter what happened, I did trust her. Even still. But there was nothing I could do except leave.

FREEDOM

We are unable to leave this place.

At the beginning of every summer, we line the side of the road, watching the parade of minivans and SUVs arriving from beyond the causeway and wondering about where they come from. The places spelled out on their license plates in strange combinations of letters: Del-a-ware, Mary-land, Virrrrrr-ginia.

Virginia is actually not far from here but we've never been: our curse forbids us to leave the small network of islands that comprise our temporary home. Or should we say prison?

Elsewhere is a popular topic of conversation for us. We speculate as to what it must be like—any elsewhere, it doesn't really matter. We long to see "Tennessee," where we imagine beautiful girls who live in elaborate castles and spend endlessly looped hours on the chore of brushing their waist-length hair while devising fiendish and unreasonable tasks for their boyfriends (dimpled, broad shouldered) to accomplish in their tribute.

We imagine "Pennsylvania," a land of warrior princesses, tan and sinewy and wild haired, running through forests with machetes and bows and arrows, faces streaked with dirt and war paint, killing their enemies without remorse.

"Connecticut." A cloud city? A land of rocks and fire? We can never make up our minds. But we are jealous of the girls

who climb into their cars at the end of the summer and are carried back to these faraway homes, shedding the ordinariness of what they call vacation and becoming more and more themselves again as the ocean—our ocean—recedes into abstraction. Even in the passenger seats of crowded sedans packed with beach towels and luggage, faces pressed to the glass as they float up the beach road, they are free.

SEVENTEEN

WHEN I WAS just a little kid, on the Fourth of July, I asked my then-normal mother what would happen if a firework forgot to burn out, if all those flares just kept on falling and falling until they floated on down and tumbled onto the grass, still glittering and alive. Could you touch one. Could you catch one and keep it. Could you hold it in your pocket.

That was before. It was back when my mother had still been a kindergarten teacher, before she'd heard of Facebook and Women's Land. And on the hill behind the middle school, the Fourth of July when I was five, Mom had warned me about the dangers of catching a stray piece of firework. "It would burn your finger off," she'd told me. "And then your whole body would explode and then you would die. But don't worry about it. It could never happen. They fly high and burn fast."

I know now that what Mom told me is not precisely true. I'm not stupid, and I've never heard of an innocent bystander's entire body exploding because of a wayward firework on the Fourth of July. But even so, ever since then, even now, I have to admit that fireworks scare me—not as much as they did when I was little, but enough that I find myself flinching and watching the first red flash of the rockets from behind closed lids every year. In these moments I imagine every single spark flying right for me, a billion of them swarming my body. With my eyes shut, fireworks exploding hundreds of feet over my head, I can feel myself burning.

In recent summers, I'd spent the Fourth with Sebastian and his older sister Sophie, along with whichever guy she was making time with and any other friends we had that didn't happen to be away on vacation. We would all cluster on a blanket on the hill, sipping booze smuggled in an old Starbucks thermos, trying to ignore the residual taste of coffee, just biding our time, really. The night always started rowdy—with Sebastian throwing popcorn at other people in the crowd and Sophie being typically distant and cool—and usually ended on a note of contemplation as we all wandered off the field, not really talking, a little drunk and maybe stoned, too, depending, the lights still flickering in our corneas, all of us just happy it was summer but at the same time sad, because the moment you remember to be happy about summer is always the same moment that you remember that it will be over pretty soon.

This year Sophie and Sebastian and the usual people were summers away; Jeff had barely looked at me since the incident with Kristle a week-ish previous; and DeeDee had cast me off like an expended Gauloise. Meanwhile, my father's quest for undiscovered metal was drawing him farther and farther down the shore and away from all of us. It was just me and Mom now.

On the beach, the Girls still stared at me as they passed, smirking and twisting their hair around their fingers, but now I didn't look back. I knew it was a game to which I didn't know the rules. None of them approached me.

I'd nearly forgotten that the Fourth of July was even happening. I barely knew it was July at all. I hadn't been invited anywhere and I had gone back to sleeping late, past the point of any parade, so it sort of slipped my mind. Yes, I'd noticed the beach was extra-crowded with an alarming number of people in star-spangled bikinis on the morning of the day that turned out to be the Fourth, but somehow it didn't register with me that it was a holiday or anything.

I wouldn't have been that interested anyway. My only patriotism was to the beach of my own on which I had somehow found myself. And even that I was sort of ambivalent about.

But then, in the late afternoon, Kristle appeared to remind me of the holiday just as I had stepped from the wooden outdoor shower and was wrapping a towel around my waist.

"Listen," she said, materializing from behind the Volvo—not flinching a bit at my nearly naked body or my surprised glare. "We're having a party. Tonight."

"Uh-huh," was all I could say.

"You should come," she said.

"Yeah, sure," I said. I had by then stopped caring what her

motives were and had decided to just think of her as a crazy person who should be avoided if possible and humored if she did happen to cross your path.

"Just come," she said. "Don't be an idiot." Then she softened: "Look. I didn't tell Jeff I was inviting you. I didn't tell anyone, actually. But you should come. It's on the beach tonight, by the pier, after the fireworks. I know DeeDee'll be happy if you come. And your brother will get over it."

Somewhere off in the distance a radio was playing that song about being "proud to be an American." It suddenly occurred to me that Kristle's shorts were starred and striped; only then did I realize the date.

"Don't you know the Fourth of July is a holiday about America?" I asked. "You guys aren't even from here. You shouldn't, like, be allowed to have a party. It's unpatriotic. How would you like it if I threw a party for Trotsky's birthday or whatever?"

She looked at me blankly and I couldn't exactly blame her. I didn't really even know who Trotsky was. "Oh please," she said. "Just trust me. Come. I mean, I know you have absolutely no reason to trust me. But trust me anyway." Then she was gone.

"Happy Fourth of July," she called over her shoulder from wherever she had disappeared to.

A few hours later I was still lost in indecision as to whether I would take her up on it. I was in my bedroom on top of the sand-crusted comforter, flipping through an ancient copy of *Her Place* that I'd found under the couch. The quiz was "Are

You Worth It?" but I decided I wasn't sure I wanted to know the answer and was instead about to read my horoscope when I smelled smoke. My mother was in the doorway with a lit cigarette. When I looked away, she knocked on the doorjamb. "Hey there," she said.

"I can't believe you're smoking in the house," I said. "Does Dad know you're smoking in the house?"

"He said it was okay," she said uncertainly. "Anyway, he's not the boss. I'm my own woman."

"They're going to keep the deposit," I said. "Who would smoke in a rental, anyway?"

"Come on," she said. "Don't be such a grump. It's the Fourth of July. Come and watch the fireworks with me."

I grunted and looked up from the horoscope only long enough to roll my eyes. But a minute later I could sense her still standing there and I looked up again, and she hadn't budged from the doorway, holding her still-burning cig at her chest, where it had grown an inch-long totem of ash.

"Please?" she asked. "I'll be lonely all by myself." And even with everything, I couldn't help but relent. (This is the main difference between a mother and a father—a father's patheticness is just pathetic, while a mother's can almost always move one to sympathy or at least acquiescence.) I gave in. I stood without a word, tossed my magazine to the floor, and followed her out to the deck with the ocean view. She had decorated: it was done up in red-white-and-blue streamers and those little flags and everything. She'd made a cake, decorated with white icing for stripes and stars, strawberries for the red, and blue-berries for the blue. Mom shoved a plastic plate and fork into my hand.

"Have some," she said, and because I felt obligated, I cut myself off a small piece while she watched eagerly. It felt preposterous.

"I thought this was what you hated," I said with a full mouth. "This domestic shit. You know, baking cakes and hanging streamers. I mean, I thought this was why you left." (The cake was actually not bad, although I myself would have preferred a seven-layer dip.)

Mom shrugged. "I just wanted to be festive," she said. "I was hoping Jeff and his friend would come. And Dad of course. But now I guess I'm kind of glad it's just you and me. You always understood me best anyway. Happy Fourth of July!" She lifted her cigarette as if cheersing.

I almost said something, but then I just could not bring myself to. I couldn't even think of where to begin. So I plopped myself into a plastic lawn chair and ate my mother's sad and perfect American cake, one small bite at a time, waiting for it to get dark.

A few minutes later, she brought me a glass of chardonnay from the box she was working on and we clanked awkwardly. "To independence," she said. Then there was a whistle from the direction of the ocean and it all started.

And sitting on the porch watching the fireworks with my drunk, tattooed, chain-smoking mother, her reclined in oblivious languor on a half-collapsing beach chaise as she sloshed at her wine and murmured unintelligible little phrases of satisfaction to herself, the rockets shot up into the black sky, and I closed my eyes until I heard the bang and then eased them open just in time to see the blue sparks burning out into smoke. For some reason all I could think about was DeeDee.

I have heard a lot of things about love. You hear different things about it, of course, depending. My personal points of reference include the opinions of Jeff and Sebastian; the insipid overheard conversations of Michelle Schwartz, who sits behind me in math class; songs by people ranging from Bruce Springsteen to Lady Gaga and everyone in between; X-Men comic books; and even the occasional short story in *The New Yorker*, as long as it's not written by a person with an aggressively foreign-sounding name. You would think all this would count as a certain broad range of knowledge in things romantic—or rather, the stupidity of all things romantic—which is why I was surprised, watching the remnants of that very first firework, when I found myself struck by a confusing, sublime infinity, and wondered, in a sort of abstract way, if it had anything to do with DeeDee.

Okay, I don't know anything. All I know is that as the rockets burst and faded against a blackening sky, the burning smell of Mom's American Spirit crawled across the deck, and—bang! bang! bang!—it was DeeDee's face that was etched onto the back of my eyelids. Her face and the way she smelled and the way she smiled and whatever. And the funny way she tilted her head when she didn't understand something, the way that made you think perhaps she understood better than she was letting on, maybe even better than you yourself understood.

Her jittery and uncertain confidence. Her anger, and the way she thought everything was funny, even the things that made her mad.

I felt a sort of nauseated sensation, similar to the feeling in the pit of your stomach when you go down a giant waterslide. It was a feeling that was starting to become fairly old hat.

Chalk that up to whatever you'd like; I have no name for it beyond the one that is both obvious and unlikely, and I'm not going to say much more about that. All I know is that suddenly everything was really exploding in rapid fire. The fireworks were, I mean. It was the finale.

At my side, my mother let out an embarrassed hiccup and I looked over at her, and she was my mom again, my mom as I'd once known her. Somehow in the strange, unnatural Independence Day light—observed through the filter of glitter and smoke—the tattoos on her chest and arms were washed away; the various piercings and the red stripes in her hair were obscured. She was the mother she'd been before. But that implies a certain diminishment, and that's not right either. She was more than a past echo of herself. She was something else entirely.

"Mom," I said.

She looked over at me and seemed just as baffled as I was, as if she too was seeing a version of me that she'd forgotten all about, and faltered and then gulped before replying. "Yeah?" she said.

"Remember when you told me you'd die if you caught a firework?" I asked.

"No," she said. "Really? I told you that you'd die?"

"And your finger would explode."

"I think you'd probably just get burned," she said. "But I knew a guy in high school who stuck a lit firecracker where he shouldn't have and could never use the bathroom properly again, if you know what I mean. I probably just didn't want you to play with the things. They're illegal in some states."

"I know," I said. "Obviously."

"You really shouldn't pay attention to anything I say," Mom said. "I usually have no idea what I'm talking about."

"You're my mother," I pointed out. She just shrugged sheepishly and looked away and tossed her cigarette into the darkness.

"I love you," I said.

I mean, I guess love is complicated. Of course I went to the party.

On the beach by the pier, they had a bonfire burning and music blaring from a pickup truck parked haphazardly in the sand. I figured on this particular night that the beach patrol chose to look the other way. There were tons of people, hundreds, it seemed like, all clustered together in an unsolvable knot. Here I was. Another fucking party. I hung back on the edge, not really knowing what to do.

Kristle saw me, and for the first time since I'd known her, there was no artifice or calculation in her expression. She looked up and met my eye and smiled, a real smile, all sincere and everything, and puckered her lips and blew me a kiss. I wondered what had changed, what had made her bring me here. I doubted I would ever really know.

Then Jeff turned around and saw me too, and at first his broad, bare shoulders clenched and he looked angry. But he brushed the hair from his eyes and shrugged a half-hello before turning back to Kristle, putting his hand on her hip, and, pulling her close to him, planting a kiss on her forehead as she sank into his chest. I guessed that was as close as he was going to get to telling me everything was okay.

I hardly recognized DeeDee at first; she approached as a blurred and glowing figure, as a nimbus that slowly collected itself into the shape of her body as it got closer. Then she was standing right there in front of me and she was herself.

"Hey," she said.

"Hey," I said.

"Here," DeeDee said. "Have a sparkler. Actually, have two. Because you're worth it."

She handed me a couple of sparklers, unlit, and had turned to walk away when I grabbed her by the wrist.

"No way," I said, yanking her back. She looked trapped and panicked for a second, like she was going to shove me off, but then she didn't.

"You shouldn't have come here," she said. "I thought we had this all settled."

"We didn't settle anything," I said. "You know that. I can't stop thinking about you. Sorry, but it's true."

She sighed and looked away. "Yeah," she said. "Same, I guess."

"I'm very confused by you," I told her.

"I know," she said. "I'm sorry if I've been confusing. If it helps, you're confusing too."

There was a pop and a whistle and a cheer and a small, busted explosion over our heads.

"Oh, sure," I said, not even really noticing the firework. "What's confusing about me?"

"There you go being confusing again—asking questions that I can't possibly answer." She grimaced in frustration. "This isn't supposed to happen to us."

"What?" I asked. "What, exactly, is 'this'?"

She gnawed at her thumbnail. "We're not supposed to care," she said.

"I really wish you would speak in the singular," I said. "Every time you start with this *we*, I know you're just about to say something that's complete bullshit. Kristle and Taffany and Olay have nothing to do with you."

"Fine," she said. "I. *I'm* not supposed to care."

"Care about what?" I asked. "Other people? Feelings? Who do you think you are?"

She took a deep breath. "It's not supposed to happen to us. It's, like, against our nature. Sorry, plural again, but sometimes the plural's important. Like when it puts everyone at risk."

"You keep saying that," I said. "But I already told you. I don't care if I get supposedly hurt. I already got hurt, so what's the difference?"

"I wasn't talking about you," she said.

I stopped. "Then I don't know what you're talking about," I said.

"Yes you do," she said. And maybe I did.

Taffany came around with a lighter. "Happy Independence Day!" she said as she lit me up. Next she waved her lighter for DeeDee, and then we were both glittering in the dark. Orange sparks shot around us in an unpredictable halo, and it didn't even occur to me to worry about being burned.

A few yards away someone lit a Roman candle and suddenly everyone was squealing and running for safety. DeeDee and I didn't move. We stood there with our sparklers, not saying anything, just showered in flame. The hairs on my arms were standing on end, and I could feel the summer seeping in through my pores. I was still pleasantly drunk from the box of wine I'd split with Mom.

Fuck it, I thought. "Fuck it," I said. At a certain point, it's just time to be a man. Actually, no. Fuck that too. Being a man is bullshit; maybe trying to *be a man* had been the problem all along. At a certain point you just have to trust someone. Even if it's only yourself.

So I dropped the sparklers to my side and kissed DeeDee. Summer and sparks and smoke curled around us into a cocoon, and then we were the only ones at the party. Everything had gone silent and she kissed me right back.

That night, DeeDee and I left the party together but stayed on the beach, wandered down the shore until we couldn't hear the music or the shouting.

We didn't do anything, really. We sat by the ocean, idly gathering sand in our fists to let it slip through our fingers, tossing it at the glowing sand crabs that scuttled toward us in the blackness of everything. Just talking some stupid shit, or not talking, or whatever, our legs barely grazing each other's. And right before it was light out we fell asleep right there, faces buried in the sand, our breathing even with the roll of the waves, bathing suits riding low on our hips. I dreamed of other summers and of beaches that I had not yet traveled to.

I was someone transformed and new, unknowable and strange. Maybe not a man, but not the boy I had come here as, either. Even in the sand, even in my sleep, I knew he was gone.

And summer was leaving too; that's the summer thing. The Fourth of July is over before the fireworks have had time to burn themselves into memories. So you just stand there with your sparkler, eyeing it as it sputters in your hand, all dumb and sunburned and sad but also happy, knowing that sometimes you have to take one last salty breath and make it worth it.

EIGHTEEN

AFTER THE FOURTH of July we started going to Ursula's most nights. Jeff and I would chug a couple of beers on the porch and then walk over together, or Kristle and DeeDee would spin by after their shift and pick us up and we'd all head out—Jeff and Kristle walking a few paces behind as DeeDee skipped on ahead, laughing and talking to me nonstop as I tried to keep up with her.

I didn't even know what DeeDee was talking about half the time. She'd be going on about some article she had read in *Her Place* or some asshole at the restaurant who'd wanted prime rib or a book one of the girls who worked as maids had brought home after it had been left behind in one of the houses. I'd just listen to her and be happy.

DeeDee was different from how I'd thought she was when I met her. She was different, honestly, from how I'd thought she was a week ago or yesterday. She kept surprising me with herself. Sometimes I got the impression that she was surprised too.

Ever since the Fourth of July—since DeeDee had resigned herself to my continued presence—I'd seen her every day. She would come over and watch TV, or I'd hang out in the Fisherman's Net while she worked and she would come sit with me when she got the chance, or we would sit on the beach even though she hated it, or when we were up early, we'd walk to the McDonald's on the bypass and get breakfast sandwiches, sometimes with Kristle and occasionally Jeff.

We played lots of cards. We assembled a jigsaw puzzle. We played Scrabble.

DeeDee was better at Scrabble than you would expect for someone who claimed not to speak English; she was judicious with her letters and knew all the tricky words like *za* and *qi* and was ruthless enough to play them when necessary. She was kind when she won, which was always. One time I looked down at the board and noticed that all her words were sad, and we didn't play Scrabble again after that.

Sometimes we would stay up till like three in the morning on the porch, just talking. She would smoke a thousand cigarettes and I would get a little drunk and then, when it was really late, she would amble off down the street into the dark, her smoke trailing behind her.

She never took me back to that cove. I started to wonder if it had ever even existed. She never took me back to Nalgene's pirate ship either. We hadn't kissed since the Fourth of July.

It's not that I didn't want to, but there was a new, invisible barrier between us. I didn't know where it had come from, and I didn't ask.

Taffany was the bartender at Ursula's on Mondays, Thursdays, and Saturdays. She was usually grumpy because she never had any customers, but she would give us free drinks anyway and when you'd try to pay, she would throw the money back at you and roll her eyes like she was all offended or something. When she was in a rare good mood, she was something else; she'd have Nalgene put some Prince on the jukebox, and then she'd ignore everyone while she freaked out, dancing alone, shimmying and jumping and tossing her hair and doing little backbends over the bar, mouthing the words to "Raspberry Beret" or whatever while everyone stopped what we were doing to stare. When the song ended, she'd just sweep her hair out of her face, and she'd head over to the cash register, punch in a few numbers, and let it clang open only to slam it back shut, a little smirk the only thing indicating she even remembered her dance.

She wasn't doing it for tips or anything. No one was really tipping anyway. She was only doing it to amuse herself, which was easier said than done around here.

One night after we'd been going there a couple of weeks, my parents showed up. As in, they showed up *together*. Taffany was just starting to groove on "Dirty Mind" and then there they were, waltzing right in through the swinging doors like they were regulars at the place. Mom was laughing and looking up at Dad, nuzzling his shoulder, and he had his arm around her waist and this big-ass grin on his face. He was wearing a clean button-down shirt and had what was left of his hair combed; it was the first time I'd seen him dressed respectably in ages.

You could feel the room get weird as soon as they walked in. Jeff was across the bar with Kristle, and he thunked his whiskey down and furrowed his brow before throwing his head back to study the ceiling fan. DeeDee carefully set her cigarette in the ashtray and reached for my leg. She scrunched her mouth to one side of her face.

Even the people I didn't know seemed to realize something was going on; I saw heads swivel to my parents and then to Jeff and finally to me, everyone with the same confused, concerned frown.

The only person who didn't notice was Taffany. Because the music had kicked in and she was starting to dance for real now, eyes closed as she swung her hips and flung her hair back and forth across her face, ecstatically mouthing the words to the song. *You just gotta let me lay ya, gotta let me lay ya, lay ya, you just gotta . . .*

Mom was waving at me across the room, smiling, and before anyone could do anything about it, she was dancing along to the song. It was just an awkward shuffle at first, her fists clenched at her chest and her elbows stretched out to her sides, but then my dad began his own soft-shoe and Mom upped the ante. She began to twirl and prance, pumping her fist in the air before putting her hands on her hips and bending over to jiggle her ass.

I assumed my dad would be mortified, but he was getting into it too, clapping and spinning on one foot, bobbling his head back and forth and wiggling his shoulders, all without taking his eyes off my mother. I myself had no clue what the fuck was going on. After having loud sex the day after she'd arrived, they'd mostly been avoiding each other—although, thinking about it, it was true that in the last few days I'd noticed a certain thawing between them.

No one had ever danced while Taffany was dancing. But my parents had broken the seal. Soon Nalgene was dancing too, and then the rest of the Girls and even the few other people at Ursula's; everyone was on their feet shaking their asses.

"Oh, fuck it," DeeDee said. "We might as well too. I mean, right?"

"No," I said. "In fact, I think I'm going to go home."

At the other end of the bar, I could see Jeff resisting also, sitting resolutely with a frown on his face and his arms folded across his chest as Kristle tried to coax him to his feet. He was not budging.

DeeDee didn't bother with trying to convince me. She just rolled her eyes and started swaying and waving her arms, and before I knew it, it was "I Feel For You."

Fuck it, I thought to myself, and then I was dancing too and everyone was dancing but most of all my parents, who were twirling and dipping and pogoing and pantomiming like they were the only ones in the bar.

And then they were kissing. They were really kissing; it

occurred to me that I had never seen them kiss like that before. It was hard to say if I'd ever seen a kiss like that in my life, including in movies. Dad had Mom up against the bar, and she was leaning backward with her leg on the stool, her head cocked back, and her mouth on his. It was pretty gross.

Then I looked to my left and Jeff and Kristle were kissing too. And then I was kissing DeeDee. Tonight, with my mother's dancing, something had come over all of us, and it suddenly felt right again. It *was* right.

It only lasted a minute, though, because soon the song was over and everyone kind of drifted back to their seats like none of it had happened in the first place. DeeDee's cig was still in the ashtray, now burned all the way to the filter.

"What the fuck was that?" we said at the same time. Then we both laughed.

"Let's go outside," I said. "I need to get the hell out of here."

So we wandered out of the bar, first onto the deck and then into the grassy plot of empty land between the beach road and the highway. It was before midnight—things happened early around here—but it felt later.

We stood and watched the cars speeding by. It was so muggy out that the beams of the headlights seemed to refract through the beads of moisture in the air into a million little rays that refracted again, and over and over, like the highway was filled with flying disco balls.

It didn't feel like we were at the beach; if not for the smell of salt water we could have been on the edge of any shitty suburban subdevelopment. Yes, the beach was only a minute's walk from here, but the strip mall was even closer. We were together, though.

DeeDee lit a cigarette and reached out her other hand for mine. She put her head on my shoulder. "That was nice," she said.

"I know," I said.

Starting to understand her was less like learning and more like forgetting. I was forgetting the DeeDee I'd created in my mind. Now, outside Ursula's, in the grass by the highway, she was just DeeDee. She was only herself.

That night, with the cars speeding past us, a few minutes after we'd kissed in the bar, DeeDee took my hand and I pulled her close to me and kissed her again, and this time she didn't push me away. She seemed nervous, maybe, tentative. But she kissed me back. I ran my hands through her hair and then let my other hand drift to her boob. Then lower.

"Sam," she said.

"Let's just do it," I said. "Let's just do it."

"Here?"

"At my place, obviously. Jeff's gonna be with Kristle. My parents won't even notice. You saw them in there. Who knows when they'll even be home."

She looked away.

"It doesn't have to be this big deal or anything."

"Sam," she said. "Come on. It is this big deal. You know it is."

"Why?" I asked. "You wanted to do it before. The night at the golf course. I know you wanted to. You would have. It was my fault. So let's do it."

"That was before. Things are different now. I'm different now. Everything's different."

"I know," I said. "I know it is. That's why we should do it. I want to. I'm not afraid anymore."

Which was a lie, obviously. I was very afraid. I don't even know what I was afraid of, but I was definitely afraid. But I was a lot of other things besides that too.

"It has this tendency to complicate everything. And I like things how they are now. Don't you?"

"Yes," I said. "I do."

"So let's not fuck things up."

"Okay," I said. I was sincere; it was okay.

LOSING

We have tried to leave this place. We consider ourselves reasonably sneaky, but these islands are sneaky too. They will not surrender us.

The last one to try leaving was Taffany. It was at the beginning of this summer and she had just turned twenty: one year to go. It wasn't much time, but all she wanted was to see something else before the end. Spend a year in another place, that's all. Eat at a restaurant she'd never heard of. It would have been enough, she said. She had been talking about it for ages, but time was running out. She said, "What do I have to lose?"

Taffany decided to take a boat. There was some logic behind this choice: she thought that by traveling over water she could go unnoticed until it was too late to stop her. The water is still ours in some ways. And although our father will do anything to keep us, we still have our brothers and our mother on our side. We still have ourselves.

So Taffany got a raft, one of those inflatable ones, but the expensive kind—sturdy, with oars—from the store between the roads, where they sell kites and sunglasses and T-shirts and tanning oil. The raft was stolen, so as to avoid detection. (Receipts and credit card statements are our father's domain.) She brought nothing with her and left right away without saying final good-byes. A shady dip. We thought, Well, maybe this will work.

Of course, we knew it wouldn't. She was back by the evening. She had paddled for hours across the bay, and when she got to the other side, having never deviated from her course, she found herself just where she had started.

Tresemmé took a car, a rusty old Topaz she'd saved for a summer to buy. She left in the middle of the night to avoid outbound traffic on the causeway. But just before she reached the bridge, the engine began to smoke. She kept driving anyway: she only had a mile to go. She could make it if she didn't panic.

She didn't panic. And still, the Topaz sputtered and died. When Tresemmé opened the hood, water spilled out. It was filled with an ocean. She hitchhiked home. No one would take her across the bridge.

Tiara thought the easiest thing would be to walk. Tiara had been unusual: she too had fallen for an out-of-towner, but this one was a girl. This happens rarely and is not approved of. Love is against our laws as it is, but at least with a boy there are some pragmatic aspects.

The girl had gone home, back to her normal life. Tiara wanted to find her, if only to say good-bye. We wondered if the girl would even remember her, but we didn't say it.

And what could go wrong with walking? There could be no room for mechanical disaster; Tiara would not be reliant on anyone else's navigation as one would on a bus or a plane. She packed supplies for several days; she bought comfortable walking shoes from one of the outlets and gathered enough money to survive after her escape.

At the end of the summer, she caught a ride to Manteo, where her plan was to walk across the island and cross the Virginia Dare Bridge on foot, finally landing on the mainland in Mann's Harbor. She didn't know what she was going to do once she got there, but she would figure it out. We are resourceful.

When her feet began to sting, she kept walking. When she couldn't walk anymore, she swallowed her pride and crawled.

Tiara's mistake was persistence. Everyone else had given up.

We found her in the sand, a few days later, lying in the parking lot of the Outback Steakhouse on the bypass, barely able to speak, unable to remember how she'd gotten there. She was never the same.

Still. Someone tries it every summer. Someone will try it again next summer. The stories become legend; they are passed along until they lose meaning. Someone always thinks she will be the one to outsmart him.

She thinks, What do I have to lose?

But there's always something.

NINETEEN

WE WENT TO the ocean. DeeDee couldn't swim and she was never really that excited about lying on the beach, but it was a Tuesday. She had the day off, and we couldn't think of anything else to do. So now we were lying on an old blanket together, her flipping idly through an old paperback she'd found and me just napping, drifting in and out of wakefulness, every now and then turning to look at her when she thought I was still sleeping. I knew it was pushing my luck, but I wanted to go in the ocean. "C'mon," I said again when she ignored me. "Let's go for a swim. It'll be fun."

DeeDee flushed without looking up from the page she was reading. "I can't swim," she said. "I know it's weird. I just can't."

"We don't have to go in deep. Just up to our waists. It won't even be swimming."

She sighed, still pretending to be absorbed in her reading. "It's not the *swimming* part I don't like. It's more like I'm afraid of the water. It's just one of those things—it's like, hereditary. Ask Kristle. Ask any of them. Don't start."

The day was hot and overcast. The sun had made cursory appearances over the course of the morning, but since lunch it had been coy behind a mountainous landscape of clouds. As the beach deepened in its monochrome, the dullness of the afternoon began to turn DeeDee more radiant, her hair and eyes burning in breathtaking relief against the gloomy backdrop. Lying in the sand in a white V-neck and denim booty-shorts, she cut through the gray like she was lit from an entirely different source, like the world was one of the doctored photos in one of her dumb magazines and DeeDee was the element that had been hastily dropped in.

"Come on," I said. I rolled onto my stomach and leaned close to her face with the same eyes that had lured her onto the blanket on the sand. "Just get your feet wet. I won't let anything happen." I kissed her on the cheek and she dropped her book and laughed, finally looking up at me from a place somewhere far beyond a heavy veil of lashes and slanty Cleopatra eyeliner. "Okay," she said, smiling tightly. Deep breath. "Fine. Let's do it. Just make fucking sure I don't drown, or Kristle'll kill you."

"I wouldn't want to get on Kristle's bad side, that's for hell of sure. She looks like she'd cut a bitch for looking at her funny."

"She would," DeeDee said. "I've seen her do it. Blood everywhere, not a pretty sight. All because someone sent his fish sticks back to the kitchen."

Since the Fourth of July, Kristle had become something like a normal person, had stopped staring at me and touching me inappropriately and climbing nude into my bed when I was sound asleep. Jeff, too, had forgotten to be mad at me and had started behaving like his usual obnoxious self again.

And DeeDee stood, stripped off her white T-shirt and tossed it aside, slid her cutoffs to the sand, and picked the wedgie of her bikini from her ass (which I couldn't help ogling). She sauntered ahead of me with a careless swing in her shoulders, but when she looked back to make sure I was following, I could see that her confidence was just a put-on. I moved to her side and she took my hand. "Forget Kristle. If you let me drown, *I'll* fucking kill you," she said.

I laughed. It was hard to take her too seriously. DeeDee looked like she belonged to the water.

"What is it about it that scares you?" I asked. We had made our way to the edge of the water, but DeeDee had paused abruptly, nervous again. "Besides that you don't know how to swim."

"Isn't that enough?"

"It just seems like there's something else," I said.

"Oh, I don't know. Just the fact that it goes on forever, I guess. The fact that you look out and you can see for miles and miles and miles but it's not even the start, not even close. The fact that it's beautiful. I know it sounds stupid, but it's the same way that you scare me. If you want the truth."

"I scare you?" I asked. But of course I was pleased. What I was really thinking was, *She thinks I'm beautiful?*

"I read somewhere that the human eye can see exactly twenty-six miles into the distance on a perfectly flat surface. So when you look out into the ocean, the point where the water blurs into the sky is twenty-six miles away. The same as a marathon. Doesn't that seem like a weird coincidence?"

"Yeah," I said. "But it also doesn't seem like it's true."

"Oh. Yeah. Maybe not. I don't even remember where I read it. Probably *Her Place*—they run 'Ripley's Believe It or Not' on the back page, you know. Anyway, I choose to believe it even if it's fake. Sometimes you can locate a truer version of the truth somewhere in a total lie. And don't you think it would be cool to watch a marathon run on the surface of the ocean? Just to stand right here and watch the runners disappearing into nothing at the horizon point, racing straight off the edge of the world?"

"Yeah," I said. "I guess it would. If it really worked that way."

"Details, details," DeeDee said. "Don't stand in the way of a pretty thought, babe."

Although we had stopped moving forward the tide was rising and was now lapping at our toes. DeeDee flinched for a second and gripped my hand tighter when the chilly ocean washed over our feet, but after the third or fourth time it had presented itself to us she seemed suddenly emboldened. When it withdrew again, DeeDee and I went with it, her pulling me forward.

The water had seemed calm from our blanket, but I could see now that it was getting choppy, and when we were in up to our knees, we had to brace ourselves not to be bowled over by the roiling of the waves. I almost lost my balance, and I felt DeeDee tense up again. She shuddered a little.

"Careful," I said. "Just hold tight."

I was surprised when she didn't listen to me, instead dropping my hand to hold steady on her own. The ocean was at our thighs and I thought she'd want to turn back, but she took another step forward and then another, straight into a drop-off, where she began to paddle her arms easily, gliding still farther out, over a swell. I dove under the water to surface at her side, shaking my hair out. It was shallow enough to stand but only barely—when the waves rolled by, you had to sort of hop over them until they passed.

DeeDee was regarding me with amusement. "You look cute," she said when we both had our bearings. "Like a wet dog." She pushed my bangs from my eyes. "I guess the water's not so bad after all. Maybe I can actually do this."

"Duh," I said. "Anyone can swim."

"Not me," DeeDee said. "I might be able to go in the water for a second, but I definitely can't swim. Trust me."

"You're safe with me," I said.

"No," she said. "No one's ever safe, babe. The minute you think you're safe is the same minute you're screwed."

"You're safe," I repeated, and in a moment of impulse I took her hips and kissed her, never feeling more sure of anything I'd ever done.

I knew she was wrong. Because in that moment, kissing her, our bodies pressed together as the water pulsed through us, I had never felt safer in my life. I felt an unfamiliar happiness swelling in my belly, a warm and twisting certainty. It didn't matter what happened in the future. It didn't matter what happened in a minute. It didn't even matter what had happened already. I didn't care about anything except right then, there with DeeDee in the water for the first time, us on a cloudy beach, content forever for a second. Then the second was over and we broke away from each other and reality intruded again, but only in the form of a cool and mostly pleasant breeze.

"I need to tell you something," she said. "I should have told you before, but I didn't know how. Actually, I still don't know how."

"What?" I asked. "You can tell me anything."

DeeDee just looked at me, twisting her mouth and sort of wincing. "You're going to kind of freak out," she said. "I mean, you probably won't even believe me."

"What?" I asked, suddenly nervous.

Before she could say anything more, a wave came out of nowhere.

We'd been safe in the steady, gentle swells beyond the surf. The minute you think you're safe is the same minute you're fucked. And we were fucked. The wave was an angry one: I saw it towering two or three feet above my head, about to break right on top of us. "Duck," I said. I reached for DeeDee but I couldn't find her. Still, wherever she was, I thought I heard her mumble something about her father just before we were taken by the wave. Then we were wrecked.

The water boiled me: flipped me heels over head and pulled my back into a painful zigzag before pummeling me shoulder-first into a rough and prickly sandbar. I came up coughing, lungs waterlogged and sinuses stinging. I'd scraped my elbow and when I looked down, I could see it was bleeding. But I wasn't worried about blood. I was worried about DeeDee, who was nowhere to be seen. She couldn't swim.

I recovered quickly and scanned the shore for DeeDee, hoping to see her lying safe (if bruised) in the sand. She was not. Using my hand as a visor, I turned again to the sea. At first I saw nothing, but then I shifted my focus to a more distant point, and there she was. Barely.

I had no idea how she'd gotten out so far, but I could see her head bobbing in the water, just beyond the waves. She was sputtering and flailing, gasping for breath.

"DeeDee!" I screamed. Or tried to scream—it came out as just a cracked and hopeless wail that I knew couldn't come close to reaching her. Even if it mattered.

So even though I'm barely a swimmer myself, I dove back into the water and swam. I pushed hard, trying to remember the swimming lessons I'd neglected to pay attention to when I was ten years old. Somehow, I found a reserve of strength within myself, a well of technique that I'd never known I'd had. I felt supercharged. Several times since I'd gotten here, I'd thought I'd felt hands grasping at my legs, trying to pull me under. This time, I felt the same thing, and I realized that they weren't trying to pull me at all. Something—or someone—was helping me.

When I caught up with her, she was treading water helplessly, her head thrown back, face barely suspended above the surface of the water, eyes barely open. "DeeDee," I said, wrapping my arm around her limp body. "What the hell are you doing?" She looked up at me, startled.

"Sam?" DeeDee was surprised to see me. "It was so weird. We were just standing there talking and then . . . how did we get so far out? It's fucking freezing!"

"Come on," I said. "Relax."

"I can't even swim!" DeeDee said. And as it dawned on her what was going on, she suddenly started struggling, paddling her legs furiously and thrashing around in my arms. She began to cough up water.

"Shh," I said. I piled her hair on top of her head with my free hand. I took the wet strand that was stuck to the side of her face and tucked it behind her ear. Her breathing got slower. "Just float on your back. I'll float with you. Just relax. We'll be fine." DeeDee halfheartedly tried to push me away, but I held her tight.

"Come on," I whispered. I let her go, rolling onto my back as an example. I looked her in the eyes until she followed my lead, and I reached out and touched her shoulder and we floated back to the shore like that, wave by wave, until we could stand, and soon we were back on the shore floundering in the cold of Kristle's glare.

"What the fuck is this?" Kristle said, before we'd even stood up. Jeff was standing beside her with his arms crossed awkwardly at his chest, looking off to the side. "DeeDee can't

216

swim, dipshit." And then, pulling DeeDee up by the hand, "What the fuck were you fucking thinking?"

"You know what I was thinking," DeeDee said. "You know exactly what I was thinking, so leave me alone."

That was when Kristle slapped her. Hard. The sound of her open palm stinging DeeDee's face was louder than it should have been; it echoed up and down the beach, and I could see vacationers turn to stare.

"Hey," I said, lunging for Kristle, but Jeff had already pulled her away.

"Okay, okay," Jeff said. "Enough. Everything's fine."

"It's not," Kristle said. "Everything is so not fine."

DeeDee took off running. I moved to follow her, but Kristle grabbed me by the elbow. "Let her go," she said, still glaring. "I want to talk to you."

BECOMING

It takes us a while to find our bodies. When we first arrive here, we are shifting and blurry at the edges, changing from moment to moment. We have to become something. So we take out our knives and carve ourselves into something that they will find becoming. We chisel and etch ourselves into the form that we will find the most useful.

We page through magazines and scrutinize the women on television, trying to find the perfect formula. We agree on generalities but sometimes argue about specifics: the ideal proportions, the right curves. We pay careful attention to the men on the streets, watching to see which way their heads turn, where their eyes drift. What makes them give in.

And so we give ourselves breasts and hips and round, perfect asses. Shining hair, glittering eyes.

We could look like anything, but we settle in this body until it becomes familiar, if not exactly our own. We might prefer a different appearance, but this is the costume we have chosen. We clothe ourselves in the shortest shorts, the tightest T-shirts. We paint our nails like movie stars. We wear things that glitter. We glitter too.

This is not beauty. We would be beautiful in any shape: our beauty is immutable. This—this is just how we get what we want.

But sometimes we feel ourselves losing our grip on the borders of our form. We find ourselves confused. What was that disguise again? We have to struggle to keep our shape.

And sometimes, more rarely, we see someone looking straight through us as if he is peeling away our mask, as if he is glimpsing what is truly beautiful: the part of us that is infinite and fiery and dark. He is seeing our strength. He is seeing our knife.

We are still becoming. But becoming what?

TWENTY

THEY WERE IN the water: there were hundreds of them—maybe thousands, maybe more—lined up hip to hip at the edge of the surf, stretching in a line for as far as I could see. It was after midnight, and I was standing on the outcropping of rocks that overlooked their secret cove. Under the full moon, the shoreline on the cove seemed to have expanded to accommodate infinity.

I had my flashlight with me, but I didn't need to use it. The Girls were glowing. Or. Maybe *glowing* isn't the right word.

Maybe none of it is the right word. Because to call them girls wasn't quite accurate either. It was them, for sure—the Girls, I mean, a whole army of them—but tonight they were different. They were all naked, their shining skin rippling with the sway of the water, in and out and in and out, half-submerged in the shallows, pointing to a horizonless horizon. Their hair was fanned out behind them in the sand in tangled clumps, no longer blond but black and iridescent, like seaweed smushed up with gasoline and tar. Every now and then one of them would stretch a little, or splash her legs—if they were even legs—but mostly they were motionless.

And they were buzzing: bluish and bright in the moonlight, like the flicker of a television in the crack under a closed door.

There was no reasonable explanation for the fact that they were glowing. The moon was full and bright, yes, but that wasn't it. It occurred to me that they were lit from within. When I squinted a little, I saw that their legs were shining most of all; they seemed to be covered in something shiny and electric, something throwing sparks. When I squinted a little more, I saw that they were covered in scales.

DeeDee was here, I was sure. I could feel her presence as a tingling in my chest. But I didn't bother looking for her; I knew it would have been impossible to pick her out. I began to feel almost dizzy.

The Girls in their repose appeared more alike than ever now, as if in a mirror: enchanted, shattered. From where I stood, they were now so much the same that I had an understanding that they were all part of the same being.

Or something.

I knew that I was not supposed to be seeing this. I could tell, somehow, that it was a secret beyond secrets. But I also knew, in some way, that there was a reason I was allowed to be here, a reason I had made it here at all. In the dark on the beach in the secret cove that DeeDee had once taken me to, the Girls were revealing themselves to me in a form that was, if not true, then as true as I could understand. If they had wanted this to be secret, I wouldn't have been able to find their beach tonight.

I tried to move closer, but I couldn't; I tried to remember how I had come to be here. The memory was hard to summon at first; I was having trouble thinking. It felt like I was revisiting a dream I'd once had. But it wasn't a dream.

Kristle had told me to come here. At the beach earlier that day, DeeDee had run away and Kristle had grabbed my arm and said, "I want to talk to you.

"The cove," she'd said. "Meet me there tonight. It's a full moon. It will be close by. You'll find it."

So a few hours later, when it was dark, I'd left the house and headed to the beach. I didn't have to worry about finding the cove. As soon as I stepped onto the beach road, I'd noticed a Girl making her way through the dunes toward the beach. She had a familiar gait, and for a second I thought it was DeeDee but then realized it wasn't. Making my way down the road I kept seeing them, Girl after Girl, all of them looking skittish but determined, all glancing over their shoulders before sneaking off into the tall grass. Finally, I decided to follow one of them onto the sand. There, I found an almost-procession of them, all heading up the beach, each of them alone.

I wasn't just meeting Kristle. I was meeting all of them. As I walked up the beach, the moon grew not just brighter but larger and lower, and when it was a half dollar scraping the water, I saw rocks emerging from the sand. The Girls were crawling over them, one by one as if in a trance, none of them acknowledging the others. I sat in the sand for a while and waited; they didn't seem to notice me as they passed me by. Then, after the parade trickled to a halt, I figured it was safe and began my own climb up the slippery rocks. At the top I looked out and started to understand.

There they were in the water, no longer girls and no longer anything I could recognize. They were just them.

Kristle had wanted me to see this. DeeDee had wanted me to see this too; it was what she had been trying to tell me in the water that afternoon (had it only been that afternoon?) just when she'd gotten sucked under by the wave.

They all wanted me to know this about them.

Well, I could see it. And still, I knew I would never, ever really understand what I was looking at. Any explanation would never be explanation enough. It was like looking at a drawing of God: it doesn't even begin.

I don't know how long I stood there watching them.

Then I felt a hand on my shoulder, but I didn't jump. It was almost like I was expecting him: Jeff was at my side. He looked different in the full moon too, both more and less than himself. His dark, curly hair was longer and wilder than I'd ever seen it and his biceps were pulsing, his shoulders cartoonishly broad. He smiled and punched me in the side.

"Fucking unbelievable, right?"

"How long have you known about it?" I asked him.

"A while. Long enough."

"What are they?" I asked.

"They are what they are," he said. "I don't even think they know, not totally at least. Why does there need to be a name for it?"

The word mattered to me, though. Names matter.

Before I knew it the moon was gone and the sun was yellow and burning, and I rubbed my eyes from sleep. I was in the sand, the rocky barrier of the cove above me. The Girls were gone.

DeeDee's face appeared first. Her hair was wet, slicked back, and she was golden, washed in sun.

"I have to tell you something," she said.

LEGEND

We are renters and borrowers and, in the end, only thieves. Our jewelry boxes are filled with things we have stolen: dangly fish-tail earrings and sea glass and little plastic figurines that we find in the sand. Bracelets left behind at tables we serve, driver's licenses abandoned in the rooms we clean. Finders keepers.

We have learned by now that our beauty does not count as a possession. The only thing we truly own is our legend.

Legend:

Once upon a time, we were happy. Once upon a time, we were home.

We had a mother and two brothers and even a father, although he was distant and saturnine. Our mother was patient and gentle and kind.

Our mother is the Deepness. She is beautiful with the wisdom of the universe, brimming with formulas and poems and books and myths and other things beyond description.

You may call her a whore. Some have. But being the Deepness, how could she be asked to draw edges around what has none? Being the Deepness, how could she be expected to turn her back on the possibilities of the world, to ignore the unfathomable caves of her being, the glittering wrecks abandoned in her honor at every turn? How could she do anything but accept *what is rightfully hers? If that makes her a whore, then we're whores too.*

Well, maybe we are.

Our father is the Endlessness. The Endlessness had grown envious of our mother's knowledge. And being the Endlessness—having an understanding of the infinite reaches of jealousy, being acquainted with the unquenchable deserts of vengeful rage—he exacted a punishment.

To punish a mother, you punish her daughters. Every king in history has known that rinky-dink little trick. It doesn't matter if her daughters are your daughters too. A father still has his sons. A father still has Speed and Calm. Most importantly, he still has his cock.

So the Endlessness banished us to this nowhere. We come here on our sixteenth birthday, spit from the ocean we're born in. We crawl naked from the water with no possessions, no memories, and no name. We come unable to swim and barely able to walk. We come bearing only our knife.

The older girls—the ones who have been here for many summers—know where and when to look for us. They are led to us by the aching in their feet. They take us in, give us clothes and Chinese slippers, and help us soothe our feet in baths of salt water. They feed us french fries and teach us the names of all the characters on soap operas.

They teach us this legend. First, they remind us of our curse—remind us why we are here before it becomes indistinct in our memories. Then they reveal the second and more important part of the curse, which is how to break it. Which is the way home.

Our sisters hate us, of course.

We hate them, too. We all hate one another. We have to hate one another: like the lost girls on Top Model and The Bachelor we are not here to make friends. We are here for one reason only, and that is to leave. But it doesn't really matter whether we're friends. We're sisters, and few of us are leaving anyway.

Well, put it a different way: only a few of us are going home. As for the rest of us—we don't like to talk about that.

All we want is to break the curse. Like any good curse, it is breakable. Like any good curse, you lose as much in the breaking as you gain. Perhaps more. But what's the alternative?

It doesn't matter. We will do whatever it takes. We don't care what we lose. Loss is our legend.

TWENTY-ONE

DEEDEE TOLD ME the legend, and the beach lost its detail. As she spoke, the tourists and the umbrellas and even the sun and the clouds overhead just faded into nothing until we were facing each other on a bright and infinite shore, only us two. Even the water at our feet was indistinct, abstract.

DeeDee was fidgety, waiting for my reaction. I noticed that she had a flower in her hair, small and pink and intricate in its composition. I didn't know where it had come from. Had it been there before?

Somewhere in the uncertain distance, on the fringes of the endless landscape, I felt the Girls hovering, watching, listening, waiting. Their eyes glowing, hair twisting, arms solemnly at their sides.

Beyond the ocean's horizon, I sensed DeeDee's other sisters beneath, reaching for the surface of the waves with slimy, grasping fingers. But right there, on the beach, it was just us.

"So how do you break the curse?" I asked finally.

I didn't waste time arguing over whether the story was true. I didn't expend a lot of thought on the idea that she was crazy, or that I was crazy, or anything. Although I did feel a little crazy. It's hard to explain why I accepted it all so easily, considering how unbelievable it was. But. Maybe it was just that I'd been at the beach so long. It all made a certain watery, logicless sense.

I had seen it with my own eyes. I had felt it. It was all as reasonable as anything could be around here.

DeeDee laughed ruefully. "Oh, it's simple, really," she said. "I mean, very simple, but complicated, too. Like all good curses."

"Well how?" I asked.

She tucked a strand of hair behind her ear, darted her eyes left and right, and then looked at me again, now steady and direct. She took a deep breath.

"You do it with a virgin," she said. "I mean, we do. I do. A virgin boy, obviously. Don't hear much about *them*, do you?"

"No," I said. "I guess you don't." I didn't smile. A virgin.

"I mean, don't get the wrong idea," she said. "You're still a *guy*. I wouldn't go trying to ride any unicorns or anything." She grinned entreatingly. "It's just this particular little bit of magic."

"Why are you acting like this is a joke?" I asked.

She crossed her arms and faced away from me, looking at the sand. "Because it *is* a joke. A bad one, but still—don't you see? Our father has always had an obnoxious sense of humor."

"I'm not following," I mumbled.

"Come on. In the book of curses it doesn't seem very serious, does it? Sex with a teenage boy. How fucking difficult can that be? Hardy har har."

I frowned.

"Should be easy, right? " She shrugged apologetically. "Look, we figured that little punch line out a long time ago. We're not as stupid as we pretend to be—we get that from our mother. Our sense of irony—that's from Dad. Anyway, it's harder than it sounds. A lot harder. You guys are picky. You only get to lose your virginity once. And there aren't actually that many of you. Children don't count, by the way, not that we would stoop that low."

I understood. Maybe I had understood all along. *Fuck a virgin.* Well that was me. They must have been able to smell it on me from the start. That explained the Girls staring at me everywhere I went, Kristle's hand on my neck at our first lunch at the Fisherman's Net, the fact that they'd all but ignored Jeff, at least at first. The visit in the middle of the night. It explained pretty much everything.

I felt sick to my stomach.

"So that's it?"

"You have to understand," she said. "We live with this. This is strange to you. It's everything to us."

It didn't matter what it was to them.

I was their ticket out. I mean, not *theirs.* I was *her* ticket out. Not even DeeDee. *Any* her. Whichever her got to me first. It was just that simple. The rest of it—the details, the explanations, the caveats, whatever—was all meaningless to me. It wasn't even my business.

Yes I had questions. Well, how could I not? But I was too angry to really ask any of them. Instead I started unbuttoning my jeans. "I guess we might as well get it over with, then."

"Sam," she said. "Come on."

"What?" I said. "This is what you want. I'll stick it in, and then you can get your ass out of here. Back to where you belong, to wear pink shells on your boobs, hang out with Ariel and the rest of them. Let's get this shit over with."

"I'm not going to do it with you," DeeDee said. "I already decided, so you can button your pants."

It was too late; I was sliding them down. "How long does it have to last to work, anyway? Do I even get to wiggle it around a little? Or is it just wham, bam, no more curse?"

"Don't humiliate me," she said. "Please?" She was touching her mouth.

My jeans were puddled at my ankles. I was standing there in just my white briefs. I tried to affect an air of defiance, but it was difficult; I suddenly remembered that the right butt cheek of this particular pair of underpants had a hole from washing them too many times.

Humiliate you? I wanted to say.

DeeDee was standing straight, shoulders back, neck long, and chin up. She had her jaw squared. She didn't look sad about any of this. She looked tired and over it, but not sad. *What, no ciga-rette?* I wanted to say.

"So then what? So we don't do it; then what happens? Then what do you do? What next?"

"I still have a few years to take care of it," she said, like it was the least important thing I could ask.

"And then?"

"Ever read a fairy tale, Sam? They never end well."

"I thought it was all *happily ever after?*"

"That just shows how many fairy tales you've read," she said. "Then again, you didn't know the Bible was filled with hos."

At that she sat down in the sand and slumped into herself. The ocean was just an indeterminate little blue-and-white swirl—a curlicue, really—coming and going at her feet.

I probably should have left her alone, but I couldn't. "But wait: I'm confused about whether I'm supposed to be the prince or what?"

"You're you," she said. "And I'm me. None of that has changed."

This was too much. "No," I said. "You can't fucking say that. When it's basically the opposite of what you mean. You don't even care who I am. Why would you? It's unimportant for your purposes."

DeeDee finally buckled. "Sam," she said.

"I fucking can't believe you. The rest of it I can believe—I don't know how, but I can. But you. I thought you were different."

She looked at me as if I'd said something she didn't understand. "Sam," she said.

"None of this was real. You were just using me."

"No," she said. "Okay, maybe at first, but—"

"Look, I get it."

I got it.

Look, the fact of the existence of life on Earth is basically unbelievable if you think about it for two seconds. You might actually call it a miracle if you get off on that sort of thing. Because what are the chances?

The fact is that if our homey, temperate, generous little planet spun just a little bit closer to the sun, we'd all be cooked. Even a tiny bit farther into space and we'd be freezing our asses to death.

And that's just one factor—the easiest one to conceptualize. It's not even taking into account the chemical unlikeliness of Earth's unique preponderance of oxygen, water, and whatever else allows us to survive here. (Look, I don't know the details, but I did actually read all this somewhere.)

The point is that you can't think about it too long; it will boggle your mind. How are we even here? At the very least it's an astonishing statistical fluke. At most—well, some people use it to make a case for the existence of God.

I don't believe God exists. Life found Earth only because of the sheer vastness of the universe; with an infinity of planets floating around out there at various distances from various stars it had to happen somewhere, right? And so here we are because here we are and that's just that, and in fact it's not such a big thing after all. It's basically just luck.

As I looked at DeeDee sitting on the beach, her elbows on her knees and her chin on her fists, her floral dress flapping a little in the wind, it occurred to me that this was also love's trick. This notion that you are somehow special: that it could only have been you and her, in this place, at this moment, in this exact way. If Mom hadn't left, if Dad hadn't quit his job. If I hadn't wandered into that party.

What if the earth were the tiniest bit closer to the sun? Instead of knowing each other, DeeDee and I would have been burned to a crisp before we even had a chance to be born.

At first, one assumes destiny has had a part in lining up all these what-ifs, all with the particular purpose of bringing you to her at the exact moment that she needed a light on the pier outside the Fisherman's Net. One begins to believe in God.

But that's all just fake. This is not actually how it all happened.

The actual actualness of it was both much more complicated and, at the same time, the fucking simplest thing in the world. DeeDee hadn't even needed a light. She already had one. She just came out there because she could smell me. Or who cares? It didn't matter who was standing there on the pier. I could have been anyone.

I was not special. They needed a virgin and a virgin appeared, the same way another one would appear after me and another after him. I wondered if these same scenes were playing themselves out elsewhere on the beach at this moment. Other virgins, other DeeDees, but still pretty much the same.

I could have been anyone and she could have been any of them.

We had never been anything. In a way it was a relief. I shrugged at her—her face in her hands, now—and I gathered my clothes as quickly as I could and turned and walked for home, the beach returning to me with every step I took.

TWENTY-TWO

THE RED FLAGS were up on the beach and the lifeguard chairs were abandoned, tipped into the sand. The water was dull and choppy, whitecaps dotting the surface, the horizon obscured by giant gray clouds. This had happened quickly— just an hour earlier it had been sunny and clear, and as I'd walked down the beach away from DeeDee, the breeze had become restless in a way that pricked the hairs on the back of my neck. A storm was on its way.

At the beach access near our cottage, a crowd of people had gathered on the shore to watch a clutch of surfers in the water. There was something about their weightless speed that implied motionlessness, a state of suspense, as they hung there in the curled bellies of towering waves and careened toward the shore in smooth, jigsawed lines.

Every one of them wiped out before making it to the sand. And then they'd pop up from the water, unfazed, and paddle back out to repeat failure.

When I reached the beach road, I found it gridlocked with cars pointed for the causeway, an endless line of them sitting in the muggy heat, honking and spewing exhaust and going nowhere, bare feet dangling from passenger windows, fingers drumming on doors. They were all headed away.

The Girls were the only ones not leaving. They couldn't leave, I knew now. They were walking on the side of the road looking both preoccupied and unburdened. Their eyes were cloudy and their hair was frizzier and more tangled than usual, bunching at their skulls like strange, futuristic hats.

They seemed as fidgety as the people in the cars, touching the sides of their faces and biting their nails as they wandered along in the sharp, yellow grass. When I'd try to catch their gazes, they'd just smile nervously and look away like they were sharing a dark joke among themselves.

The little grocery store on the beach road was crowded with people, the shelves half-empty, the lines winding through the aisles. Everyone was chattering with an inflection of cheerful mania, but the checkout girls were untouched by the excitement, going through their motions with slow and liquid languor, pausing to stretch their necks to the left and then the right, rolling their shoulders in between ringing up items, blinking long and hard, and taking slow, deep breaths every few seconds. I'd stopped to get a Gatorade but quickly decided it was a lost cause and retreated.

I missed DeeDee already.

At home, everyone was on the porch: Jeff, Dad, even Mom. When I spotted them from the street, the three of them standing there all casual and summery—Jeff smoking, Mom with her glass of wine, and Dad's bald head bobbing here and there—I had an unsettling double-take feeling. There was something off about the tableau they created, something about their unguarded postures and the easiness of their movements that was both familiar and very odd.

Everything looked right, but at the same time I had this feeling it wasn't. I looked harder as I got closer. Jeff was sitting precariously on the guardrail, a cigarette dangling from his mouth and his shoulder slumped toward Mom, his face pointing to the ocean. Mom was gesticulating madly with her glass of wine, looking back and forth from Jeff to Dad, who appeared from a middle distance to be puttering and paying no attention. They all looked absolutely normal.

That was it, of course. It was just the fact that they were together at all, bored and natural and just whatever. For the first time in I don't know how long, they looked like a family.

Then again, it wasn't normal, not exactly. If we were going by the standards of truly normal, or at least the old version of normal, Jeff would not be smoking in front of them, Mom would not have been drinking a glass of wine at noon, and Dad would have been wearing at least some form of shirt. But still. There they were. They were waiting for me to complete the picture.

"We've decided to stay," my father said, grinning, when I'd

climbed the steps to the porch.

"Where would we be going?" I said.

"Evacuation," Mom said. "There's a hurricane on the way."

"We'd be going home, Tiger," Dad said. "But we're not. We're not the types to throw in the towel like that. If there's a storm, we'll weather it."

Where is home? I wanted to ask.

My brother puffed on his cigarette and didn't say anything. I could sense him trying to catch my eye, but I avoided meeting his gaze.

He knew. I could tell. He had known all along. I couldn't look at his face.

"So why are we staying?" I looked from Dad to Mom. "If we're supposed to leave?" Everyone just sort of shrugged. "Are we all going to die?" I asked.

"Pfft," my mom whistled, waving me off. "People make such a big deal about death. It's just a *passage*." She put an arm around Dad's shoulder and he pulled her close, kissing her on the cheek.

"Anyway, we're not going to die," Dad said.

"I vote to leave," I said. The sooner we left, the sooner we could forget everything that had happened here. But no one answered me.

I hadn't been paying as much attention to Mom and Dad as I probably should have since the night of their epic dance at Ursula's. It was partly that I had been wrapped up in DeeDee and partly that I just didn't want to think about it very hard because it was gross, not to mention confusing. Now, though, seeing them all hugged up on each other, Mom giggling as Dad whispered impishly in her ear, I had no choice but to wonder what was going on with them. (I did manage to refrain from speculating on what Dad was whispering.)

When Mom reacted to Dad by pulling out of his grip and slapping him on the butt, I accidentally looked at Jeff. He ashed over the deck and looked back at me like, *don't fucking ask me.*

Overhead, the sky was closing in. I went inside.

I was lying in bed on top of the quilt a few minutes later, not doing anything except trying to ignore the blare of the hurricane coverage from the television in the other room—trying not to think at all, really—when Jeff came in. He stood in the doorway for a second before flopping on the other bed without a word. I didn't say hello, but continued to stare at the ceiling.

We stayed there like that for a few minutes.

"So how pissed are you at me?" he finally said. I turned and faced him; he was on his back with his arms folded. Then he rolled over and faced me right back.

"What am I supposed to say?" I said.

"Should I have told you?"

"I mean, yes?" I said. "Obviously?"

"They made me promise," Jeff said.

"Bros before hos?" I said. Thinking: *How could he of all people argue with that?*

But he did. "Dude," he said. "I mean, bro. Bro! You are my number one bro. Literally and figuratively. You know. But you know it's not like that. You of all bros should know that, right?"

Me of all bros. "You should have told me," I said.

"I know," Jeff said. "But, you know, they're good people. Or whatever they are. Maybe it's rude to call them *people*, like that's disrespecting their identity. I don't know. The point is they're good. They really are. After you take it all away. They're, like, the embodiment of everything good."

The idea that Kristle was a living vessel for the universe's goodness was something that I couldn't even begin to grapple with. But.

"How long have you known?" I asked. "I mean known everything."

"Since that night," Jeff said. "The night I found Kristle and you . . ." He trailed off.

"Sorry about that," I said.

"Bro, I get it now. She shouldn't have done that, but I get it. I'm definitely not mad at you or anything."

"So that's when she told you?"

"I mean, I sort of knew a little before that. Some of it. Or something. I just had this feeling. But that night was when Kristle told me the whole fucking fucked-up story."

"At least she was honest with you. Why was she, exactly? Honest, I mean."

"I guess she knew I'd understand."

"What did she say?" I asked. "As in, what exactly?"

"I can't really talk about it," he said.

"Well fuck you," I said.

"Yeah," he said. "Fuck all of us, I guess."

I rolled onto my back. Jeff didn't say anything else but he didn't leave either. I wasn't actually mad at him. I was trying hard, and he certainly deserved it, but I didn't really have the energy. But what I wanted to know was why they thought he would understand and not me?

And I know this sounds insane. I know, I know, I know it does. But there was a part of me that wanted to crawl into bed with him and just curl up at his side, the way I used to—once or twice at least—during lightning storms when I was little. Just gather my knees to my chest and bury my face in the crook of his arm.

I didn't do that. It was just one of those things that flashed in my brain long enough for me to feel like a crazy person.

An hour later, my mother was still on the porch. The sky had turned a muddy yellow gray that faded downward into a thin line of radiant and unexpected periwinkle at the horizon. A beautiful but troubling Rothko. It wasn't raining yet. But it was coming.

Mom, like the sky, appeared as an unexpected painting. Her bright red hair was loose, hanging in salty curls to her bare shoulders. When had it gotten so long? Her eyes in this light were a color I'd never really seen before.

"Rough day?" she said.

"How'd you know?" I asked.

"I'm a mom," she said. "I know these things. It's my job."

I let out a hoot.

"Well it is," she said. "Need someone to lend an ear? My advice might not be that bad, you know."

"I'll pass," I said. I didn't really want to talk about myself with Mom. She stared at me expectantly, which was probably a trick she had learned in some parenting book. Not that I figured she had read one of those in a while, but they used to be one of her main hobbies. Finally she was making me so nervous that I had no choice but to speak, which must be the point.

"So, like, what's up with you and Dad? Are you back together or whatever? Are you back for good?"

I didn't want to talk about her and Dad any more than I wanted to talk about myself, but it was the best way I could think of to change the subject.

"Oh," she said. "If you figure it out, tell me please! I don't know anything!" She slapped her forehead and frowned clownishly. I noticed then for the first time that she'd painted her fingernails black.

"Why did you leave?" I asked. "The real reason. Especially if you were just going to come back. Are you really back, even? Are you even my mother?" I wanted to stop but I couldn't. "Are you going to stay?"

Mom looked taken off guard, rolling backward onto her heels into an awkward step toward the porch rail and frowning a bit before recovering her smile.

"Sam," she said. "Sam. Pal of mine. I don't know what's going to happen. But I'm here right now, and there's a hurricane on the way."

STORM

When the hurricanes come, we are among the few who stay behind. We have nowhere to go and no way to get there anyway. We're not afraid of a little rain. Actually, we kind of like it.

During the hurricanes—and only during the hurricanes—we find that we have certain immunities. We can step outside into the worst of it and feel suddenly steadier on our feet. We feel the maelstrom passing through our bodies, leaving us with electricity sparking from the center of our chests, shooting out to our fingertips and toes.

Our mother tries to help us where she can.

So when the storm arrives, we make our way out into the streets, off to the bars, unfazed by the rain and wind. We let ourselves inside and turn the jukebox on—at least for as long as the electricity lasts—but we don't dance. We don't really talk, either; when we are alone like this—truly alone—conversation becomes superfluous.

We take our shoes off. We put our feet up on the bar and lean back as we sip bizarre and generally disgusting cocktails. We twist our hair around our fingers and feel it twisting back. The Stones sing "Ruby Tuesday."

The wind rages outside. The walls begin to shake. The floor vibrates like an angry lady downstairs is banging on the ceiling with a broom. There is whistling and crashing, and then the music on the jukebox cuts out along with the lights. We let our eyes adjust to the darkness and hunker down for as long as it lasts. It could go all night and we will not get tired. We settle in. We clink our drinks with each other and know that we are in no danger.

All over these islands, houses are flying away, falling into the ocean, splitting in two, but wherever we stand will remain untouched. We have no doubt about this. The locals know it too, which is why we are allowed in here in the first place, why we are drinking for free.

It's just the way it is. We are good luck, at least during hurricanes.

They're when we are happiest. They're when this place feels the closest to being a home.

And when the storm has passed, when everyone else is sifting through the wreckage, taking stock, rebuilding, we make our way to the beach, stepping over downed power lines and trash and misplaced tree branches, to the shore, where we will sit in quiet, observant clusters, feeling the power that we had for a few hours slipping away.

Junk floats in the water. Sometimes entire homes have been swallowed. Lives have been destroyed; people have sometimes been killed. But the ocean is still here, and so are we. Nothing feels that different.

TWENTY-THREE

"HERE," DAD SAID. "Take this. Go find some treasure, okay?" He was brandishing his metal detector at me almost like a threat. It was the next day and the hurricane still hadn't come. It was supposed to hit in the late afternoon, according to the news, but they kept changing the prediction. Upgrading, downgrading, pushing, and pulling. I wished it would hurry up and come so we could get it over with.

Mom was on the couch reading a book about meditation; Jeff was sleeping in a ball on a La-Z-Boy, snoring, his mouth gaping, while the local news anchor droned on about weather predictions. Someone had suggested going to stock up on supplies, but no one was in the mood to deal with the lines. At some point Dad had spotted me gazing longingly into the kitchen cabinet for the thousandth time, hoping something interesting to eat had somehow materialized, and had gone to fetch his device. Now he was shoving it into my hands.

"You've got to be kidding," I said, taking it from him. It was lighter than I expected. It felt right in my hands.

"You need something to do."

"What about the hurricane?"

"I don't think anyone's going to be worried about a little hurricane when you come back with Blackbeard's legendary booty. Anyway, the hurricane won't be here for a few hours at least. Just come back if it starts to get really dicey out there."

"What do you think I'll really find?"

"Who knows, Tiger? Could be nothing. It's not really that important anyway. The journey is the destination, as they say."

"I've heard that."

"But you know," he said. "I haven't been able to find anything. And I know it's out there. It occurs to me that maybe you might have a little more luck."

I surprised myself by taking his suggestion. I guess I just liked the idea of having no fixed destination, of being carried on the waves of blips and bloops until I looked up and found myself somewhere new. It seemed like it could lead me anywhere, even someplace secret—which is to say a secret place that could be my own, unlike the other secret place that wasn't mine at all. I also liked the idea of having something to do. So I took the metal detector, put in the headphones, and went out to find whatever it was that I was supposed to find.

Outside, the dunes were keeling over. The oceanfront buildings were boarded up; the parking lots of the motels were empty. The only people on the street were packs of drunk, shouting bicycle riders—locals, I figured—speeding into the wind, falling over, then getting back up and mounting their bikes again.

It was already pouring when I stepped onto the beach. The rain soaked me, spilling down from my hair into my face in rivulets so thick I could barely see. It ran down my shoulders and my back and my spine and my chest into the waistband of my underpants, then down my legs. I ignored it and just powered on the metal detector—knowing the water was probably bad for it but whatever—and started my trek. The downpour didn't last anyway; it was over a few minutes after it started, and though it was windier than ever, it became suddenly dryish, the sky gray but clear.

So I walked and walked, sweeping my arm back and forth in a slow, repeating arc like a blind man with a cane. I let the thing lead me, not worrying about the fact that I wasn't moving in anything near to a straight line. Here and there it would beep, and then the beeping would get louder before stopping suddenly, like to say, *Oops, sorry about that, no big deal.*

So I'd just keep going, choosing my own path until the beeping suddenly started again and led me a little farther. At first I thought it was being indecisive, but as I made my way farther down the beach in whatever direction, it started to dawn on me that this was how the metal detector wanted it. It was not content to be my guide. Yes, it would give me hints, but I had to act on my own instincts if I was going to find my way.

As it started to rain again—this time as more of a horizontal drizzle—I thought of the first time DeeDee had taken me to her secret cove. About the way it had just seemed to drop itself in front of us, summoned by an esoteric combination of footsteps. I thought about the fact that when Jeff and I had gone back looking for it on our own, it had obstinately refused to exist.

The rain got harder. I kept wandering.

I thought about the night we'd spent in the belly of Nalgene's fiberglass ship, wrecked on the green-carpeted shoals of the golf course. I thought about how little I'd known DeeDee then, and the fact that I still barely knew her now. I wondered if that really mattered.

And I wondered what had happened to the Girl we'd seen in the surf on our first night here. Whether she'd found DeeDee and Kristle; whether I had met her without knowing it. I wondered what her name was.

I thought about whether DeeDee would ever make it home. Around that time, the machine started to beep, and I looked up and saw that I was standing on a part of the beach that I hadn't seen before. The shoreline was mostly all the same around here, but this section was different. It was broader and greener, and the dunes were so high that they looked like grassy little mountains and were bordered with squat and gnarled trees that were twisted over with vines flowering in tiny lavender stars. Even wet, the sand was a bright, clean white, and the water had a cerulean tint not native to the place. It was as if I'd found myself on another planet, which was virtually the same but not quite.

And the machine was going crazy, beeping and blooping louder than it seemed like it was supposed to. It was practically vibrating in my hand, and then it was pulling me to a spot on the beach, dragging me with it like a stubborn dog until it came to rest in a place that was nothing special.

The metal detector was quivering with excitement. It wanted me to stop here. So I set it aside and began to dig. At first I felt silly doing it—what was I really going to find, anyway?—but the more I dug the more it felt important, the more it felt like I couldn't stop until I hit something.

I started with one hand, scooping damp sand and tossing it to the side, and then when the earth got firmer, I began to use two. I still didn't know what I was looking for—didn't even consider it, really—but soon the hole was deep enough and wide enough that I had to climb inside it to keep digging. So I did.

The rain started getting harder again. The water started to fill up around me in my pit, but I kept going.

Time seemed to have stopped, or at least I had stopped caring about it. The metal detector, placated that I was digging, wasn't screaming anymore and had settled into a robotic purr.

What I didn't realize was that the beach was shrinking around me. How could I know, absorbed as I was in my dig, that the water was rising around me on every side, that I now stood in something like an island, five feet by five feet, as the hurricane raged and the water flooded? How could I know that the metal detector had been swept away, that I was alone now, and that there was no way home?

All I knew was that I was digging. That there was something here and that I needed to find it. Maybe it was what my dad had been searching for all along.

Or. Maybe it was something else.

The wind was raging around me, but I was dug in deep enough that I was safe from it. The rain didn't bother me anymore. I was about to toss another handful of dirt to the side when I felt a lump in my hand.

I was uncertain that I'd found what I was supposed to be looking for. At first, it looked like nothing more than a crappy shell.

But then I looked closer and saw that it wasn't a shell at all but a silver, clam-shaped something—man-made and barely bigger than a large coin or the face of a watch, crusted in sand and grime and greenish mossy stuff. I turned it over in my hand, examining the scalloped grooves on the back, running my fingers over the slimy fuzz. Dad's discoveries had mostly been stuff that had probably been dropped by people on the beach the same afternoon and been covered over by an inch of sand, but this had been here a long time. He had never found anything like this. It seemed likely that it could have been buried here forever.

Then I noticed that it was hinged at the bottom edge, with a deep groove around the outside rim, like a locket or a pocket watch.

I pushed at the groove with my thumbnail. I didn't really expect it to open, but all I did was pry it a little and it yielded easily: with a click, it flipped right open. There was a minor flash of brightness that could have been my imagination, but I flinched as a fractured bit of what might have been sunlight, if it had been sunny, bounced into my eyes. When I opened them, I realized that I was looking at a mirror.

The glass was unscuffed and gleaming like new, and was framed by five tiny green jewels, each set into a recess in the intricate silver molding. It looked expensive. But I didn't take the time to examine it. I was too busy staring at the person who was staring up at me.

It was me. And I couldn't help it: I caught my breath. It took me a beat to realize it was me.

I looked so different. I had changed since we'd come to this beach, and somehow I had missed it. Now I could see myself all at once as a re-created person.

When we'd left home in May, my hair had been short enough that you'd barely know it was technically curly; now it had grown out into wild rings that spiraled into my face, weighted by rainwater. I had changed color, too. My skin was burnished gold and splattered with a confused matrix of orangey-brown freckles that crawled out across my cheekbones from the broad bridge of my nose. My jaw looked wider; my eyes were deeper set and ringed with dark circles. I was heavier, more substantial, but there was a definition in my face that was new.

In the mirror, my mouth was open, and I realized I was

smiling, just a little, revealing a small sliver of this one snaggly tooth I have.

I'd never really looked at myself before, not like this.

I was seeing myself for the first time, not as a stranger would see me, but like when you meet someone and have that zing of déjà vu. It was almost how I'd felt when I'd opened that door and found DeeDee in the bedroom of that beach house at Kristle's birthday.

It recalled another feeling too, and a night I'd almost forgotten about. Back in October—it was less than a year ago, but it seemed longer now—Sebastian's parents had been out of town, and he'd had this great idea to catch a ride into the city with his sister, to sneak into this club where they were having some dance party type of thing he'd read about on the internet.

I'm not much of a dancer, but I'd gone along with him because Sebastian thought it was such a great idea and I didn't want to chicken out. Anyway, I'd figured there was no way we'd be able to get in; we were underage.

But I'd forgotten that Sebastian was Sebastian. It only took him a few seconds to work some kind of magic with the bouncer, and then we were walking inside the club, where we got ourselves beers and stood in the corner, watching the crowd swell and shift around us, watching the girls waving their arms in the air, flashing their midriffs and tossing their hair, laughing and slugging drinks. Sebastian and I didn't really say much to each other; he seemed as much at a loss for what to do next as I was. But after a few minutes, he shrugged and took a last chug of his drink before plunking the glass down on the bar. "Dude. I'm gonna see what's up in this place," he said. "I'll find you later. Don't get in too much trouble."

I waited for him for a while, drinking beer after beer—feeling bold, I'd started experimenting with fruity microbrews—until I was definitely buzzed, and then, when it seemed like I'd given him plenty of time on his own, I went to find him.

I squished into the center of the dance floor, where I found myself in a mass of bodies that twisted and pumped around me as they threw themselves into one another and into the air, all operating as one big indistinguishable organism.

The music was nothing I'd ever heard before, just a swirling funnel of guitars and synths and voices that pushed forward into someplace new and then looped back on itself. I felt like I was staring out the end of a long tunnel, and realized I was probably drunk.

Then I was dancing. I don't know how I knew how to do it or anything, but my body was moving itself. Driven by the pulsing around me, the thump of the bass that now seemed to be coming from inside my chest.

I closed my eyes and kept going.

The strobe was flashing on the backs of my eyelids, and then it was as if they weren't closed at all. It was as if I was watching myself from above, pink and green flecks whirling on my face, the vapor from the smoke machine curling at my feet, my beer sloshing as my shoulders rocked and swayed, and the music just shooting through me.

I lost track of where one song ended and the next one began, of where I ended and the music started.

I felt beautiful, like a battery absorbing lights and sound and sweat and rhythm and throwing it back out into the crowd.

It was sort of like being in love, I think—but a different kind of love than most people usually talk about. I was in love with everything and with nothing. I remember feeling very far away from myself, but more myself than ever too.

Eventually Sebastian found me, alone and just moving and not caring who saw me or what they thought. He tapped me on the shoulder and I turned to face him, but kept dancing, unashamed, before slowing to a stop as he looked me up and down with a bemused smile that suggested that he thought I'd gone completely nuts. "Dude," he said. "This place kind of sucks. Let's get the fuck out of here."

So we left together and called Sebastian's sister, who was annoyed to have to take us home so early. She lectured us the whole way about "knowing our limits" and "pacing ourselves." The next morning I had expected to be wrecked, headachy and hungover, but I was fine.

But the feeling I'd had when I was dancing that night, alone and surrounded by all those people—the feeling that I was trying to reach out to another, truer version of myself across some kind of infinite and unbridgeable divide—remained with me. It was the same feeling I had on the beach in the hurricane, gazing into the shell mirror I'd dug from the sand.

I was looking at myself with this sadness and hunger and love that was mixed together and shaken up until it was all basically the same thing. And the image I stared at was shedding layers, just sloughing them off. I forgot about my parents, about the beach and the hurricane, and even about the mirror itself. I forgot about DeeDee.

I forgot everything except the person who stared back at me, stripped to an essential but incomprehensible core and wishing that I could be that person.

I don't know how long I stood there, just looking at myself in the mirror, caught up in the weird rapture of knowledge, the drunkenness of unexpected recognition. But after a while I felt water at my thighs and looked down and saw that the hole I was standing in had entirely filled. I climbed out and looked up and down the beach—or what was left of it.

It was just gone. It had been swallowed by the storm.

Then I felt the wind, in the form of falling on my ass. I was swept over backward onto the sliver of mud that was still left to me. When I tried to stand, I stumbled a little and then fell right back down. Well, fuck, it was a hurricane after all. Had it just started? Or had I simply missed it up until now? It occurred to me that I didn't even really know what a hurricane was. Wasn't there supposed to be lightning or something?

I sat there, stuck, trying to survey the beach with the wind and rain in my eyes. Somehow, mysteriously, the water had risen so high that the mud I sat was the only spot as far as I could see—from the ocean to the battered outcrop of the dunes—that remained above the flood. Of course I couldn't actually see that far, so it was hard to know for sure. But at least for now it seemed that I was stuck. Worse, it seemed that it was only a matter of time before the water got me, too.

I figured I had to try to get to the dunes, although with the wind so strong I couldn't even get to my feet; it didn't seem promising. But I was going to try to wade or swim or crawl until I could grab on to the dune grass and somehow climb to safety. I was just about to do it when I saw them coming for me.

It was DeeDee and Kristle, walking down the beach as if the storm was nothing, moving easily through the curtain of rain, totally unbowed by the gale that was keeping me on my ass.

They were both usually so afraid of the ocean, but now they seemed unbothered by the fact that it was taking over and that they were walking right through it. At first it looked like they were walking on the water, but as they moved closer I saw that they were following one of their unseen paths, their feet only finding purchase at the exact spots where the flood was at its shallowest.

They looked otherworldly. You couldn't even see the sky through the weather, but even in the distance I could see the sisters clearly as they approached, like a separate image that had been overlaid on top of reality. Their hair was twirling around their bodies in twisty, jumping crowns of brilliant neon. Their gait was loping, their faces peaceful and resolute. It was impossible to tell how far away they were; their proportions relative to the landscape were all out of whack, their faces big as hovering moons, their eyes piercing green, green, green through the trouble.

I could hear them speaking like they were right next to me, like they were whispering in my ear—a trick, I guessed, of the howling wind. But they didn't sound like themselves. They were speaking with one voice, a voice that was low and droning and cool:

Our mother is the Deepness. Our father is the Endlessness. Our brothers are Speed and Calm. We are . . .

I'd had the mirror in my hand the whole time I'd been sitting here. Though I'd half forgotten it, I'd been clutching it so hard that my palm was beginning to hurt. Without thinking, I shoved it into the pocket of my swimsuit.

We have always known you. We knew you the moment we saw you. We will know you the next time. You will always break our hearts.

They were coming to rescue me. And one moment they seemed miles in the distance, and then they were just a few paces off, wading through an ankle-deep tide. "What the hell are you doing out here?" DeeDee said. Her voice was louder than it should've been, but at least it sounded like her again.

Kristle didn't say anything. She looked frightening, fierce and alien, as she reached out and pulled me to my feet.

"Here. Come." As my hand touched hers I felt a warmth coursing through my body. I found that now I could stand without being knocked down.

"How did you find me?" I asked.

"The hurricane told us," Kristle said. She smiled like it was a joke, but I had this weird feeling it might not have been. "Half of this will be gone tomorrow."

"Half of what?" I said.

"Come on," she said.

We walked home together, in the storm. It was strange passing through it with them; I had the sensation of moving through an illusion. I could tell that they felt it differently, though. They weren't talking anymore, but they seemed invigorated by every step we took.

The beach churned, the waves resembling a looped newsreel of buildings collapsing under the weight of a wrecking ball. The dunes lay flattened and panicked and almost invisible. There was no distance or horizon. Just rain and rain and wind and waves and more rain and wind.

"It's the eye," Kristle remarked when we turned the corner into our cul-de-sac, past the Seashell Shoals sign. I looked into the sky and realized she was right; the sky was white, and a ray of sun pierced through a break in the clouds, streaking my face. The rain had stopped around us. The wind had stopped too. There was a stillness.

I was tempted to whisper.

Kristle stood there, hands in the pockets of her soaking shorts, looking off with a blank expression like she'd forgotten who she was or how we'd gotten here. I looked at her for a minute, wondering what I was supposed to do, but DeeDee just motioned for me to leave her.

"What were you doing out there anyway?" she asked. "Were

you looking for something?"

"I don't know," I said, and it was basically the truth. Then we were back at my house. It was still standing.

"Thanks for saving me," I told DeeDee at the end of the driveway. "I don't know what would have happened to me. How did you do that?"

"It's not important, babe. None of it is. Just be with me," she said. "It doesn't matter how. Please?"

"I don't know," I said.

The calm of the eye felt like its own kind of chaos. The black clouds whirled in a ring, and we were in the center of it, standing in a small bright circle.

The world moved just a tiny, undetectable fraction of a light-year closer to the sun. We were all of our different selves. DeeDee was beautiful, inscrutable, prickly and wise and angry still. She was a mermaid, complete with tacky hot-pink shells on her boobs. She was a girl. She was with me.

"Okay," I said. "Fine."

I still had the mirror in my pocket. I'd forgotten it already.

GIRLS

We are not girls. At least, we don't think we are. Girls do not do what we do.

Once a month at the full moon, from June to September, we make our way through the dunes, across the sand and rocks to our beach.

There, we undress wordlessly and venture into the water as our bodies begin to transform.

We set our knife to the side, where it lies angry and glittering, waiting for us to pick it up again.

We shed our skin and find scales, oily and hard and slick. We shed answers and find questions.

We lie in the tide and let the waves wash over us. It feels good, this small taste of the home we can't imagine returning to. This is how we feed the summer. What would become of it if we just stayed home?

We can't do that. We need it as much as it needs us.

But the water is cold. It is endless. It reminds us as much of our father as of our mother. We know what's down there. We know how dangerous it is. Still, we don't move.

We lean back and feel the deepness creeping on us as the tide rises. We feel it first at our ankles and calves and then between our thighs. We feel it lapping at our breasts. Our arms and legs twist and contract, curling slowly into slimy tentacles that sink themselves into the sand like the roots of a tree.

The world rushes through us. We are peaceful. We are as deep and black as space. Staring up at the stars, we see only our own image reflected back at us.

We are infinite and we are ravenous.

TWENTY-FOUR

IT WAS BRIGHT and hazy on the beach. Figures more than a handful of paces away appeared first in formless silhouettes and then emerged from the cloud of distance like they were climbing down out of a spaceship, still steaming from a fiery entry into the atmosphere.

As they got closer they gained color, took shape. They kept on walking, drifting through the end of July and into August. Out past the pier, more figures floated into view.

DeeDee and I were sitting on a blanket, watching them appear and then disappear and appear again, each time with different bodies, different lives. She was in a pair of shorts and a T-shirt, and I had just come in from the ocean and was salty and sore from swimming. I had my arm draped around her shoulder and she was leaning into me in an easy slump.

Summer was moving along to a slow finish, but there was still time left. For now we could put it aside.

So DeeDee was saying something funny, and I was probably laughing. Kristle and Jeff were playing a game with a Frisbee that involved chasing each other in circles, laughing hysterically, and then tackling each other into the sand, where they would lie, pawing at each other, before picking up the Frisbee and repeating it all over again. Dad had dragged a beach chair to the edge of the water, where he was reading *Her Place* as the waves came in and out.

Somewhere out in the water my mother was swimming a backstroke. All I could make out of her were her fingers surfacing and sinking in a windmill. She had been at it for ages.

The damage from the hurricane hadn't been so bad. Most of the buildings had survived, and news of what hadn't had been accepted by the people who lived here as the inevitable way of the world. Around here, where everything already hung precariously over the ocean's edge, a thing's very existence guaranteed its eventual destruction. Life would be washed away, then built over basically the same as before, then washed away again.

For everyone, things were mostly back to what passed for normal, at least for the end of July.

It was very hot. Since the storm, the heat had become constant and slimy and a little bit sinister. Things had slowed down: every day felt like swimming through a pool of Jell-O. Words dribbled out of our mouths at half speed; it sometimes took a full minute to climb the stairs up to the cottage. At night on the back porch the air was so thick that Kristle's cigarette smoke left her lungs and just hung in front of her face as a dense and listless cloud that needed to be waved off every few seconds.

Mosquitoes were everywhere. And flies, too, big, black, fearless things that orbited your head in a sickening halo. You couldn't stop moving, because if you paused for just the tiniest second the flies would all land on you and start crawling on your skin. It wasn't worth trying to swat them; they were the only thing that still seemed to be able to move quickly. Anyway, we didn't mind them all that much. They had started to feel like part of our bodies.

By now I was immune to the sun. All summer I had been shedding layer after layer of skin from sunburn, and then one day I crawled from the sand brown and new, finally a creature of the beach. I jumped into the water without hesitation now, never noticing the cold, never flinching at the sight of jellyfish. I was unbowed by even the biggest waves.

DeeDee had quit smoking, but had taken to constantly touching her mouth, still searching for a phantom cig.

It was like we'd entered a dream somewhere in the middle. Days spent in the sand now had that blur around the edges that signifies not the end, but the part just before—the golden hour before sunset, the glittering bridge of the song.

One day, DeeDee took me to the cove. She paused at the top of the rocks and I was climbing behind her. "Look," she said.

In the distance, a horse was wandering in the surf.

"A Banker pony," DeeDee said. "They have them all over in Corolla and Rodanthe, but you never see them around here. I wonder how it made it so far."

The pony was gray and small, squat with a bowlegged gait, and had an air of amused indifference about it. Its pelt was threadbare and patchy, its mane a frizzy tangle of knots. The thing was less than majestic, not exactly the Black Stallion or even Misty of Chincoteague. But it was still a horse alone on the beach, and DeeDee and I just stood there watching it.

We jumped from the rocks onto the sand, and the horse looked up at us curiously but didn't startle. The horse began to move toward us. "Um," I asked. "Are they dangerous? What if it has rabies?" Other than squirrels, wild animals are not something I have a lot of experience with in general.

She laughed. "Don't be stupid," she said. "Look at it. Does that thing look dangerous to you?"

It didn't.

The horse was not afraid of us. In fact, it seemed to like me—it came right up to me and almost knelt, bowed its head like it was waiting for something. "Go ahead," DeeDee said. And I reached out and rubbed my hand across its face. Then DeeDee did. And the horse turned around and trotted away before breaking into a surprisingly swift gallop and disappearing into the dunes.

"I wonder if there will be a new one tonight," DeeDee was saying. Seeing the horse had made her contemplative. "I have this feeling there will be. We usually get a sense. We can feel it in our feet."

"A new what?" I asked, brushing a stray strand of hair from her face.

"A new girl," she said. "A new one of us. They keep coming until September. It's always weird when they get here close to the end like this. Like an afterthought. Kristle was born at the end, you know. I've always wondered what it was like when she got here—who found her. She never talks about it."

I was getting used to the idea of all this. I still didn't quite believe any of it. Except that I did. "Jeff and I saw one the night we got here," I said. "Back at the beginning. I wonder who it was?"

"Saw one what?" DeeDee asked, and I told her about the Girl we'd seen that first night at the beach, the one crawling from the water. It was the first time I'd been able to talk about her. A spell of silence had been broken.

"Maybe I know her," DeeDee said. "But maybe not. There are hundreds of us, you know—who knows, maybe thousands, maybe even at other beaches."

"I wonder," I said.

"I wonder what name she chose," DeeDee said. She leaned down and flicked a handful of sand into my lap. "I wonder if she's happy."

"Are you happy?" I asked.

"I don't know," she said. "I mean, I would have said no. But I think I am, actually. Right now, at least, like at this minute, I guess I am."

"I've been thinking about the Lost Colony," I said. "Where do you think they went?"

"Oh," DeeDee said. "I'm sure they're still around here some- where. They probably just want some peace and quiet. Now that they're local celebrities and all."

We lay in the sand for a while; we didn't have towels with us, but it didn't matter. I went for a swim while DeeDee sat on the beach and watched. I tried to do tricks to amuse her—standing on my hands, doing backflips into the waves. None of those things are really so impressive-looking, though, and I couldn't tell if she really noticed. But she seemed content to watch.

"Can I ask a question?" I asked her when we were walking home. It had been a long day spent all outside, and I was sun sore and peaceful. I was holding her hand. There had been so many things I wanted to know about, but it had never felt quite right to ask.

"Sure," she said.

"All summer, I saw these girls looking at me. Smiling at me and stuff. Not saying anything but just like glittering in my direction. It was like they *knew*. Who I am. Like, what I am to them or whatever."

"We can tell," she said. "We can feel it. It's almost like a smell, except that it's not a smell at all."

"I thought so," I said. "And don't take this the wrong way, but why was it just you and Kristle? Why were you the only ones who ever really talked to me? All the other ones just stared. You would think if I had this thing—this valuable thing—you would think they would have tried harder. In terms of sheer practicality or whatever."

"Yeah." DeeDee looked embarrassed. She hemmed and hawed. "Oh, you know, well, it's funny."

"But why?" I asked. "Is there an actual reason?"

DeeDee dropped my hand and looked me in the eye. "We're not allowed to talk to you first," she said. "It's one of the rules. You have to be the one. You said hello to me. You said hello to Kristle. So we were allowed. It's as simple as that."

"I've talked to Taffany," I said. "I've had a million conversations with her at the bar. She always acted pretty normal though."

"Taffany's different," DeeDee said. "She doesn't really care about breaking the curse. She, like, refuses to participate. Sometimes I think she's the only one around here who knows what she's actually talking about. Sometimes I think maybe to just say fuck it is the way to go. But at the same time, I want to go home, right? I miss it. Think about what it must be like. How can you just say fuck it to all that? But Taffany's Taffany. You've seen the way she dances. I wish I were like her. It would make everything simpler. But I'm not. I'm just not. What can I do?"

"You guys make this big deal about *we*. It's always *we we we*. You act like you're all the same, like you all want the same things. It's like you think with the same mind or something. But you don't. Sometimes you're really not alike at all, other than all having basically the same hairstyle. Which I hate to tell you, but blond is not technically a personality trait."

"Yeah," DeeDee said, like she was uncertain. From her tone I could tell she wasn't really hearing what I was saying. "I guess," she said. "It's sort of hard to explain. We're not like regular people."

"Who?" I asked.

"Kristle," she said. "All of us, actually. I just close my eyes and . . ."

She closed her eyes and a distant look came over her face. Then she began to laugh.

"What?" I asked. "Why are you laughing?"

"They're watching *The Price Is Right*," she said.

"So you're, like, psychic?" I wondered why she had never told me this before. It seemed like a useful and potentially important piece of information.

"Not really. We're connected to each other. We always are; it's just a matter of whether we choose to pay attention. We usually don't—it can get confusing. Sometimes even I forget which one of us I am."

"That explains some things, I guess," I said. "You should have told me that before."

"I didn't want to weird you out."

"Yeah," I said. "I get it."

"We're connected to other things too," she said.

"Like what?" I asked.

"Like everything," she said. "But everything is a lot of things. You have to be careful. You can't do much more than dip a toe into it or you get washed away."

"The ho with the apple," I said.

"Now you get it," she said.

When we were back on the main stretch of beach, it was getting late. Most people had gone home, but there were some stragglers left. There was a family with small children, two little boys. Their father was chasing them around in the almost-dark while the mom laughed and egged them on. I couldn't decide whether it made me sad or happy; both I guess.

"It's sort of a strange curse, isn't it?" I asked DeeDee.

"What do you mean?"

"I just mean, isn't it unusual that your father wants to punish you by making you have sex? It's sick. I thought that was the opposite of how fathers were supposed to be. And why does he want to punish *you* anyway. You didn't do shit to him."

"Read a Greek myth sometime," she said. "Read a fairy tale. Read *Her Place*, for that matter. It's how the world works."

"It still seems weird to me."

"Yeah, well. Sometimes I think it's not a curse at all," she said. "Sometimes I think, maybe we don't know the first thing about it. Maybe parts of it have gotten lost in the translation, or maybe we're only seeing half of it—the obvious part. It could mean something else entirely than what we think it means. And maybe it's not a curse at all. Maybe it's a lesson. Or something."

"What kind of lesson?"

"Who knows," she said. "I'm talking out of my ass. But the thing is, we don't even really know how we know about it. It's just been passed down. I'm not saying it's not real—it's definitely real. But maybe there's more to it. Sometimes I wonder if it doesn't come from our father at all. It could be our mother's doing. You never know, really."

Then I noticed two figures moving toward us, shadows. It was Jeff and Kristle. "Come home," Jeff called. "Dad's barbecuing."

So we all went home for dinner. Dad toiled happily over the barbecue on the porch while the rest of us hung out. My mother sat by herself on a chair a few feet away, speaking up only to read little silly bits of poetry aloud from her book every now and then.

After dinner, Kristle and Jeff went to the movies, and DeeDee and I decided to go back to the beach. It was getting chilly out, and I had gone into the bedroom to get a sweatshirt. I was surprised to find my father there, standing next to my bed, holding my swimsuit in a clenched fist. He looked up at me guiltily, like I'd caught him at something, then dropped the suit to the floor.

"What's up?" I asked.

"Oh," he said. "I was just looking for something. I thought maybe—never mind." There was a note of panic in his voice, but I didn't press him on it. And then a funny thing happened. His face opened up, blossomed into this endless, knowing grin.

I knew what he had been looking for. He had found what he'd been looking for all summer. But he had left it with me: when I looked in the pocket of my bathing suit, it was still there. I picked my sweatshirt off the floor and left him still standing there, and went to get DeeDee to walk to the dunes.

We were going to wait for her. DeeDee had grown more certain throughout the day that a new Girl would be coming, so although it felt somehow forbidden, we found ourselves crouched in a bare sandy patch, peering through the tall dune grass out at the ocean. I wasn't quite sure why we were doing this, but it seemed important to DeeDee, and I have to say that I was sort of curious myself.

We weren't really supposed to be here. DeeDee had told me that it was an unspoken thing: even when you knew they were coming, you waited for them to find you. They would find you, or you would find them by accident, but you didn't go out looking for them. It was important that each of them make their way on their own. It was just how it had always been; it was just how it was supposed to be.

I was holding DeeDee's hand while she built little hills of sand and talked. Her voice was rote and distant, but not unhappy. We had settled into some kind of something, but it was hard to say what, except that it was comfortable as long as I didn't think about it for too long.

It was almost midnight, but the sky was brighter than it should have been, considering the hour. The way night looks on a sitcom when they step outside the living room into a front yard lit by klieg lights.

There was a sticky breeze that rustled the dunes around us. The sound of the ocean was roaring and musical, like the experimental-noise bands that Sebastian's into, which I'd always considered crappy and stupid until that exact moment. The stars seemed to be humming too, singing with brightness.

And then she appeared: at first, the Girl was just a shimmer in a wave, barely noticeable. She was really just a feeling, a hollow wanting in the pit of my stomach. DeeDee saw it—felt it—too. She squeezed my palm and held her breath.

It wasn't our imagination. It was her: the wave crashed down, and then a figure was rising from the tide, white and glowing, a piece at a time. She was assembling her own body out of sea foam and salt.

For a moment she was upright, and she turned one way and then the other, trying to get her bearings, before she stumbled back into the water, face-first, and lay there for a moment, motionless.

"Should we do something?" I asked DeeDee.

DeeDee just shook her head and put a finger to her lips. She placed a gentle hand on my knee: *Be still. Watch.*

After a few minutes, the Girl got up again, wavering a little, and then steadied herself. She was naked and skeletal, and if I hadn't known, I would have had a hard time deciding whether she was a young girl or an old lady. Or even whether she was human at all. She limped slowly forward, putting one foot uncertainly in front of the other, her arms tentatively stretched to her sides, then tripped again. And again she stood.

"What will happen to her?" I asked. "We should help her before she goes wandering naked up the highway."

"Someone'll find her," DeeDee said. "One of us will take her in. Or, I mean, she could wander into the street and get hit by a car, or be murdered or whatever. Or anything. But nothing can help that. It's not our place to interfere. This is the way it's

274

supposed to go. She won't even remember this soon."

"Do you remember?" I asked.

"Not really," she said. "Little bits. I remember being cold. I remember feeling wet; I had never felt wetness before and it was weird, like seeing a new color for the first time. But the first thing I really remember is Kristle finding me. I was hiding behind the Dumpster at the Fisherman's Net, and she was throwing out the trash at the end of her shift."

"What did she do?"

"She took me inside and wrapped me in a towel from the gift shop and let me use her lip gloss and gave me some tomato bisque and a magazine to read while she closed up. I couldn't read yet—that took me a few days—but I looked at the pictures. I thought Beyoncé was the most beautiful person I'd ever seen. Then she brought me home and helped me fix my hair."

"Were you scared?"

"I don't know," DeeDee said after thinking about it for a minute. "I don't know what I was."

The Girl was still moving forward. As she got closer, I could see that she was grimacing in pain.

"Her feet hurt," DeeDee said, explaining the pained expression. "It never goes away, but it's the worst at first. This one's strong, though. I can tell. She's mad—look how pissed off she is. She's going to be a real handful. I hope she doesn't end up working at the restaurant—we've had those types before; it always ends with a customer getting a drink poured over his head."

The Girl had finally given up on trying to walk. She collapsed to her hands and knees, defeated, and began to crawl. She was faster like that. We watched her.

"She's not quite here yet," DeeDee said. "She's still changing. She's still part of *there*."

"Do you ever get here? I mean, totally become part of here? Are you ever totally transformed?"

"Don't ask me things I can't answer, babe," DeeDee said. Her voice was small and quiet. She wasn't touching me anymore; she had her hands folded in her lap. She was slumped toward the ocean.

The Girl was gone now, off for whatever life waited for her. And DeeDee was elsewhere too, staring into the distance with oceans in her eyes.

"You could go home," I said. My voice cracked a little, but I wasn't really embarrassed by that sort of thing with DeeDee anymore. "You know you could go back. You can break the curse whenever you want. I'm right here."

She didn't answer me.

SEPTEMBER GIRLS

When the season is over—when the tourists have all gone home and half the shops are boarded up—we remain behind. We are the same but diminished. Time begins to move at an uneven clip, sometimes racing forward, sometimes slowing almost to a standstill.

September feels strange; we go to bed early and develop a perpetual sour taste in our mouths. In October our skin turns grayish and our shoulders begin to feel sore at the smallest exertion. By November the gold rings around our pupils have faded. We walk around half-asleep; we double our cigarette consumption. Our hair becomes limp and knotted.

Now our knife is dull.

Even television ceases to interest us. We leave it on in the background anyway. We stop speaking to one another, although we might nod politely every now and then as we slump side by side on the couch after a long day.

Language, always hard to hold, is now liquid slipping through our fingers.

We are unbothered by all this. In fact, we luxuriate in our malaise, taking sick pleasure in the empty feeling in our stomachs, the rawness of our cuticles, the dark circles under our eyes. It pleases us when we run our fingers through our hair and come away grasping a thick clump.

We find ourselves on the beach more often than usual now, wrapped in scarves and sweaters, staring out at the gray and choppy ocean, the sky the color of our curling smoke.

We don't spend much time mourning the loss of those who have gone. We know it's the natural order of things, and anyway, it makes the beds less crowded. For now we can sleep alone.

Our feet are the worst in February, so in March we buy new shoes. By now the old shoes are so stained with blood that they are beyond use.

And then in April we feel a prickling in our cheeks and chest. In May certain facts begin to dawn on us all over again. We might be struck by a sudden, unexpected memory of one of our departed sisters. We might be visited by a forbidden glimpse of love.

Summer is coming; we can feel it. The sensation is not unlike waking up from a hungover sleep—we feel groggy but restless. We get dizzy easily and have to be careful when we stand.

We know that the first of the new girls will arrive around Memorial Day. We are all born in the summer.

It would be tempting to suspect that we are summer's children. We are not. Our mother is the Deepness. Our father is the Endlessness. Summer is what we have made.

And once it's here, it certainly couldn't get by without us. After all, who but us would change the sheets in the beach cottages?

TWENTY-FIVE

WE WERE STILL at the beach. I'd stopped asking my father if we were ever going home. I figured I didn't really want to know.

August in the suburbs is one thing: the yellowing lawns and sprinklers that spray you like warm sweat when you pass them on the way up the block, the scattered and picked-over back-to-school displays at CVS that remind you of an abandoned funeral. That humid loneliness—the feeling that the world is out of town forever even when you know most everyone's just holed up in their bedrooms smoking thin and solitary joints, avoiding both summer reading lists and phone calls.

Under the hum of the central AC, you sit in your underwear, wrapped in a blanket with a bowl of soggy cereal curdling at your side and some dumb Spanish soap opera on TV even though you don't like or even understand soap operas and you don't speak Spanish. You decide to get out of the house, so you walk to the park, where you plan on lying by the narrow, toxic creek that borders the bike path, where you intend to stare up at the unwavering leaves on the trees to enjoy them, knowing that soon they'll be yellow, then red, then brown, then shaking and gone. On the way there you pass by the high school, your feet already blistering because you didn't wear socks, and you get a sick feeling in the pit of your stomach.

In August, in the suburbs, life crawls by at an alarming pace. I know from past summers. You are both too hot and too cold. And as bored and depressed as you are, and as shitty as August is, you know you have to enjoy it while it lasts, because soon it's all over. So you pour another bowl of cereal, even though the bowls are piling up around you and it's starting to sort of smell. Maybe there will be something besides a soap opera on TV today.

That was August in the suburbs. I sort of missed it—just the familiar, bored dread. Because August at the beach was different. Especially at this beach, which felt precariously balanced at the edge of the world. I was starting to wonder if my family and I would be the next Lost Colony, if someone might soon show up at our cottage to find it empty and us gone without a trace. A pencil resting by the half-completed daily crossword in the local paper, a hot dog cooked and uneaten, still in the skillet. Kidnapped by Indians. If I might look down at my hands one day and find myself staring straight through to the floor.

The CVS here at the beach was putting up its back-to-school displays all right, but they were pristine and orderly, untouched—a barely noticed formality dictated by some corporate office, because surely no one went to school here. There were no lawns, no sprinklers, no central air, and the television in my room was so old that it didn't really work. It definitely didn't get Univision.

The feeling was different here too: it was the novel dread of the unknown rather than the familiar dread of the familiar.

DeeDee and I spent days wandering the beach together, just walking. When we couldn't walk anymore, we'd lie down in the sand, curled in each other, and just sleep.

It was the nineteenth, and Kristle was having another birthday party. She was twenty-one again, for real this time. This party wasn't going to be any big thing like the last one; she seemed too depressed by her impending old age to bother with a gala affair. It was just going to be us and her and DeeDee and a few of the Girls at Ursula's.

Jeff had been listless and quiet all day, or actually for the last week when I really thought about it. I found him on the back deck as the sun was going down, smoking a cigarette.

Jeff had dressed up for the party, sort of. He had an oxford shirt tucked into his jeans and his hair slicked back in a way that gave him a Dennis the Menace–y look.

"What?" he said testily when he saw me looking him up and down, suppressing a smirk. "You never heard of looking nice?"

"Wanna head over now?" I asked.

"Yeah," he said, stubbing his cigarette into the rail. "Sure.

Why not. Let's go." And we started out down the steps and into the street on the now-familiar path to the bar.

At the end of the block, as we were about to turn out onto the beach road, I was inexplicably moved to look over my shoulder, back at our cottage. Mom had come outside and was watching us go, and as she saw me turn, she grinned and waved good-bye. I smiled and waved back and Jeff swiveled to see who it was, and then he was waving too.

DeeDee wasn't at the bar yet when we got there. Kristle had said she was "running late," which wasn't like her—they were never running late. They had no concept of late. But there it was. A drink somehow materialized in front of Jeff and he slid in next to Kristle at a table, and I went to the bar, where Taffany sidled up to me from the other side.

I wished I had gotten to know Taffany better. I had always liked her; I liked how her hair was always messier than the others', her eye makeup always a little smudged. She applied her lip liner haphazardly, and the outline sometimes seemed to bear little relation to the actual shape of her lips. Sometimes she kind of smelled. From time to time she was moved to dance alone.

"What can I get you tonight?" she asked, tossing her hair offhandedly. Fuck it.

"Just a beer, I guess," I said.

"Nah." Taffany plopped two shot glasses down and got to work pulling out bottle after bottle, constructing some concoction in a shaker with perfunctory speed. "It's a *Cocktail* night," she said. "One Kokomo coming up. My secret recipe."

"Thanks," I said.

"So when are you guys going home?" she asked. "Summer's almost over, in case you hadn't noticed."

"I don't know. Never? Tomorrow? I really have no actual clue."

"Must be nice," Taffany said. "Not a fuckin' care in the world."

"What are you talking about? I have a fuckin' care. I have so many fuckin' cares. You don't even know." But it occurred to me that I was actually pretty happy. It had crept up on me, but now that I noticed it, I realized that it was the first time I'd been recognizably happy since at least when my mother left and probably before.

Taffany laughed and seemed about to say something before she stopped herself. She poured the booze from the metal shaker into the shot glasses, sloshing a little onto the bar. The elixir was pink and translucent and oddly bubbly. "Sorry," she said. "I'm just being a bitch. Don't mind me or anything. I'm just sad about Kristle, I guess."

"Why?" I asked. "It's her birthday. Why is that supposed to be sad? Aren't people supposed to be happy to turn twenty-one? You can, like, drink and everything."

Taffany looked me up and down. "We aren't people," she said coldly. "You know that."

"What?" I asked. "I mean, it's just a birthday. Why's everyone acting like it's the end of the world?"

Taffany seemed taken aback. "You really don't know," she said. "Do you really not know?"

"Know what?" I asked.

Instead of answering me, Taffany raised a glass and nodded at the one still on the bar, and I picked it up and raised it and we clanked. Taffany smiled a wistful smile. "You're a good guy," she said. "You really are, Sam. Cheers."

She threw back her drink and I did too. It was the weirdest thing I'd ever tasted; it tasted like grass and mint and salt, with only the faintest burn of alcohol. It tasted like summer. Well, mostly. It tasted like the end of summer. Taffany was wiping her mouth with the back of her hand and I did the same. When she took it away, her chin was shiny with smeared lip gloss.

"Well," she said, and turned to walk away.

"No," I said. "What? They told me—I thought they told me everything. What don't I know?"

We were alone at the end of the bar. Everyone else was clustered at a table in the corner, smoking in violation of the No Smoking sign that hung directly above Kristle's head. Jeff had his arm around her, a burning cigarette dangling from his mouth, and I saw him lean into her, push her hair away, and whisper into her ear. Her eyes brightened and she smiled and then burst out laughing. In that moment she was the most beautiful that I had ever seen her; she was joyful in a way that she had never been before. There was something about it that made me want to cry.

Taffany didn't answer my question. "It's not so bad here," she said. "We make a big deal about how terrible it is, how much we hate it, how much we miss home. But the thing is, this *is* home. It's the only home we remember at least. It would be nice to have a choice, of course, but it could be worse."

"I've actually thought about that," I said. "But it seemed rude to point it out. I have no idea what it's really like."

"It wouldn't be so bad to stay here forever. Get old here. Maybe save up some money and buy a place like this. Go into business. Something like that. There's a lot we could do—if we could stay."

"What do you mean if? I thought you *had* to stay. I thought that was like the thing."

"Kristle's leaving," Taffany said.

"Leaving?" I asked. "Where's she going?"

"She's *leaving*," she said. Her voice was firm and her eyes were sharp. "The kind of leaving where you don't come back. She's going—" Her voice wavered. "She's going, like, to the place of great uncertainty. The place of *final* uncertainty. We all go there eventually. Even you. But I'll be going a lot sooner. And Kristle's going tonight."

I didn't quite see what she was saying.

"It's her birthday," Taffany said. "Twenty-one. It's a big birthday, all right? Haven't you ever noticed that none of us are older than twenty-one?"

It started to dawn on me.

"You mean?"

"On our twenty-first birthday, we go back to the water. We

can't help it; it's just something we do. We're always drawn to the water, but when we turn twenty-one it just gets to be too much. Just one little problem."

"You can't swim."

"Bingo. And what happens in the ocean to girls who can't swim?"

Suddenly I understood. Kristle was going to die. Tonight.

"Oh," I said.

We just looked at each other. Taffany held my eyes so long that I had to look away, but when I averted my gaze, it settled on Kristle, which was even worse. She was now nestled into my brother's shoulder with her eyes closed. He was looking down at the top of her head with a distant fondness. He knew. Why hadn't he told me? Why hadn't I figured it out? I was fucking stupid, that's why.

"Aren't you fucking upset?" I asked. I wanted to scream.

Taffany looked at me. "Upset? Of course I'm fucking upset. But you don't understand. You have no idea. I mean no idea. Kristle will be the third this summer. Fontaine went at the beginning of June. Or was her name Aquavit? Kristle's first birthday was really a going-away party for Fiesta. We get used to it. The parties at the end of the summer are more low-key. It just gets to be overkill."

"I'm sorry," I said.

"Next year there will be six of us," Taffany said. "That's Chanterelle, Blair, Serena, Tresemmé, and Visa. All twenty-one. And me, of course. My birthday's the Fourth of July. Send me a present if you want. No books or gift certificates."

"There's still time," I said. "You could still—"

"Nah." Taffany shrugged. "It seems impossible now to think that there's time to stop it. Nothing much happens after August here. Anyway—I don't want to play the game. Call me a conscientious objector."

"I'm sorry," I said again. "I can't even—I don't know. I'm sorry."

"I'm sure you are," Taffany said. "Why shouldn't you be? Everyone's always sorry. But there's nothing anyone can do about it." She turned her back to me and started arranging bottles. "This is how we live. We try to make the most of it."

Then it came to me. "I can stop it," I said. "I can—I mean, Kristle. I could totally . . ."

"You could," Taffany said. "But you probably shouldn't. And you won't. Like I said, I've seen it all before. That's why *I* get to be the bartender. Kristle understands too. She tried to fight it. That's why she gets to be Kristle. She knows better than anyone that there's no fighting it, but she fights anyway."

"Yeah," I said, thinking about Kristle naked over me in my bed, about the way she'd looked at me. About her on the porch, a gin and tonic in her hand, sweat on her chest, and hair glittering in the summer sun, brittle and determined. They were always talking about how they were the same, how there was barely any difference between them, but it was the furthest thing from the truth.

"I mean, this could be the first time she's ever failed. When

Kristle puts her heart into it, she usually gets what she wants. It's what makes her a bitch, but it's also why she gets to have the big bed. Maybe her heart wasn't actually into it after all, come to think of it. Look, even your brother understands."

The jukebox had flipped over to some shitty synth-country ballad, and Kristle and Jeff had stood and were dancing, her head against his chest, his hands on her hips, both of them swaying back and forth, looking oddly peaceful, oddly at ease with each other. Normally I would have thought it was ridiculous. He looked like a total schmuck. But he was not a schmuck at all. It was hard for me to decide whether he had been one in the first place, or whether the summer had changed him. I supposed it had changed everyone.

Then DeeDee appeared. Like Jeff, she was dressed for an occasion. She was wearing a simple blue dress, the kind that ties at the neck, and had smeared her eyes with eyeliner and sparkly blue eye shadow. She had braided her hair and twisted the plaits in rings around her head. Everyone turned to look at her, but she didn't say hello to any of them; she headed to an empty corner of the room where she sat down at a table alone. Without me even asking, Taffany had already pushed another drink across the bar to me. I took it and made a move to pay and she just waved me off.

"You didn't tell me," I said to DeeDee, plunking the drink down in front of her and sitting. She was already lighting a cigarette, although she had supposedly quit weeks ago, and the music from the jukebox was whirling around us. "How could you have not told me?"

"I thought about it," she said. "I almost told you. But Kristle didn't want me to. And, really, I guess I didn't want to either. Maybe that was selfish."

"Maybe it was," I said.

"We have a hard time understanding selfishness," DeeDee mused. "It's one of those words that doesn't quite translate. It gets all confused with *selflessness*."

"I've never actually noticed your English being as bad as you're always saying it is. Kind of the opposite, actually."

"Maybe every time you've understood me, I was actually trying to say something completely different from what you thought?"

I shook my head. "Nope."

We finished our drinks and then got another round and wandered over to the table where everyone was sitting.

There wasn't like a whole thing or anything. No one said a toast for Kristle; no one got too sentimental. Even Nalgene, who I'd heard had a reputation for being a weepy drunk, seemed happy and relaxed. Kristle was swaying along with the music and tossing her hair and brandishing her Gauloises with languorous panache. Every now and then I saw her looking sideways at Jeff as he talked. She was smiling peacefully. The last time I caught her, she looked up after a few seconds and saw me watching her, and she just took a drag of her cigarette and kicked me under the table, then tossed her head back and laughed.

After a few hours, when the songs on the jukebox were all starting to seem terrible and no one wanted to drink anymore, we went down to the beach: me, DeeDee, Jeff, Kristle, Nalgene, Chanterelle, Tresemmé, Activia, Jessamee, Blair, Serena, Visa—even Taffany, who didn't bother locking up.

WANT

What we want:

High-heeled shoes. Patent leather. Sharp enough to slit throats. We want them so tall you can't tell the difference between our hair and the sun.

A bedroom of our own, with a down comforter and striped Todd Oldham pillowcases from Target, and a window that looks out over anything except a parking lot. With a bathroom with a door that locks. And a bulletin board with tacked-up photos of ourselves and our friends, which are another thing we want.

And a mother.

And a home karaoke system with dual microphones and lots of songs.

And a taste of snow.

And a red Camaro, a checking account with a plastic card, a trip to Paris. A break from all this work. A glimpse of clouds as they appear from above, as they appear from an airplane. And, and, and.

We want a name.

We want a choice.

You might say that we want a lot of things. Of course there's really only one thing that we want. We thought we knew what it was. We were told what it was. We were deceived.

We're not asking for sympathy. We're just trying to explain where we're coming from. But by now you know exactly where we come from.

For want of a home we've lost everything we ever wanted. We lost one another. We lost you. You: our home.

What we want. What we really wanted. What we gave up, not knowing—thinking we knew exactly what it was that we pursued.

And what we overlooked in our wanting: the absolute home of your uncertain smile. Your steady, familiar embrace in the sand before dusk when you were peaceful and near sleep; the rising and falling of your chest, with its little hairs starting to grow in their uneven spiral. The wild, dark curls at your temples, the broadness of your shoulders and ropy muscles of your arms. Even the gnarled and undersized big toe on your right foot. The glint in your eyes from one angle is mischievous and bold—reckless—and from another so vulnerable that it would break our hearts, if our hearts were capable of being broken.

You have appeared many times, with many faces. You are always, always, always just exactly the same.

You always surprise us. It's hard to surprise us—like heartbreak, surprise is against our general nature—but every moment with you is a revelation. The things you find troubling and the things you find funny. Your jammed-together and slightly crooked teeth and the way they blossom into a smile that is warm and unguarded and beautiful. Your unexpected freckles and your prickly gentleness, just as unexpected. And

292

then there is the final surprise that didn't strike us until it was too late.

This is the home we are leaving; this is what we give up. What we will miss. This is what we wanted after all. We never had a choice. Or did we? Well, we want to think we didn't.

We never get what we want.

But who does, really?

TWENTY-SIX

THE TEN-MINUTE WALK to the ocean somehow took the form of a procession, with DeeDee leading the way and each of us following behind her in a sloppy single file with no one speaking. When we made it through the dunes, we stood in a row, still silent for a few minutes, all looking out at the water before Jeff let out a roar and ran, stripping his clothes as he went until he was down to his pink boxers and then they were off too. He swung them over his head like a lasso and tossed them onto the sand, then cannonballed into the breakers in triumph.

"Oh, for fuck's sake." Kristle laughed. The momentary tension broke and we all dispersed, Kristle to the water's edge, where she yelled shit at Jeff while he vamped and frolicked, shouting a stupid, tuneless song he'd made up right there. The rest of the Girls drifted together to a spot in the sand, but DeeDee came to me and took my hand, leading me ahead to where the shore was still damp.

"So this is it," DeeDee said. "The end of the summer."

"Summer doesn't officially end until September twenty-third," I said. "Autumnal equinox. I looked it up."

"Be real," DeeDee said. "Summer ends now. Feel the breeze."

I don't particularly believe in magic, but where the air had just been perfectly still, there was suddenly a breeze out of nowhere. It was cool and dry and smelled a bit like smoke. But for once, no one was smoking. Then it was gone and all I could smell was salt and fruity shampoo.

"Bye," DeeDee said to no one, waving at nothing.

Jeff had finally stumbled out of the water and he and Kristle were a few paces off, just talking. I knew I shouldn't watch—it was private and also Jeff was completely naked, not that you could see anything—but I couldn't look away either. DeeDee put a hand on my hip and I could feel her staring in the same direction, watching them with me. They were saying good-bye.

They were laughing and leaning into each other, touching each other with casual intimacy, almost like it was no big deal, and then they were kissing and they lit up the beach. I realized that DeeDee and I were not the only ones staring. We were all watching. But Jeff and Kristle didn't seem to know or care.

Then Kristle was walking off down the beach, and Jeff was standing alone in the surf.

He ran his hands through his hair, then sank to his ass, still watching her go. A wave came in and pooled around him. I wanted to go to him, wanted to say something, but DeeDee grabbed me by the elbow before I could move.

"You have to do it," she said. "Find her. It's gotta be you, babe."

I couldn't see Kristle anymore, but I knew she was moving just outside of the frame. She was going to the cove.

"I know," I said. "But what about you?"

DeeDee sighed. "Listen. She's the one who found me," DeeDee said. "She's the one who gave me clothes. She's my sister. She's me and I'm her. You have to do it. Just try not to think of it as some big deal, you know? Think of it like you're doing it for me."

I looked at DeeDee, then back up the shore into a distance I couldn't see, where I could picture Kristle venturing forward, her feet aching, a traveler now as always, embarking on a new and strange journey, alone for the first time since she'd arrived here. She had always seemed a lot of things to me, but never lonely. There was something I couldn't bear about picturing her like that.

So I went after her. When I found her, she was standing at the rocky barrier at the edge of the cove, staring up at it, her hands on her hips like she was trying to summon the strength to start climbing. "Hey," I said. I was sort of expecting her to jump or something, but she didn't; she just turned around and gave me a stupid, embarrassed wave.

"I've been waiting for you," she said. "I knew you'd come after me. You're actually kind of predictable, you know?"

"Yep," I said. This was it. I hadn't thought to be nervous. I hadn't actually put much thought into what I was going to do. But now here I was, and I was scared. "So, uh," I said. "Okay, then. Here we go."

I was blushing as I pulled my shirt over my head. Kristle just let out a halfhearted giggle. Her face was hard to interpret. Suddenly I wasn't totally sure it was even her. It could have been any of them. She could have been all of them.

"Put your shirt on," she said. "I'm not going to have sex with you."

"Why not?" I asked. "It's the only way."

"'Cause I think you're gross."

She must have seen my face fall. "I'm kidding," she said. "You're totally a hot little number. I'm not because I'm just not."

"Don't you want to live?" I asked.

"Yes," Kristle said. "But I won't do it."

"You will," I said. "Come on. It's not a big deal. It's worth it."

"It's not," Kristle said. She folded her arms at her chest. "I can't. It's too fucked-up. It's what he wants. I don't want to give him the satisfaction. It's starting to seem to me that the best way to break a curse is just to ignore it."

"He?"

"Our father. The Endlessness."

I was disgusted by the whole thing. All of this. It occurred to me that I probably wouldn't even be able to pop a boner to get the job done anyway. Or maybe I would; it's one thing I've never had an issue with. But I'd never been in a situation quite like this.

"Kristle," I said. "This is what DeeDee wants."

"I know," she said. "I knew she'd send you. I felt her do it. But I made up my mind a long time ago, okay? Or a little while ago, at least. Anyway, I've been thinking, and here's the thing: I'm pretty sure it might not work anyway."

"What do you mean it wouldn't work? How can it not work? Isn't the whole point of things like this that they have rules? That they *work*?"

"The whole point of curses is that there are always loopholes. They're always trying to trip you up. Where do you think that 'be careful what you wish for' thing came from? Sneaky genies—duh. And we've never totally understood the curse, you know. It's not like we have it written down anywhere or anything; we haven't had a chance to have our lawyers review it. But the older I get—the closer I get to, you know"—she gestured at the ocean—"this—it's like my mind is expanding or something. I'm already starting to leave my body. It's like I'm starting to have a deeper understanding. I'm losing my human self, becoming more whatever I was before. Things that didn't make sense are starting to seem more and more obvious. Not that *obvious* is probably the right word. The point is that we've been operating under the assumption that sex with someone like you is all it takes. I don't think it is. It's just a feeling I have, you know; I could be wrong. But I think there has to be something more than plain old sex. There's another component, there has to be. For it to work."

"Well what then? What else does there need to be? What *component*?"

"You tell me," she said. "I think you're the one who knows. I'll tell you this, though. I kind of don't even think the *sex* is the most important part. I think it's important, okay, sure, but it seems to me that it's just the last step. It's dotting the *i*. Fuck, who knows?"

Just make sense, I wanted to say. *Just tell me what I need to do.* I had been angry all summer, angry since we had gotten here, all at something I couldn't identify. Now I wasn't mad anymore and I missed it. Anger was a tool to get you what you wanted, and without it I felt powerless. So I tried to summon it back. For the first time in as long as I could remember, I couldn't find it. It was like someone asking you your name and being unable to come up with a good answer.

"You have to live," I said. I meant to shout it, but it came out nearer to a whisper. Still, even whispering, my voice bounced off the waves and hit me in the gut. "What about DeeDee? Fuck, what about Jeff? What about the whole fucking world? You're just going to give up all of this?"

"It's not the world," Kristle said. "And I'm not giving up. We don't even actually know what happens next. We've only been speculating." And then: "Come on. Dude, you know what you need to do. And it doesn't involve me." She started for the rocks, and I tried to stammer out a good-bye, but couldn't find one. Then I remembered what I had in my pocket.

Suddenly, I knew exactly why I had found it, and who it was for.

"Wait," I said. "I have a birthday present for you." And I dug into the pocket of my shorts and pulled out the mirror I'd found buried on the beach during the hurricane. I held it in my hand for a moment and looked at it. It was glowing and oil-slick iridescent, pink and green and black, and I realized it wasn't made of silver or any other metal but of something that can probably only be found at the bottom of the ocean. I'd been carrying it with me everywhere I went since I'd found it without knowing why. I didn't actually want to give it away. But I handed it to her anyway.

"Take this," I said, standing there with my open palm out-stretched. "It's for you."

She looked at it for a second and seemed to hesitate. Her mouth twitched with recognition and then again with disbelief.

Kristle took the mirror, clicked it open, and held it up. As she stared at herself, she looked at first curious, then aston-ished, and then troubled. I saw a flicker and a spark and then a flame ignite in her. She stayed like that for a minute, and then laughed with pleasure and surprise. But tears were also rolling down her cheeks now.

She flicked the mirror closed and palmed it, dropping her hand back to her side. She tossed her hair and shrugged. "You're fucking sweet, Sam. Okay, I guess what I mean to say is that I fucking love you."

"What did you see?" I couldn't help asking.

"Nothing," she said. "Well, a lot of things, but nothing I'd never seen before. Nothing I hadn't realized by now. Still. I love it. I've been looking for it. It's pretty much the best present you could have given me. I think it belonged to our mother when she was younger. She must have sent it to us."

Then she leaned over and kissed me, on the lips, close-mouthed but lingering, slick and sweet with strawberry-kiwi gloss. It was a kiss for friendship.

When she pulled away, she looked different. I couldn't identify what it was that had changed, but she seemed more solid, somehow. When I'd kissed her on the deck on the night that was supposed to have been her birthday, her face had seemed to shift before my eyes, rearranging itself as I took it in, like one of those sliding puzzles. Now it had settled into place. It was just a feeling. I opened my mouth to say something, but she put a finger to my lips. I noticed that her nails were unpainted; they were short and jagged like she'd been biting them.

"Shhh," she said. "I already said good-bye to your brother. But say good-bye to him for me anyway."

"What about DeeDee?" I asked.

"Dude," Kristle said "You two are on your own now. I don't know what you need to do. I thought I did and now I don't anymore. But you'll do the right thing. Even if you don't, she will. She's always been different, you know. We're all supposed to be the same, but we're not really, and DeeDee's always been the most different of all. More confident or something. Angrier, maybe, although who could be angrier than me? It doesn't matter. From the minute she got here, I knew she would be the one who would get to leave in one piece. Even if

I didn't want to admit it."

We just stood there. "All righty," she said. She looked at her watch, and then laughed a silent laugh when she realized she wasn't wearing a watch. She slapped me on the ass and then cocked her head, looked me up and down with a happy smirk, and let the mirror drop to the sand. It spun through the air like in slow motion as it fell, catching the moonlight and whirling it around. I looked down to where it had fallen, thinking I'd bring it to DeeDee, but it had disappeared.

"Nah," Kristle said, reading my mind. "She doesn't need it. I don't think she ever did. Leave it for someone who does." Then she walked off toward the water.

That was the last time I saw her. Or at least I think it was. Maybe it was my imagination, but as she walked away, even though it was impossible, I almost thought I heard her whispering in my ear. *My mother is the Deepness. My father is the Endlessness. I am something else. You will see me again in commercial breaks and in the bridges of songs and the change of seasons and in the moments just before sleep. You will see me in the spaces between.*

I knew less about love than I had when I'd gotten to this place. Not that I'd known much then, either; honestly I hadn't really thought about it a lot until I'd met DeeDee and Kristle. But the more I'd thought about it the more I'd gotten tangled up in what it all really meant, and while at the beginning of the summer I think I would have been able to identify at least two or three incontrovertible facts on the topic, I no longer felt equipped even for that. Summer was ending.

The one thing I knew was that I loved Kristle. It was unexpected. It occurred to me just as she was walking away from me, as I heard her alien voice in my head. I didn't know what it meant. But there are a lot of different kinds of love, right?

RAPTURE

Before we leave this place, we wade into the water one last time. Or maybe it's for the first time. Ankles, thighs, hips, chests, waves crashing around us. We feel the weather in our eyelashes, the summer in our hair. We feel the cold air on our bare shoulders. Then we don't.

Our younger sisters are waiting just beyond the waves to encircle us as we enter the deep. They grasp at our green and floating hair. They run their slimy fingers curiously along the curves of our breasts and kiss us tenderly at our necks. Our lungs fill with water. Bubbles swirl around us as the moon shines in from the surface like light streaming into a dusty bar during daytime. Our sisters bat at the bubbles and laugh, and we clutch our chests, beginning to panic.

Our sisters know nothing. They don't even know that almost every one of them will someday be in our place. They're too young to understand. But we know, now. We know almost everything, now. (Almost.)

We know that we aren't joining them. We know that we aren't staying here. We are going where the forgotten ones have gone: Donna, Kelly, Brenda. The L'Oréals. The ones whose names we can no longer summon. We don't know where we are going, but we are not going home. We will never go home. We are on our way to elsewhere. We feel like we are drifting off to sleep.

Our father is the Endlessness. Our mother is the Deepness. Our brothers are Speed and Calm. We didn't know who we were. Soon we will find out.

We leave this place by wading into the water one last time. Our sisters encircle us. They reach out for us in underwater slow motion, but we understand that it's simple fascination that draws them to us rather than affection. Our eyes begin to close. We feel our muscles slackening. And just as we're about to drift off, they begin to swarm us—what suddenly seems like hundreds of them coming from every direction, the water pulsing with their excitement—and they lean in, all together, to whisper our true name into our ear. The name we had forgotten. The name we were never even sure we had. And our eyes pop open. We gasp in recognition with our last fist of air. Even though it's not possible, I speak.

"No," I say. "My name is Kristle."

Then I'm gone.

I am not returning to the water. I was banished from this place long ago; it is no longer my home. If it ever was. I have no home now, and home is not where I'm going. But this is not death, either, not in the way we understood it before. That would be punishment, and the punishment is over. My father no longer has any power over me.

I know this because the last thing I see is my mother's face, a face I thought I had forgotten but which I remember as soon as it appears to me. It isn't what I expected, not how I imagined it all the times I tried to imagine and not the face that sometimes used to come to me in dreams.

It's a face and it is faceless; there is no nose, no mouth. My mother's eyes are filled with the reflection of a universe of stars. She is beautiful, but it would be easy to call her ugly or at least terrifying. She holds no knife.

She is covered with tattoos upon tattoos, her skin so black that it circles back to brilliance. Every one of them bears another legend. I am not scared.

She kisses me.

"I love you," she says. All this time, we thought she had been powerless. But she was just holding back, letting us find our own way.

Magic is full of loopholes; one might say it's all loopholes. All curses have more than one way out. There's always a back door. I found it. I stepped through the mirror.

I am going somewhere else now. I don't know where. I don't know how long it will take. When I get there, I will be something else. But I will never forget my name.

TWENTY-SEVEN

I FOUND DEEDEE on the pier. She knew I would look for her there. I walked out to where she was sitting, halfway out into the ocean, her feet dangling off the edge. The night was black and cloudless and there was a breeze. Her back was to me. Her hair was tangled with stars.

"So did you do it?" she asked without moving as I neared her.

"No," I said. I sat down next to her and she turned her face to me. It was dark and bitter; she had been crying.

"You fuck!" she said. "You piece of shit. You guys are good for exactly one thing, and you can't even make yourself useful when it counts." It would have hurt my feelings except that she didn't sound like she meant it. She was trying to summon her old anger and it wasn't coming to her. "I told you to fucking do it," she said. "I fucking fucking told you. If you loved me you would have done it."

"I mean, I wanted to," I said.

"I knew you wouldn't," DeeDee said. "I knew she wouldn't, too."

"Yeah," I said. "She wouldn't. I would have. I was totally ready."

DeeDee rolled her eyes. "I should have known. Men!" Even now, even this. She couldn't bring herself to be really mad, but she was still able to find it funny.

We both started laughing, and then we were laughing so hard that we couldn't stop. I put my arm around her, and then we collapsed on our backs onto the wooden pier, still cracking up.

"So she's gone, huh?" she asked when we were out of breath.

"I guess she is," I said. "Whatever that really means. It's not like I have a lot of experience dealing with this. With, you know, magic or whatever."

"Damn. She was one crazy bitch. She was pretty much the best."

"I'm going to miss her too," I said. "She's really nothing like I thought she was."

"I know," DeeDee said. "She's nothing like anyone could think. I mean, she taught me basically everything. I don't know what I would have done without her. She was the closest thing I had to a mother." She caught herself and sat up. "What did she say to you anyway?"

"Oh, I don't know. Just good-bye." I thought about telling her about the voice I'd heard in my head as Kristle had waded into the water. She deserved to know. But it was something between Kristle and me. Kristle deserved to have her last secret.

Something that was just hers.

DeeDee left it. She pulled her fist through her hair. She arched her back, stretching her arms to the sky, stretched her fingers until they looked like they were scraping the moon. They were translucent; you could see right through the tips of them and out into space.

"Look what I found," she said. She turned and picked up something next to her, something she'd had with her on the pier all along, a small black box with a retracted metal antenna. "It was in the sand; I tripped over it when I was coming here. It's a radio. You never see these anymore. It's always a surprise what you end up finding on the beach. Sometimes it's just a weird shell; sometimes it's a radio. Or something else."

I took it from her and fiddled with the knobs. It felt odd in my hands, mechanical and old-fashioned, like something from a long-ago beach. "Does it work?"

Before she could answer, I flipped it on and it began to buzz. At first all that came out was static, but I pulled the antenna up and then music was coming in perfectly clear. It hovered above the roar of the waves. It was like nothing I'd ever heard on any radio in the past, nothing like I'd ever heard before, actually. It was barely music at all: it had no melody or rhythm or lyrics or instruments, but it was music anyway, the most perfect music I'd ever heard, being broadcast from someplace very far away. It sounded like it was coming from the other end of the universe, traveling all the way here just for us at this moment. It was the same song Kristle and DeeDee had sung together that night at Ursula's.

"I guess it works," DeeDee said. "You'd think the batteries would be dead by now. Like I say, you never know what you're going to find around here."

We lay back together and just listened. After a few minutes I felt a warmth moving through my body, my muscles rippling like water from my toes to my chest to my fingers and then out again and back. It was sort of like the time Sebastian got supposedly really good weed from this person named King Koopa in exchange for a binder full of Ms. Smith's quizzes from last year (she never changed them) and we accidentally smoked too much of it and spent an hour with MTV on in the background while we tried to say the alphabet to each other, except that DeeDee and I weren't talking at all. We were just listening.

And then I had this sudden urge to jump in the water and start swimming, to swim out past where the marathon runners could run, out past where the ocean dropped off with the horizon, swim out into space and keep going, arm over arm, kicking, breathing.

I was almost about to do it. I could feel my toes scraping the water. It felt like home. I was just about to push off when DeeDee grabbed my hand and sat back up, pulling me with her.

"So you're going home soon, huh?" she said. "You have to be, right? You can't stay here forever."

The music was still playing, but it felt distant now. Buried. It felt like music from another room.

"Yeah," I said. "No one's said anything, exactly, but I get the sense. This morning I saw the keys sitting on the table in the kitchen and I could tell they wanted someone to pick them up. I passed the car in the driveway on the way to the beach and it was like an animal that had been tied up for too long. I know that sounds stupid. But I think you're basically right."

"I don't know what to say," she said. "I wish you would stay. But I know you can't."

"I have to ask you something," I said. "It's important."

"Okay," she said. "Go for it, I guess."

"Is this real?" I asked.

DeeDee laughed. "What's reality, dude? That seems like a bigger question than I can answer. That's some serious graduate-level philosophy shit, don't you think?"

"What I mean is, like, is this part of the spell? Is this really how I feel or is it, like, you know . . . magic?"

"You mean do you like me because I put some kind of ancient love spell on you?"

"On karaoke night. When you and Kristle were singing. That was when you did it, right? It was like a siren song or whatever. Right?"

She hooted. "Sam. Is it that impossible that I'm just really good at karaoke?"

"I don't know," I said. "It seems pretty spooky in retrospect. It seems like something was going on."

DeeDee sighed. "Would you believe me if I said I don't really know?"

I shrugged.

"Well believe it," she said. "Because I don't. It's possible. I'm pretty sure that we can do things we don't even know about. How could we not? Does it really matter though?"

Of course it mattered. Didn't it matter?

Oh, fuck it.

I was ready. We both were. This had been inevitable, of course, but it came to me that there was no way it could have actually happened until now.

I wasn't thinking about the curse anymore. Everything that had happened this summer was gone, over for good. All I was thinking about was how much I wanted to know who she was. I wanted to finally understand her. I wanted her to understand me. Not that I understood myself. Maybe I thought she could help.

I was taking my shirt off. I was untying the halter of DeeDee's dress. She stood and turned her back to me and let it drop to her ankles and looked out at the ocean before facing me again.

Naked in front of me, on the pier, she looked surprisingly shy, but she didn't cover herself. I should have been shy too, but I wasn't.

"There are so many things that don't matter," she was saying. *Is this real?* I had asked. But naked, she looked realer than ever; she was not magic. At that moment, she wasn't a mermaid. She was real; she was a girl; she was flawed and singular and more beautiful than I could have possibly imagined.

"Isn't that what all of this has been?" she asked, sinking down next to me. "Just sifting through all the different things that don't matter, tossing them aside and trying to figure out what we're actually left with?"

"What are we left with?"

"This," she said. She touched my face and made a circle with her thumb, letting it drift over my lips.

"I'm going to miss you," I said, and I touched her side and moved on top of her as she leaned back. She was very warm. I kissed her neck. "I mean, a lot."

"Same," she said. "I'm going to miss you so much. But I don't want this to be sad. I don't want it to be about missing. It's not about good-bye, or about magic, or about anything else that doesn't matter. I just want it to be exactly what it is."

I kissed her forehead and kissed her breast. I had always wondered how you were supposed to actually do this, but I knew what to do. "I feel like I've always known you," I said.

"I know," she said. "Same."

TWENTY-EIGHT

THE DAMP, HEAVY blanket of air that had been draped over all of us since the hurricane was starting to lift. Even on the sunniest days, there was a new coolness everywhere I went. The skin on the backs of my arms tingled with it whenever I stepped outside. The beach was carefully knitting itself into something different, something both lighter and darker, something ocean blue that smelled of smoke and patchouli.

It had been a week since Kristle's birthday, and although I hadn't seen DeeDee since then, I still had this feeling that she was around somewhere, lingering in the air, changing with the weather. I knew that I shouldn't go looking for her now. She would find me when she found me. I was sure she would, but I also accepted the possibility that when it happened I might not recognize her anymore.

I'd stopped my long walks on the beach, stopped swimming, stopped mostly everything. I spent most of my time watching

TV now. I didn't have the energy to do anything else. It wasn't that I was depressed. I was just resting.

Jeff and I hadn't really talked to each other about what had happened to Kristle. We hadn't actually talked about anything. I was giving him space. He had become obsessed with the Housewives and spent entire days parked in front of the TV, immersing himself in their petty dramas. If it hadn't been for the happy smile on his face as they bickered over flowers and tried to pull out each other's extensions, I would have tried to get him to snap out of it. But I knew it reminded him of her, so I left him alone.

One afternoon I was lying on the porch when my father and mother came wandering out and announced their intention for us to finally leave. "Pack your stuff," my dad said. "We're out of here tomorrow."

"Why?" I asked. "Why now?"

"Summer's over," Mom said, snapping her fingers cheerfully at her sides. She looked over at my dad. "Time to go home."

"All good things come to an end, Tiger," Dad said, smiling too.

I decided he could call me Tiger if he wanted to. He would grow out of it eventually.

As I stuffed my clothes into my bag a few hours later, I thought of the boy I'd met outside the 7-Eleven, the kid with the shattered, haunted look on his face. I understood him now, knew what had happened to him to make him like that. I had mostly stopped wearing shoes myself. Whatever had happened to him was different from what had happened to me, even if we had both gotten caught up in the same curse. He had never found the mirror, I don't think, and I'm pretty sure that had made some small difference.

But it wasn't just the mirror. The boy at the 7-Eleven had never found DeeDee, either. I had to think she and I were different not because of any curses or enchanted items or magic spells, but just because of who we were. Who we had made each other and who we would still become.

I did a quick sweep around my room, wondering if I had forgotten anything, when I saw it lying in the corner next to the bedside table: the white, ribbed tank top DeeDee had been wearing the day I'd met her.

I walked over to it, opened it up, and put it up to my face and breathed it in. It smelled like salt water and summer. It smelled like her, of course. After a few moments I was tempted to take another breath, just keep smelling her as long as I could, but instead I balled it up and shoved it into my bag on my bed, into the farthest crevice underneath my dirty old socks and underwear and junk. I knew I'd forget about it there, but that maybe I'd find it again someday when it really counted.

I went to the ocean by myself.

All I could think about that night was how different it was from the first one on the beach, when Jeff and I had come down here together with our handle of vodka and our flashlight and we'd seen the girl in the surf, back when Jeff had seemed like the biggest douche bag who would never understand anything. That night, the shore had been pitch-black and mysterious and infinite and empty, empty, empty. Tonight there was a full moon, and it was bright enough to map the shades of delineation between the silvery-purple sky and the silvery-black ocean and the silvery-white crashing of the waves and the silvery-silver of the sand. Tonight, I wondered again who that girl had actually been. I wondered who DeeDee had been when she'd first arrived here, what she had been thinking as she'd stumbled up to the dunes.

Although the beach wasn't crowded, there were more people than I'd expected, more than there usually were after dark. Teenagers were milling around here and there, and although no one seemed to be actually talking it all felt sort of convivial, like we were at a party where everyone had known each other so long that they didn't feel the need to speak to each other. There was a certain air of celebratory finality in the air—that Roman candle mix of sadness and oh-fuck-it-let's-get-drunk. I figured it was other people's last night here too.

Even without talking there were noises everywhere. Up and down the beach I could hear the hissing crackle of beer cans popping and the crunching of lighters as a couple of girls in hoodies flicked pointlessly, sprawled together on an overturned lifeguard chair. By the dunes, a group of guys were setting off sputtering, barely there firecrackers so lame that their laughter was louder than the pop of the rockets, and elsewhere a clumsy Bob Marley on an acoustic guitar wandered listlessly into the night. And at the edge of the surf, a couple was making out with such enthusiasm that I thought I could hear their slurping over the rumble of the waves. I had to say good-bye.

I wasn't surprised anymore at how easy it was to stumble upon her; by then I had learned how this place worked. If you wanted to be found, you would be found. And then there she was, just sitting ten feet behind the tide, her knees folded to her chest, her arms wrapped around her shins, and her hair flapping in the breeze, which was everywhere now. I sat down next to her.

"Hey," I said. She looked over at me and I almost doubted it was her; she looked so different. Her hair was darker, her jaw was broader, her eyes deeper set and now tilted downward in a new slant. Even though it was hard to tell in the moonlight, I could see that they were darker too, had lost their unearthly glow as well as most of the eyeliner. She looked smaller and more human. But it was DeeDee. She was transforming, just a girl now. I decided that I would choose to remember her just like this.

"Hey," she said.

I had sort of expected something more from her after what had happened a week ago. But "hey" was okay too.

"What's up?" I asked.

"Oh, nothing," she said.

"We're leaving tomorrow," I said.

"I know."

"I knew you would. You've always been a know-it-all. I guess you haven't lost your connection to the cosmic font of all useless knowledge."

"Yeah, well, I don't know most of the important stuff. There must be two different fonts, one for the stuff that actually makes a difference and one for stupid things like weather patterns and time zones and names of actresses on soap operas. Do I have any clue about the meaning of life or how to get a stain out? Of course not."

"It always goes like that."

"Still. It's not nothing. When you go on *Millionaire*, be sure to make me your phone-a-friend."

"You'd have to give me your number first. Is that show even still on?"

"It comes on really late at night," she said.

We didn't have a lot of time. With no time for small talk it was typically annoying that it was all we could manage. I wanted something more now.

"DeeDee," I said.

"Yeah?" she said. "Let me have it."

"I'm leaving tomorrow. I'm probably not going to see you again."

"I know," she said. "I'm going to miss you."

"So let's not waste our time talking about stupid-ass shit."

"Okay," she said. "I always thought he was overrated anyway. That Meredith person's just as good."

"Look, I love you, okay?" I said. There, I'd said it. I hadn't realized I was going to say it until it came out of my mouth. "I just want you to know that. It's just, like, important to me to say."

DeeDee didn't react. She looked at her hands.

"I know you do," she said. "Thank you."

"I just thought—," I said, but DeeDee wasn't finished.

"But, listen, do you really? I mean, I know you do in a way. But in another way you don't. I mean, you can't, really. You don't know the first thing about me."

I felt a catch in my throat. "How can you say that? DeeDee, look at me. I love you so much. How can I not? I know you so well. How can you think that?"

"Because I don't know the first thing about myself," she said. "I'm not sure if it's because I'm different now or because I didn't really know before or what. But I woke up this morning and saw myself in the mirror and—well, you know. It was like I needed to learn a new word for *mirror*. I had to look it up in the dictionary to make sure it wasn't the same as *window* or *balustrade*. It was so weird. Who am I? I mean, really?"

"You're DeeDee," I said. And then she finally turned and looked at me for the first time since I'd sat down. Her cheeks were streaked with mascara. Her eyes were sharp and probing and she regarded me with a concerned squint that seemed nearly wounded. I wondered if I had said something wrong.

"No," she said. At first she sounded sad, and then she turned angry. "Of course I'm not. DeeDee. God. That's not even my real name."

"Sure it is," I said. "It's what everyone calls you, so it's your name."

"That's not my name," she said, more firmly now. "It's just something I called myself. Before. It doesn't seem right anymore. And it's *not* my name. It never was."

"I didn't know you felt that way," I said.

"That's exactly what I mean. There's a lot of things you don't know about me. There were a lot of things you didn't know about me to start with, and there's even more you don't know about me now that I'm different. DeeDee. It was never my name. None of us remember our real names. We come here without names. We choose our own names. They're not our names. They're just a pose."

"It's still your name," I said. "It's still who you are. You can be whoever you want to be. You can just decide. This is America."

She was looking at the moon now, and sort of talking to herself. "It just sounded pretty. Exotic. The night I got here, Kristle gave me a towel and some old clothes and showed me how to work the remote, and we watched TV and thought of names together. It's strange not to have a name, so you have to come up with one quickly or you start to go a little crazy. What were the other ones we thought about? I can't remember. Jenuvia. Carlotta. Oh—Francie. I liked that one. Have you ever been to France?"

"Yes," I said. "We went on a field trip for French class in eighth grade. I had to room with Andrew Carlton and Ian Wang. It was completely terrible."

"Really? I hear it's nice. I always wanted to go. I saw this thing on the Travel Channel and it seemed great. Was the airplane at least fun?"

"Why does this matter?" I asked.

"See? You don't know the first thing about me. Of course it matters."

I touched her leg, and she jerked away, but only for a second before she relaxed and bowed her head to my shoulder. She put her arm around me and I could feel her breast against my side, and her breath in her chest in time with the waves.

Right before we had sex, right before we'd broken the curse, she'd asked if it really mattered why I felt the way I did. At the time I didn't know the answer. It could have been magic, some kind of watery voodoo. Or it could have just been the way the light was hitting her eyes when I first saw her. It could have been some magical pheromone drawing me to her, something in that song, or something purely chemical. I didn't even know her that well.

There were a million things I loved about her. But none of them were the real reason I loved her. I loved her just because I did. Because we'd had this summer together. So maybe I *was* under some kind of spell. Maybe, technically speaking, I wasn't in love with her. There was actually no difference as far as I was concerned.

Because isn't the whole point of loving someone—being in love with someone—that you understand her as well as you understand yourself? Isn't loving someone almost like becoming that person, and them becoming you? I mean, isn't that the point, at least in a way?

That's what I had thought before, or what I had been led to believe. I didn't know anymore.

Do you really know anyone? My father had thought he had known my mother, and he had been totally wrong. I had thought I had known her, and it was only now that I understood that I would never know her at all. Did that mean we had never loved her?

No. She was my mom. I had loved her and I still loved her and I would continue to love her even if she was a crazy person with tattoos all over her body, a person who was fundamentally, eternally unknowable. Maybe that made me love her more, even.

"I love you no matter what," I said. "I wouldn't have done it if I didn't."

DeeDee squeezed me. "I know you do," she said. "And I know you wouldn't have."

"I wasn't even doing it because of the curse. I mean, I wanted to help you and everything. I'm glad I was able to. But that wasn't why I did it."

"I know," she said. "Same, basically."

And then, "Listen, Sam: You're the best person I ever met. Even if you seem a little bitchy at first. You are so good in every way. I may not know the first thing about you, but I know that much."

"I think you're the only person who knows it, then," I said.

"No," she said. "Jeff knows it. Kristle knows it. Knew it, I mean. I keep forgetting that Kristle's gone now. I wonder where she is. She was really nice to me. She treated me like a sister—I mean, a real sister. I'll miss her."

"I'm sorry," I said.

"You should never be sorry for anything," DeeDee said. "And I love you too. Of course I love you. You've given me all this." She fluttered her hand in the air to indicate I don't know what. It was a gesture that was both expansive and dismissive. *Everything, nothing, what's the difference?* Or something like that. "I mean, this is all thanks to you."

She turned and looked at me. "I love you," she said. "But I can't love anyone right now. Except Kristle, maybe, and she's gone. I can't love anyone for a while. Maybe forever. You knew that. And I'm going home. You knew that, too. You knew all of this would happen."

She was right. I had known everything. I don't know when I had known it, or how I had known it, but I had known it, and I hadn't cared. Maybe I had known it the first time I saw her; who could say? It had been worth it of course.

"Yes," I said. "I knew all of that. I love you anyway."

"I know," she said. "And I love you for that."

"When do you go?" I asked. "Like, tonight? I actually thought you would have been gone already."

"Oh," she said. "I can go whenever I want, I guess. I can do whatever I want now. The curse is, like, totally broken. For me, I mean. I'm free. I'm my own woman." She forced a thin smile and pulled her fingers through her hair all the way down to the ends. "It feels totally weird. I don't know anything except this dump. Everything's different now. What'll become of me?"

"Yeah," I said. I didn't understand. "I guess. So what will you do?"

"I think I'll stay on through the winter," she said. "It would be strange to leave right away. And winter is nice here. It's peaceful and the colors are totally different."

"Then what?"

"Then I guess—I don't know. I guess I'll buy a car or something. And just get out of here. I'm going home."

"A car?" Now I was really confused. "Why do you need a car? I thought you were going—you know. Back down there."

"That's what I thought too," DeeDee said. "That's what we all thought. But home isn't where I thought it was. We got everything all wrong. That's where we came from, yeah. It was home once, or a kind of home. I don't know if a place like that can really be a home, actually. It's wet and very cold and no one's particularly friendly. One way or another, it's not home anymore. There's nothing down there for me, or for any of us. Not anymore." She paused, considered something, and amended herself: "I mean any of *them*. But I can leave here now."

"I thought—," I started.

"I know." DeeDee cut me off. "Me too. We were just wrong. These stories—they get passed down; they get retold. We don't even know who started them. Our memories—their memories—they're all fucked-up anyway. Things get very confused. A legend can be wrong. Actually, I think they're wrong

325

more often than not. Or at least wrongish. I guess." I was still sort of unsure what it all meant, but she seemed to be struggling with the notion herself, so I didn't press her.

"But the legend was right, too; it was just confused," she continued. "I can go home now; it's just not the same home I came from. I don't know where I'll go. But wherever I go—that'll be home, right? I can have whatever home I want. I can be anyone. It could be anywhere."

"It could be somewhere in the suburbs," I said. "Somewhere north, following I-95. Nearish to me. And you could be DeeDee."

"It could be," DeeDee said. "And I could be. You never know. But I wouldn't count on it."

"I know," I said. "I wasn't."

"I just wish I knew my real name," she said. "That seems like it would make everything easier, somehow."

I didn't reply. I didn't care what she said. Her real name was DeeDee.

"You know," she said. "We have this legend. It's different from the other legend. It's related, I guess, but it's its own legend too. Maybe even older than ours, if that's actually possible."

"What is it?"

"It has to do with a mirror."

I tried not to show any trace of recognition or surprise, but she was tilting her head and smirking a little bit, staring right into me. "You know," she said. "A mermaid's mirror. Total old-magic shit. Very powerful."

"Oh," I said carefully. "What does it do?"

"It's hard to say. There are different versions of the story. And legends can be wrong. But they say that if you find it, you'll see the person you really are, the truest version of yourself. The one that really matters."

I decided it was better not to mention the mirror I'd given to Kristle. Why bring it up? I wasn't sure if I believed in this kind of magic anyway. It seemed too easy. I had looked at the mirror myself, and it's not like I'd had some huge revelation. Although maybe I just needed to listen harder.

"Maybe you'll find it someday," I said. "It's not too late."

"I have this theory that part of the spell is you can't find it unless you don't need it anymore. The only way you can find the mirror is if you already know what it's going to tell you."

"Why is magic always so useless?" I asked.

"Fuck if I know. But maybe it's not totally useless. I wonder . . ." she said. She gave me a sly look, and I knew I was bearing a guilty expression. "Not for me, I don't think. But I bet Kristle could have found a use for it."

I shrugged, noncommittal, and I knew she knew. "So let's just say you found the mirror now," I asked. "What do you think it would show you? Just try to guess."

She didn't have to consider it for long before answering. She had already considered it. "I think it would show me on the beach with you a few weeks ago, when we saw that horse."

I felt a surge of happiness as the memory of that day came to me. I reached out for her hand. "Well that's not so bad, is it?"

"I guess not. But it's not enough for me either. That's why the mirror wouldn't do me any good at this point anyway. Do you get that?"

"I think so," I said, although I wasn't sure I did. Magic was complicated, but it was nothing compared to how complicated people were.

"I can change my reflection now," she said. "I can make it whatever I want it to be."

She sounded so much more grown-up now than she had the first time I had met her, and I knew that she had been right. I hadn't known her at all. No—I had. She was changing, yes, but so was I. She was different and the same, and I had known her insofar as you can really know anyone, which is to say not much. But the not much was more than enough. It was everything. She had been a mirror.

"You should go," she said.

"Yeah," I said. "I guess I should."

And I kissed DeeDee for the last time. It was unmistakably final, which is not at all to say perfunctory. It wasn't that I was holding back, or even that she was. She was kissing me and she meant it. The *it* that she meant was just a different *it* now.

There was a weird comfort in that too. Just in knowing for sure. The first time I had kissed DeeDee, I'd felt the world unfurling at my feet, and now I felt nothing but the limitlessness of my own self. I felt myself expanding past the edges of my own body, past the boundaries of the ocean, out to the brink of a flat earth where the water spills out into big nothing in bright and crashing cascades.

"Well, bye," I said, when we had finally separated.

I was about to go when she jumped to her feet.

"Wait," she said. "I want to show you something." Before I could stop her she was shedding her clothes and racing into the water.

"Hey!" I shouted, but she didn't listen. She dove into the surf and I started to run in after her, still in my shoes and all my clothes, to save her, when it became clear that it wasn't necessary. She came up from the water ten feet in front of me and tossed her hair in a spray, a big grin on her face. "Check it out!" she yelled. "I can totally swim now. Awesome, right?" She flipped backward in a somersault and stuck her legs straight up in the air, then surfaced again on her back to glide around in an untrained backstroke. "It's not like I'll be going to the Olympics any time soon," she said, dog-paddling toward me. "But still. It's really not that hard."

All I could do was smile. As she got closer, I splashed a handful of water in her face. She splashed me back and soon I was soaking wet, freezing, still in my sweatshirt and jeans and sneakers. I didn't really care.

"Well," she said. "Bye. I'll think of you a lot. I promise." She wrapped her dripping arms around me and leaned her head on my shoulder for the last time. Then I was standing in the surf and she was walking up the beach in her wet underwear, carrying her clothes in a bundle under her arm. She was going away.

And then all I wanted was for her to look back, to look at me one more time. All I wanted was to be written on her, a final answer tattooed onto the tiniest aspect of her person. Say, to become a ring of gold in just one of her green eyes. But her path was already decided for her. Even if it was still invisible to her, I knew that she had taken a step, and that it was the right one. Every step would be the right one for her now.

She didn't remember the word for regret anymore; it was now just something baffling and troublesome that blocked her from moving in any direction except straight ahead. And with 123 ways of saying it, how can an Eskimo walking up the beach ever truly express: *What is cold; what is white; what is ancient; what falls from endless gray and then just*, I don't know, *lingers?*

When I got home and flopped into bed, my phone rang for the first time all summer. The horrifying mariachi of my ringtone jarred me, and I made a note to change it to something else. It was Sebastian.

"Dude, dude, *dude!*" he said before I'd said hello. I barely recognized his voice. "Are you *ever* coming home? Where have you been? I'm going crazy here. I don't even know what I'm doing with myself!"

"Hey," I said. "I mean, you could have called."

"Dude, I *did!*" Sebastian said. "Like five hundred and twenty fuckin' thousand times. What, you don't get service down there? Wherever that even is? Everyone's fucking out of town! You, Val, Nick Whitney—I've been talking to the fucking wall. I jerked off four times today, bro. Four times! It's not even fun anymore; I just don't have anything better to do. My dick's about to fall off."

"What about Alexis?" I asked. "Isn't she keeping you busy?"

"Who?"

"Alexis," I said. "Your girlfriend."

"Oh, *her*. I don't know. I haven't seen her in months. She had, like, some *issue*. It made no sense. Anyway, who cares, yo? Bros before hos, right?"

I knew too much about hos by now to respond to that in any concise or reasonable way, but Sebastian was barreling on anyway.

"Dude, what happened? Did you have fun? Are you coming home? Did you finally get your ass laid? Don't answer that; I don't want to make you feel worse than you already do. It's okay. I've seen some of the new freshmen already and some of them are hot as shit. You're going to have plenty of opportunities."

I just laughed.

TWENTY-NINE

I WOKE UP earlier than ever the next morning and decided to wander down to the beach for one last swim. There was probably a part of me that was hoping DeeDee would be waiting for me there again, but I guess I knew that there was really no way.

The sun was just rising and I decided to get naked. It was a little chilly out, but I didn't care. I ventured into the water, knowing it would be the last time for a while.

As soon as it touched my feet, the ocean felt different. It was cold, but that wasn't it; the ocean is always cold, especially at first. It sort of tingled, sent a static shock through my body, all the way to the tips of my fingers and my nose and my dick, which had retreated into itself upon exposure.

I took another step and felt the strange sizzle again. It felt like a warning, but I didn't take it; I jogged forward into the surf and dove right into the first wave that came at me, just launched myself into it without hesitating. I wasn't afraid of anything anymore.

The water chewed me up. The water entered my nose and mouth as if it was trying to flood my lungs. I waved my arms furiously, trying to paddle, but found that I no longer knew how. All I could do was try to find my legs and stand.

I managed to get my head above water a few seconds later, flailing and sputtering and gasping for breath. The water was not deep and I was finally on my feet, but I felt like I was drowning.

Then an image entered my mind. It was DeeDee on a clear and sunny day, somewhere in a place beyond the waves, a place with no land in sight, floating on her back. Her face was radiant and resolute and complicated and different than I'd known it, older, maybe, or more solid.

I saw her doing a little somersault into the water, then coming up, hair plastered to her body, laughing. I laughed too. I was happy for a second.

Like the Girls—like my father—I could no longer swim.

When I made it back to the shore, I felt a sharp, stabbing pain in my foot, like I'd stepped on a shell and gotten it stuck in my heel. I lifted my foot up to examine it, and it was bleeding. There was no sign of a shell.

We left a few hours later: me, Dad, and Jeff in the Accord, with Mom trailing somewhere behind in her Volvo. I'm not sure where she was going. It wasn't out of the question that she would be coming back to Connecticut with us, but it also wasn't unlikely that she would be headed off to somewhere else again. If she came home with us, I couldn't say who she would be this time; I couldn't say what shape she would take. Animal, vegetable, mineral; maiden, mother, crone. None of it was really my business anyway.

So we three put the beach behind us, Dad in the driver's seat and the ocean at our backs, the breeze through the windows salty and cool and the sun just starting to come up. Traffic hadn't broken out yet and Dad was speeding. He was whistling as usual, but I didn't mind anymore. Jeff wasn't saying anything, but I turned to look at him and he smiled at me, a smile that was very far away.

I was glad he was in the front and I was in the back, because if I'd been able to, I probably would have embarrassed myself by leaning over and giving him a hug. I just don't think I would have been able to help it.

I tried to picture DeeDee: what she was doing, how she was spending her day, what she was thinking about. It took a while for me to summon her, but when I closed my eyes and concentrated, she appeared, fatigued and somewhat monochrome, climbing out of her bunk bed and stepping over her sisters strewn out in sleeping bags and blankets on the floor, yawning on her way to the shower, turning the spigot and then hesitating before stepping in, shutting it off again and dressing lazily, and then leaving the apartment onto the open walkway outside, where the air was gray and cool and heavy with dampness and she pulled a cigarette from thin air and lit it and sucked it down, staring at the ocean for what felt like the first time.

Then the weather swirled around her and it was winter. The sky on the balcony was so white you could hardly look at it. Then it was nearly spring, and she was in a pilled wool sweater in the driver's seat of her own busted junker—probably something maroon and ancient with the passenger-side door secured with a fraying cable of twine—her hand dangling out the window with a burning cigarette as she hit this highway herself, hurtling off to a lonely destination where she could begin her next journey, a quest to pick up the trail of the girl she thought she had been looking for. I thought it could have been a pretty short quest if she wanted it to be, but I knew there was no convincing her of that.

She sighed and tossed her cigarette, the last one she would smoke, and she began to sing along to the radio. I couldn't hear her, but I imagined it was James Taylor.

I can't say I wasn't sad. To see her like that: headed off for a life that was beyond my knowledge. I was sad. But as soon as we hit the interstate and rolled up the windows—as soon as the dusty, cutting smell of AC replaced the saltwater air—I found that I had a hard time remembering her face. Sea foam bubbling into wet sand.

At a traffic light, Mom pulled up next to us and waved from the Volvo, and when the light turned green, she honked twice, jauntily, and sped off ahead of us into her future.

"You know," my father said. "I went on vacation here when I was your age." He smiled at me. "Best summer of my life. It's where I forgot how to swim."

"I know," I said.

I was glad to be leaving. I was eager to get back home, back to our place in the exact center of the circumference of the round part of the planet, knowing now that, like my father, I would carry with me a certain understanding in my gut: a knowledge of a place where the earth was flat, where there was no dimension to reason, where water fell into space and sprayed off into stars. Where the Deepness and the Endlessness could have a daughter who thought they were both real assholes.

WHAT HAPPENED TO THE SOCK

I'm becoming certain that I've hidden myself away somewhere. For safekeeping. Unfortunately, I've forgotten the hiding place.

Please bear with me as I try to explain. If I sound stilted or confused, remember that language still sometimes comes funny to me. Being not from around here. But I am getting better about it. And what I'm trying to say is important.

There's a jewelry box in the freezer in the restaurant, behind the Hershey's ice cream where no one would ever think to look. (Because Kristle always made me scoop the ice cream.) It's in this box that I keep a few things I picked up after my arrival at this edge of your world. A few things I didn't want to share:

1. *A blue, irregularly shaped shell I found on the beach*
2. *A bracelet I stole from the gift shop, with horseshoe and clover charms; plastic, never worn*
3. *A few strange coins I got in tips, which may or may not have any value and probably don't, but who cares?*
4. *One dangly earring to which I've lost the pair, and— although this is kind of embarrassing to admit—*

5. *The sock you thought you lost, which I took from your foot when you were asleep in the fake pirate ship, just to have something of yours, even something small and stupid and frankly smelly; you had to go home with only one sock, but it was foolish of you to be wearing socks in the first place, as who wears socks at the beach?*

Well, I could have just asked you, and you would have given me something else. I'm sure you would have given me anything. But I didn't want to ask, so I just have your dirty sock with a hole in the heel. I'm sorry I took it like that, but I'm happy I have it. If you asked for it back I would not return it, because I cannot afford generosity the way you can. It's beyond my means, and the sock belongs to me.

I do have other things of course, besides the crap in my jewelry box. I mean, in a sense. I have some clothes and a blue lighter and a pack of Gauloises, and several earrings (with pairs!), and things like that. But the clothes and earrings will be loaned out before I know it, the lighter will be stolen (because, see, I'm not the only one who steals around here), and the cigarettes will probably all be bummed by tomorrow, which is fine because I'm not going to smoke anyway. Cigarettes, like beauty, don't really count as a possession.

The things in my jewelry box are the things that I know are mine for a while. They are the sum of it. I know the other girls have their own jewelry boxes, too. We don't talk about it.

I never even look in the box much. I just like to know it's there. But a few months ago, the week before Kristle's final birthday, I had to open it up. She was out on a smoke break, and I had a little bit of privacy for a few minutes. So I dug into the back of the freezer and looked inside, hoping to find something that had slipped my mind. It wouldn't be the first time something escaped me; we are practical but scatterbrained.

I don't know what I was looking for. It could have been anything. A photograph, maybe, of the thing I once was? A nameplate necklace bearing the name that belonged to me, before I took this name that isn't really mine? I don't know.

All I found was a blue shell, one earring, strange coins, a plastic charm bracelet, and a smelly sock. And I knew then that if I had somehow been forced to choose—if I'd really had to make a decision—I would have sacrificed all the other items in order to keep the sock.

Because in rifling through my jewelry box I was looking for the thing I love most. Although it was not in there, the closest thing I have ever had to myself is you, which makes your old sock a clue or maybe even something like a treasure map.

What you have to understand is that I'd never even considered most of this until I saw you for the first time—or rather, until you saw me. It's not that I was content before, exactly— we are not content—but rather that I was unquestioning in my ignorance. It did not occur to me that I could be anything beyond "we." It just did not occur to me that I could be something other than "one."

Then at some point you looked at me, and somewhere in the space of your gaze (your gaze that is bold and unguarded and searching, both sharp and vulnerable), I saw a shape unfurl itself. It was a ghost-impression of something unraveling and reforming into a girl who resembled me and only me. In a voice I didn't even know I had, I thought, I could be her. For the first time, I thought, I.

It took me a while to figure out that this was the reason I was following you. I thought you could lead me to myself.

There were other reasons, anyway. Because you are handsome. Because you are kind, in a brittle and irritable sort of way. And of course, much as I would like to, I cannot discount the unfortunate specifics of our curse. It would be a lie to say that didn't play a part.

But then, on the Fourth of July, we were sitting on the shore after the party, and we were peaceful and happy.

I could have done it then. I could have broken the curse right there. It was the moment all of us pursued. Me, Kristle, the Donnas and Brendas and Kellys and L'Oréals who have gone before me, and the ones who will follow me, summer after summer, spit naked from the waves.

I didn't do it. Instead, I asked you, "Why me? What's the difference between us?" I knew I sounded stupid and weak and I didn't like it, but I asked because I actually wanted to know the answer. I'm actually smart enough to know when to keep my mouth shut, but I'm also smart enough to ignore my own judgment a lot of the time.

And you said, "DeeDee, you make things too fuckin' compli-
cated."

And I said, "Well make it simple for me please; I'm not from
around here."

And you said, "I can't just lay it out there. It doesn't work like
that."

And I said, "Yeah, see?"

You said nothing. I didn't say anything either. But I think we
both understood.

I wanted to ask you the same question but different: Why do
you love me? Who am I to be loved? But I didn't ask, because
then I understood that I should have the patience to let you
reveal your reasons.

We are not patient. But maybe I am?

So I waited, and it happened. Slowly. The way you put your
hand on my shoulder. The way you smiled at me when I was
talking, the way I'd tell a joke and not even realize it was a joke
until you were laughing. The way you kissed me, the way I saw
you ambling toward me down the beach, still in the distance. In
your small movements and gestures, something happened: the
girl you thought I was began to acquire form—the way we con-
struct our physical bodies from waves and foam when we arrive
here—and she was beautiful in a way that had nothing to do
with what I'd thought of as beauty. She was beautiful in a way
that had nothing to do with our knife: she was odd and clever
and angry and talkative and bold and full of opinions, kind but
maybe a little irritable. She was a bit like you.

And I saw that she was me, sort of. I was her. I am those things that she is. It's unclear to me whether I am those things because you could see something that no one else could—something I couldn't see before I met you—or if I am those things because you made it true by seeing it.

It doesn't matter anyway. Either way, it would not be enough. I am no longer just "one," and I am more than the many to which I no longer belong. I am more than some accumulation of difference. I know this now.

I mean, I may not know who I am. But I know a few things. And although I love you (in a way), I know that I am more than who you think I am. This is not your fault. I loved you. I love you.

All of this is to tell you that I am keeping the sock. It's mine now, and I will keep it close to me until I no longer need it, along with the other items in my jewelry box. I will take it with me to a home I'll find for myself in a place I can't yet imagine. I'm not going to hide it this time. I will keep it not just to remember you—although it's important to me to remember you—but to remember the girl that I am now.

Because soon I will be different; soon I will be in my car, alone for the first time and driving away from here, heading toward a destination that I'm certain will be familiar upon my arrival.

ACKNOWLEDGMENTS

THIS BOOK TOOK me a really long time to write, and for much of that time I was often a complete personal wreck. As a result I owe even more effusive thanks to even more people than usual, especially:

My editor, Tara Weikum, without whom I would likely be lying in a gutter somewhere. To enumerate everything for which I owe her would likely just embarrass us both, but the short version is that I'm incredibly grateful for her wise, patient, and insightful editorial guidance, and—no less importantly—for her friendship.

My agent, Cathy Hemming, who has saved my ass on so many occasions and whose loyalty, guts, and dogged (perhaps irrational!) belief in me made all the difference.

My parents, Jane Clark and Chris Madison, who warned me at a young age not to become a writer and then did their best to make sure I became one anyway. Thank you for dealing with the consequences of your poor parenting.

My sisters, Lucy and Devon Madison, who are the best.

My grandmother, Mitzi Clark, who made the horrible winter afternoons of 2009 somewhat bearable by drinking black coffee and eating cheeseburgers with me at T.G.I. Friday's.

Emily Gould, who talked me down from many ledges, made her couch constantly available, provided several much-needed pep talks on the manuscript and other things, and spent hours writing next to me. She also cooked me a bunch of meals, including the best poached egg I've ever had.

And the rest of the Goulds! Especially Rob, Kate, and Ben Gould, but also all the Gould-Deshler-Delaplaines who generously welcomed me into their family and provided me with several beaches: Ila, Walter, Sara, Bruce, Cody, Dave, Jesse, Steve, Dylan, Andrew, Joanne, Allison, and Kaylie.

Frank Griggs, who paid me to blog about nude celebrities when nude celebrities were all I had.

Elisa Nader, without whom I would have gone barefoot.

My writer friends, who provided me with gossip, meals, advice, and encouragement and generously read this book in various unfinished drafts, especially Elise Broach, Natalie Standiford, Justine Larbalestier, and Donna Freitas.

Bob Berens, the smartest and most tolerant story consultant a person could dream of having available to him on Gchat.

All those who cheerfully harbored me during my terrible period of quasi-homelessness: James Dreiss, Olivia Good, James Freedland, Mike Wang, and a few others who would probably be weirded out to see their names here.

Margaret Wright, for the lucky charm and for guiding me from afar.

Chris Hernandez, Christina Colangelo, Mary Ann Zissimos, Erin Fitzsimmons, and everyone else at HarperCollins—all of whom are modest enough to pretend that their unusual combination of enthusiasm, creativity, skill, and dedication is just a normal course-of-business thing.

Genevieve, Maggie, and Imogene Miles: Beach Women.

Laird Adamson, who put up with a lot of crap while I was writing this.

James Frey, Jessica Almon, Matt Hudson, and Judy Goldschmidt, my companions on the Island of Misfit Toys.

And finally, thank you to John Koblin, whom I love.

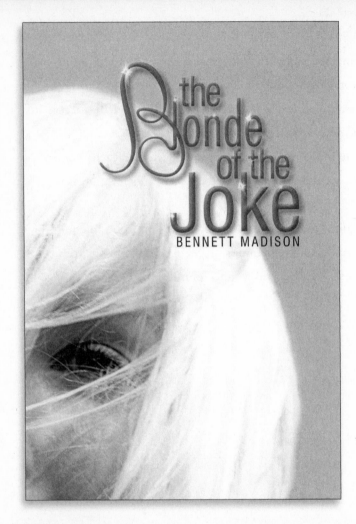